PROTECTION

Paul Hersey

Otago Publishing

Published by Otago Publishing
www.otago.ca/publishing

Library and Archives Canada Cataloguing in Publication
Hersey, Paul
Protection / Paul Hersey

ISBN 978-1-7772421-0-7

I: Title. II. Title: Protection.

Publisher and Editor: Jerry Auld
Cover photo: Shelley Hersey, The colour of ice inside a crevasse in Antarctica, 10 metres beneath the surface.
Layout: Jerry Auld

1 2 3 4 5 24 23 22 21 20

The characters and events in these stories are works of fiction. Any similarity to real persons, living or dead, is coincidental and not intended by the author.

to Jamie

Knowing the truth
is no protection against it

Zoe snuggles into the beanbag. It is a red beanbag, oversized and faded from the sun, and Zoe wriggles right on in until it looks like she has been half swallowed. These days I do not use it much. Being well into my 70s, once I am in there I have a heck of a time getting out again.

The beanbag is one of Zoe's favourite spots to sit when she comes to visit, especially with warm sunlight streaming through the lounge window like it is now. Zoe is a good name. It means 'Life' in Greek. She has just turned fifteen and is full of beans, a lot like her mother Tyler at the same age. I feel myself slipping, just for a moment, remembering a young Tyler. She was keen to give everything a go. There is that familiar twist to the gut again, and I force myself to focus on Zoe - on the now - until it passes.

Apart from Zoe, these days I get little experience dealing with teenagers, especially smart, independent ones. Zoe knows it too. But that is fine by me, well most of the time, as I tend not to deny her anything. Usually we sit and chat about what she likes or doesn't like at home or at school, who her best friends are and what they all get up to. Although I've slowed down considerably, she still enjoys going for walks with me along the beach and following trails in the nearby forest. Sometimes we row across the estuary in my dinghy if the water is calm to watch wading birds in the shallows.

Occasionally, but only if Zoe encourages me, I might retell a story from our family's past. This can be a bit of a conundrum. Even a curse, I guess, one that comes with the fragility of age. Sometimes the remembering takes up more time than the actual day to day stuff, so much so that there are moments when I feel like I am surrounded by the past and with no means to escape it.

Living vicariously, you could call it, and a bit precariously when Zoe comes to visit. Especially when she goes and asks me about her mother.

'You know,' she might say in an offhand manner that instantly makes me cautious. 'What about that time you had to rescue Mum from the mountains?'

Or even a story about my older brother.

'Go on, tell me about Granddad Duncan again,' she says respectfully, but with enough of a glint in her eye to suggest that an old family tragedy is still to be mused over.

No doubt Zoe would have already been told something by Tyler, enough to pique her interest but clearly not satiate it. I wonder how much to explain. Of course, there is no way I can tell her everything. Some details are better off staying out of harm's way, left in the past where they should remain.

But, today, I am sitting in a chair by the window and Zoe is next to me, rustling around in the beanbag. She is frowning.

I lean forward. 'What's chewing on your mind, Sawn Off?'

Zoe pushes the hair back from her eyes, thick hair the colour of sunlight on sand that reminds me so much of her grandmother. There is an odd expression on her face. I haven't the faintest idea what she is about to say.

'We found a box of stuff in the shed the other day, Mum and I did.'

'Oh, yeah?' There's another twist to my gut, and this one sharper than the first.

3

Zoe nods, clearly deep in thought. 'The box looked like it hadn't been opened for years.'

'Anything interesting?'

'Mostly books and papers,' she replies. 'Old documents. But we also found this.'

Zoe takes a photograph from her pocket. She stares at it for a few seconds before handing it to me. The photograph is dog-eared. One corner looks like it has been burned, as if someone might have set it alight and then changed their mind.

I am focusing on Zoe so much that, at first, I only glance at the grainy, black and white image. The setting appears to be a typical New Zealand restaurant or a pub, and a group of people I do not recognise are facing the camera and laughing. It is the sight of another, younger couple in the background that soon focuses my attention. The two are partly shadowed from the light, but you can see enough of their faces and that they are leaning over a bar table towards each other. They are holding hands. It looks like they are about to kiss.

It takes me a moment to recognise what - or more accurately who - I am looking at. And then I cannot tear my eyes away. The hand I am holding the photograph with starts to shake. My heartbeat speeds up. For a few, long, heart-wrenching moments I am unable to speak.

'I found it in one of the old books,' Zoe says. 'Just by accident. It was stuck behind a dust jacket with tape.'

She points to the photograph, the one that I am now holding in my hand like it's a loaded gun. 'That's my Nanna Kate, isn't it? There, at the back. Her... and someone else. But that's not Granddad Duncan. Least I don't think so.'

It is a while before I can answer. 'No,' I finally mutter.

Zoe reaches to take the photograph back. She looks at it for a while, holding the image close so she can study the young faces that were captured all those years ago.

'I wonder who it might be,' she says in a quieter voice, as if she's speaking only to herself.

These days, when certain memories surface they do much more than trap me in a bubble. Some memories can make my emotions feel so tangled, so raw, it's as if what I'm recalling might have happened only yesterday.

The moment captured in the photograph that Zoe has just shown to me is certainly one of them. I feel a sudden urge to stand up. My mind struggles to figure out all of the connotations, not least of all how in hell can something like this turn up after so much time has passed.

'It…it was a long time ago,' I stammer, struggling to get my voice to sound normal.

'I can see that,' Zoe replies. 'I mean, look how young Nanna Kate is. What was she like back then? What can you remember about this? Do you know who that young man is with her? I want to know everything.'

'Hang on,' I say, holding both of my hands up. 'So many questions all at once. Ease up, Sawn Off. Has your mother seen the photo?'

Zoe nods.

I look out the window at the rātā in the backyard. It's a tree I planted as a memorial to Duncan many decades ago. Bellbirds and tūī are skipping between its branches and sipping nectar from bright red flowers that bloom every summer, or in spring if the warmth comes early like it has this year. As I stand there and watch, they take turns puffing up their chests before beginning to sing. Their clicks and whistles are a soothing melody to my ears, a natural music that reminds me of a lifetime spent in the forested back country of our most precious land.

I focus on the birdsong for as long as I can. Then I make sure to wipe the corner of my eyes before turning back to Zoe. Judging by the look on her face, I can tell she recognises how much this unexpected discovery has affected me.

Wondering how I'm going to explain everything to Tyler later, for now I realise I have to deal with an overly perceptive fifteen-year-old. What shall I say? What can I say?

Zoe gives a small smile. She speaks to break the growing silence that has come between us. 'You look like you've seen a ghost.'

Clearly, she is trying to show that she is empathetic. But she doesn't look away. She stays sitting in the beanbag, both hands resting on her lap. Waiting patiently. Expectantly.

Of course, there is much about the past that Zoe deserves to know. After all, this is the history of her family as much as it is mine. I take a few steps and lower myself back into my chair, my favourite spot closest to the window, and that catches the perfect amount of sunlight this time of day. Positioned at just the right angle so that I can still see the rātā and hear the birdsong through my good ear.

I turn to Zoe, and I take a deep breath.

PART
ONE

I

If I had to question, defer to, or blame anything from my past it would be my own fear and love. Fear of love. Fear of not being in love. Fear of love not being enough.

But that is not how to start telling this story, especially not to someone like Zoe. I wonder for a few moments where is the best place to begin.

'I was a wee bit younger than you are now,' I finally say. 'That first day. The day I met your grandmother for the very first time, it was also the first time I met a kea.'

Zoe leans forward. 'You met a kea?'

'Well, I saw a kea.'

In a different life I reckon Zoe could have been a kea, mischievous mountain parrot that she is. With a thick, green cloak to protect from the cold and a call that sounds either raucous or eerie depending on your perspective. A call that perhaps a ghost in pain might make if ghosts feel pain, and the memory of which I still find myself succumbing to occasionally.

'You know a kea has powerful claws,' I tell Zoe, scrunching up my fingers and trying to pull a scary face to help ease my own tension as much as hers. 'And she has a long, sharp beak that could easily fight off a stoat or a weasel that might come to plunder her young or even a wild cat making its way up from the lows.'

I explain that the kea doesn't know how to fight. She knows

how to fly and the best places to fossick for food. Sometimes, she knows how to discover or solve problems like few other animals can.

The kea watches the violence unfolding in her nest - to her young family - and then she unfolds her wings and takes to the air. Small, suddenly stilled voices that could have been the final cries of her offspring echo through the valley's shadows. She climbs and falls. Flies and calls.

Her view of the country below, the West Coast of the South Island, is as always. Seeing her backyard - what would become my mountains - rumpled in steep clusters and bordered on one side by the seemingly endless, shimmering blue of the ocean.

Despite my roundabout way of starting to explain the photo, Zoe appears to be listening attentively. That's something at least. The kea keeps flying west, I say, raising one arm and taking it in a long arc, further than she usually ventures for some reason, beyond her mountain home and now almost out over the edge of the Tasman Sea. She looks down again. Perhaps she can see me staring up at her, and me trying to make up my mind between waving a greeting and flicking through the pages of my Complete Bird Book to understand who I am seeing for the first time.

In this memory I am fourteen years old. Just younger than Zoe, but both of us still of an age where we might become dictated to by our inquisitive naivety.

'Kea are very curious,' I tell her. Then I give a sly grin. 'They can be quite the troublemaker too.'

Zoe likes the insinuation. She lets out a small giggle, and I feel myself beginning to ease into the telling of a story that I have probably needed to share with her for a long time.

This particular memory I am starting with is of a time when I was woken to a strange and new uncertainty. To a new land that seemed so wild to my young mind. To a new life, and me left feeling lost and claustrophobic because of the suddenness with which I was thrust into it. The closeness of the mountains didn't help me, well not at first.

There were no over-parched plains that I had become used to while growing up in the city on the other, eastern coastline. No distant horizon of tiny, snowy mountain summits gleaming in the early sunlight like freshly cleaned teeth. Here, they rose before me as some intimidating presence or force, towering and monolithic and back lit by the sun so that their morning moods remained hidden from a young mind.

And then from this strange, new perspective emerged a flying bird I didn't recognise. It was something to focus on at least. I could see that it was a parrot, well I thought so and we don't have many of those, do we?

Zoe shakes her head. She knows her bird life pretty well.

The unidentified bird's call carried over the stilled morning air. It seemed so sad. Lonely. Even now, the memory of that sound still reminds me of my own youthful uncertainty. My own fears.

Of course, back then, I needed to know what it was. My well-thumbed bird book got thumbed some more. If someone else had been on that beach that morning no doubt they would have had a decent chuckle watching a skinny kid with a large mop of hair, flicking through the pages of his book and talking aloud to himself.

Is it a kākāpō?

No stupid they don't fly.

Perhaps a kākā, a tree parrot with a loud call and a rowdy nature.

Yes, that seems likely as there are thick forests cloaking the nearest hills.

But, no. A kākā's coat is reddy brown, and this has more of a green to its body. But with bright flashes of orange like sunbeams under its wings.

A kea then? Is it a kea?

Yes, surely that must be the one.

Excited at my detective work leading to the new discovery, I couldn't stop myself from waving and shouting out as loud as I could.

'Hello Kea Bird!'

As the kea in my memory flies over the mountains and the sea there are moments I imagine, or at least I did back then, that she would also have had a telling perspective over the disparaging landscape of my parents. Duncan once joked that our father was of the ocean and our mother the mountains. And he was probably not far from the truth.

Together, they took on the relationship of water and earth, forces of nature always in conflict or so it seemed to us when we were kids. Their personalities could only exist that way. Crush the immovable. Smother that which can't be smothered. Ebb and flow. Erode. Fragment. Re-deposit and rise again. Any calmness we might have experienced at home, back in the city on the edge of the plains, was little more than a momentary respite. A sharpness already catching in the next gathering of their breath.

It was the silence that weighed on me more than the sound of them arguing. How the force of it against my chest stopped me breathing. And then the not knowing. My thoughts rampant with worry over what hushed, harsh words they were uttering behind the closed door to the lounge. Or, worse still I imagined, the silence between them acting like a boiler without a thermostat. The longer the pressure built the worse it was going to be when it exploded again. At least when they shouted at each other I knew what was going on. All of the neighbours most likely knew.

Perhaps there had once been love between my parents. Love has its own ebb and flow after all. Its own measurement. Its tendency for unpredictable outcomes. But partway along their journey either the effort or the cost became too much. There could be no other result. And they both must have known it.

So, an old crib on the West Coast was where my mother, brother and I retreated to in the spring. To a small, seaside village located on the other side of the same, distant mountain range I had looked at so many times from my bedroom window in the city. To hopefully rediscover what was lost, or perhaps had always been missing, from our lives.

To get to the Coast we needed to drive over the mountains, taking a narrowed alpine crossing that becomes impassable in the winter snows. But that first time I didn't get to see the crossing or any of the mountains up close. It was evening by the time we had left home which meant most of the road trip would be completed in darkness.

Our family car was packed so full that there was hardly enough room for me and our dog Sugar in the backseat. My mother reversed down the driveway without as much as a glance back towards my father who had remained standing at the front door of our home. He didn't offer to help pack the car, but then he didn't try to stop us either.

Duncan was sitting in the front passenger seat, staring into a space that only he could see. My father noticed me looking back at him out the side window. We waved at each other. I felt a strong urge to hug Sugar, and she gave a small whimper as our car sped off down the road.

It was sometime in the early hours before we arrived at our new home on the Coast. The crib we pulled up to was cold and the walls smelled of mould. There were scatterings of mouse poo on the floor. My mother pointed out the two tiny bedrooms and then in the direction of the long-drop toilet near the back of the section.

'Be sure and look for spiders under the seat before you use it,' she said. 'It can be a bit scary feeling them against your backside.'

Zoe giggles when I tell her that my mother's toilet seat-checking comment gave me nightmares for weeks.

Neither my brother nor I had ever been to the crib before. Which is odd thinking about it all these years later, as it was the home where my mother and her older brother had grown up. I don't know why my mother had never taken us there. Maybe it was a part of her life that she preferred to keep secret, protected from the city and everything that represented.

Duncan tied Sugar up in the woodshed out the back, and he carried in an armful of split logs to start a fire and try to warm the place up. My mother brought bedding and extra clothes from the car. We had just enough food for breakfast.

Even now, I can still recall how weird it all was. I try to explain this feeling to Zoe. Everything was happening in such a rush that it seemed like I had nothing solid to cling to. I could hear Sugar barking outside as if she didn't understand what was going on either, and then Duncan stuck his head out the door and yelled at her to shut up which was something our father used to do all the time. Dad never even liked having a dog as a pet.

My mother must have seen the look on my face. She moved close and gave me a long hug. Then she took my hand. She led me to our new bedroom, helped me climb up into the top bunk, drew the sleeping bag around me and zipped it into a warming cocoon.

'Don't worry,' she said, leaning forward to kiss me on the forehead and then gently ruffling my hair. 'You'll see, Jase. Everything will work out just fine.'

'Were you frightened?' Zoe asks. 'Of being somewhere strange and new?'

'I was more disorientated. And sad.'

Zoe nods to herself. 'Because you'd been separated from your father,' she says. 'Your normal life at home.'

'Sad, because I knew that I should be.'

I remember waking before the dawn. I lay there in the dark and listened to what sounded like the thunder of an approaching storm. It took me a few moments to work out where I was again, and that the sound must have been the nearby ocean.

Duncan was snoring noisily in the bunk below - 'yes, your grandfather was a great snorer', I tell Zoe, my voice almost faltering when I say 'your'. I glance at her, but her face remains impassive.

Once it was light enough to see, I managed to get out of my sleeping bag and the top bunk without waking my brother or my mother in the next room. I don't know why but at the time it seemed like a good idea to go exploring. Something to focus on, I guess. Discover what was new. A way to start afresh.

Following the sound of the waves, I soon discovered a path between the sand dunes that led down to a beach. There was a dark forest of tall, thin trees covering hills to the south, while northwards a strip of white sand stretched unbroken up the coast. Behind me, to the east, rose more foothills covered in forest and then high above them the much sharper crests of mountains. Looking up, covering my face against the glare of the early sunlight, I could see that the very tops of the mountains had a mantle of snow.

The first time I saw the mountains from that perspective they seemed so close and more than a bit intimidating. A huge barrier between the old life I had left behind and the new one I was about to discover. It felt voyeuristic staring up at them, as if I was waiting for something bad to happen before my eyes. Part of me felt that they were staring back, even judging me. After a while I made myself turn away.

The coastline appeared to be empty. Driftwood lolled in the shore break, but then I suddenly needed to skirt one piece of wood that transformed into a seal which woke in fright at the sound of my footsteps. It barked at me, before humping back to the sanctity of water. I could certainly understand the animal's feeling of vulnerability.

Birdsong filtered from the nearest trees and this turned my attention to a more pleasant and familiar topic. I tightened the grip on my Complete Bird Book, straining to hear properly and trying to distinguish each call. There were bellbirds competing against each other with their morning chorus, and they were easy to make out. One or two grey warblers sounded as lonely as ever. Was that the rising whistle of a shining cuckoo nearby? Or just a common starling trying its best to mimic the cuckoo and fool me in the process.

I have always had a fascination with birds. Something about their calls and their flight and even their movement on land seems to occupy a space which remains just beyond me. Luckily, this is an interest that Zoe and I can share. When we go for walks close to home - the same walks I did in my youth and that I am describing to her now - I encourage her to identify every bird we might see or hear.

Birds have their own way of interpreting and interacting with the outdoors, I tell Zoe. Even back when I was a lad, I realised there was much we humans with our heavy footprints upon the land could still learn from them. Walking along the Coast for the first time that morning, their presence certainly helped to provide some feeling of security. Their familiarity was a comforting layer of protection.

On sand dunes covered with marram grass the dotterels, little tūturiwhatu, scuttled between the makeshift cover of speckled stones. They created tiny tracks in the sand, and their mottled feathers acted as a camouflage whenever they paused.

Overhead, flocks of gulls complained like they always tend to, red and the rarer black billed and also the larger black backed stalling, turning away and stalling again in the rising breeze. The old people, the people of the land, called them karoro and sometimes used to keep them as pets. To see a karoro too far from the coast could be taken as a sign that bad weather was on its way. A sighting might also be considered bad luck. Likely the old people would have called my father a karoro, someone who needed to live by the sea, who had to drink from its tides. Perhaps someone who carried bad luck with them.

But it was the flying kea which really captured my attention, a first new feathered friend that I had seen and eventually been able to identify. It was a land bird rather than a sea bird, or more accurately a bird of the mountains. I kept watching the same space in the sky long after she disappeared from view, thinking about what her life must be like here amongst the highest country of this strange, western land.

Then I started to wonder again about the broken life of my family, and why it was that my mother, Duncan and I had been forced to move to what felt like to me at the time as such a lonely place. A tightness came to my breathing. My legs felt wobbly and I needed to sit down in the sand. I thought about my father and how he must be feeling. Was he sad? Angry? How could he let this happen? The horizon became blurry in my sight, and it took me a while to calm down.

Blinking back the tears, I noticed someone in the distance. They were walking close to the water's edge, moving slowly, sometimes pausing to select a seashell from detritus on the sand and then tossing it flat into the air, standing and watching as it tumbled in a low arc out across the smoothed surface of the ocean.

I didn't think the person had seen me yet. I wiped my eyes, then stood up and brushed the sand from my pants.

'Hi,' I called out when they seemed close enough to hear me.

I wondered if maybe it was a girl. Yes. She looked up, no doubt surprised that there was someone hidden amongst the driftwood. Then she gave a small wave back.

Perhaps she was a year or two older than me, although it was hard to tell as she was wearing long pants, a bright red long-sleeved top and a woolly hat with a ridiculously large pom-pom. I couldn't see much more than her face and her hands, and a few wisps of sandy coloured hair that the soft rays of early morning sunshine were filtering through.

'Hello,' the girl said with a smile as she walked closer. Even then, I recognised it as a smile that also must surely contain sunlight. Or birdsong. Or both. There was a strange stabbing feeling in my chest.

Zoe interrupts me. 'Is that my grandmother?'

'Just wait,' I say, trying to act put out by her impatience. 'Don't go spoiling the story already. I'm hardly getting started.'

Zoe gives another small giggle. 'But it is, isn't it,' she says quietly and nodding to herself.

I make a point of clearing my throat.

'I'm Jase,' I said to the girl on the beach. 'I'm new here. I guess I'm a bit lost.'

'I know who you are,' the girl replied straight away.

I must have had a confused look on my face because she gave what I took at the time to be a cheeky yet reassuring smile.

'Oh yeah, sorry,' she added. 'My parents were friends with your mother back when she used to live here, her and Frank.'

'Who?'

'You must know Frank. Old Frank? Short, stocky guy. Scowls all day long, well makes out he does but everyone who knows him well knows it's only make believe.'

I shook my head.

'Really? Well, that's odd isn't it? Never mind. Anyway, my father and your mother were in the same class through school, long ago now of course. Don't know about your folks but my Dad seems like beyond ancient these days.'

I still felt confused. How did this girl who I had never seen before know so much about my family? About me. And who was this Old Frank?

I also realised that I had been nodding too enthusiastically. As the girl kept speaking I decided that I really liked the sound of her voice.

'I think they hung out after school and stuff too,' she said.

'Who did?'

'Our parents! Well, my Dad and your Mum.' Then she giggled. 'Who knows. Maybe they even made out. That'd be a complete gas, wouldn't it? What a twisted world we live in.'

Now I was totally baffled.

There was a small gust of wind that swirled sand along the beach, and the girl pulled her hat closer over her ears.

'Yeah, we found out you lot were moving back over to the Coast,' she said. 'Not much goes on round here without someone hearing about it. Gossip spreads quicker than a swarm of sand flies, you know?'

I couldn't decide whether to shrug or nod, and ended up doing an awkward combination of both.

The girl stuck her hand out towards me. Her grip was strong. 'I guess I should say welcome to the official middle of nowhere. To our very own Coast of Misfits.'

I grinned. 'So, you live out here too?'

'Just a few houses along. Over there.' She pointed at another clump of cribs set back behind the sand dunes.

'See that old browny place? The one with the flaking paint. That's Jackson's. He's a grumpy old so and so. Real grumpy. Always cussing really loud and flicking his cigarette butts over the fence when we walk past. Ours is the section in behind. With all the trees. Not too far from yours, eh.'

'You know where I live?'

She laughed quite loudly, and it sounded a bit harsh. I couldn't tell if it was at me or with me.

'Everyone knows where everyone else here lives, stupid.'

Unsure what to say, I turned and stared out across the ocean. A strip of cloud sat low over the water like a frown. Offshore it was starting to get choppy. The girl stood next to me. I wondered why she was studying me for so long, but then she turned seawards also.

'It's alright, you'll get used to it,' she continued in a softer, more understanding voice. 'The emptiness I mean. Like there's no one around for miles and you can do just about anything you want. Or, you could go and get lost, and it feels like no one would even know where to start looking for you. But then, somehow, everyone still knows about everyone else's personal lives. Right?'

I nodded. 'Yeah, I guess. I don't really know.'

'Don't worry,' she added. 'It can all seem a bit overwhelming, for newbies anyway. Especially coming from the big smoke like you guys have. But the place will grow on you, I reckon. I like it. Well, most of the time.'

'I think I will too,' I replied, trying to sound convinced as I looked both ways along the beach. 'So, we might be seeing a lot more of each other.'

The girl peered at me. She had an odd expression on her face, and I felt my cheeks getting hot again.

'I mean, with school and stuff,' I hurriedly added. 'You do have school here, don't you?'

She grinned, like she was in on a secret that I hadn't quite managed to figure out.

'Yeah, there's a school,' she said. 'Back in town. Just don't go getting on the wrong side of Owl Face Tupuna. That's probably the best advice I can give you right now.'

'What?'

'One of our teachers. Mr Tupuna. His family has lived around these parts as long as anyone can remember. He and his brothers used to represent the Coast in squash. They all went to Nationals and everything. You can't miss any of them. They've got forearms the size of hams, especially Owl Face. You'll see.'

The girl made an alarmingly wide circle with her fingers and thumbs. I was sure she must have been exaggerating.

'That's why he canes so flipping well,' she added, whooshing her arm through the air and pulling a face like she was straining too hard. 'I swear. Whacko! You won't be able to sit down for a week. At least.'

I couldn't help but flinch, mostly at her sound effect.

'And he sees everything,' she continued, pointing two fingers first at her eyes while squinting them and then at mine. 'Every thing. We call him Owl Face behind his back. Will catch you, even in the dark. Get it?'

It must have been the look on my face that made her laugh again.

'Don't stress,' she said. 'I'm sure you'll work it all out one way or the other. Just come and ask me if you're not sure.'

Then the girl with the smile and the nice sounding voice and the way about her that has always stayed with me started to carry on walking along the beach.

'So…,' I said, momentarily at a loss but knowing I needed to do something. Say something. 'What do I get to call you? I don't even know what your name is.'

The girl didn't stop walking. But she slowed just enough to be able to look back over her shoulder. She pushed her hair off her face so she could see me better. Or let me see her.

And then she smiled, again.

'Oh, sure. That. I'm Kate. Nice to meet you, City Jase.'

II

Zoe does not say anything after I finish describing meeting her grandmother for the first time. I wonder what she might be thinking. I imagine that finding this photo will have raised so many questions in her mind, some that I'm not sure how to begin to explain.

Telling her about that first meeting with Kate has my mind racing over so many other childhood and then adult memories, both good and bad. There are those which have the potential to haunt me even now. I'm fearful that some could hurt Zoe and her mother if they ever find out, and it's up to me to make sure they don't. I guess you can call it the conditions of love that come with having a family.

What is the cause of our worst fear? The measurement of it? Is it that moment in our childhood when something incomprehensible and scary happens like our parents separating and we're left believing without a doubt in our young mind that we're the sole or main reason for it occurring? That it only happened because of a particular thing we did wrong? Or didn't do right? Of all that's left in my control now, I want to protect Zoe from ever having to experience a fear - or a hurt - as bad as that. Or, at the very least, be able to help her through it as best I can.

Sometimes, I wonder whether all of this navel gazing is bad for my health. It probably is. And, now, thinking about that first time on the West Coast by the sea I find that I can't help recalling one of my earliest, fear filled memories. One that has remained stuck in my mind like a splinter. Of a cold, blustery morning a short drive from our old home in the city to a beach up the coast, a drive when our parents argued over something or other like they always tended to.

It would have been barely into summer, and the weather seemingly needed to be reminded even of that. The day started overcast and only managed to deteriorate from there. Like our parents, both the landscape and seascape were moody and grey, and what would otherwise have been a gentle sea swell was chopped up by a strengthening onshore wind.

Something about that day still troubles me. Haunts me more likely. I know it shouldn't, but it does. It might have been a test that I did not understand. And, in the eyes of my father, it was a test that I failed.

I would have been younger than Zoe by ten years at least. Maybe not even started school. Now, looking at her sitting in the bean bag and fully focussed on whichever part of the story of our family's complicated history I am able or willing to share, I again realise the level of responsibility I am burdened with.

My brother Duncan and I had been split up by our parents, a divide and conquer technique that was often employed on the few family outings we did in the weekends. As if each parent was trying to convert us to their preferred environment. Their outlook on life. Forcing us, even if unintentionally, to pick a side.

Duncan and my mother were off to walk a track that climbed above clay cliffs north of the beach.

'To get a decent view of the countryside,' my mother had said before leaving, the tone in her voice suggesting that actually finding a view had nothing to do with it.

Duncan, however, was less than impressed with the plan. 'What planet is she on?' he whispered to me, scowling like he tended to when he couldn't get his own way. 'The weather is so absolute shite we won't be able to see a bleeding thing from up there. All I'm going to be doing is freezing my arse off.'

'Come on, Duncan,' she called out. 'Don't dilly dally. Anyone would think you can't keep up with your old, frail mother.'

She knew how to manipulate him, and my brother dutifully turned and followed her along the beach. At least they were wearing raincoats, Duncan in black which was his colour of choice and my mother in clear-sky blue. Up until that day or, more accurately, what was about to happen that day, blue had been my favourite colour.

My father and I remained on the beach. I was also wearing a jacket – blue of course – but my father had not bothered to put his on. The sand swirled beneath my shorts, stinging where it struck my bare skin. I couldn't tell if water specks in the air were the first of many raindrops or just accumulating salt spray. Even the gulls appeared put out by the conditions. A few battled away in the sky, searching for breakfast, but most of them preferred to hunker down in the lee of sand dunes.

As always, my father was keen to enter his element. But, in my mind, this was not a day to be going anywhere near the ocean.

'Perfect conditions,' he said with a broad grin, at the same time easily dragging our old wooden dinghy off the trailer on his own and down to the water's edge.

I looked at the sea of froth and then back towards my father, at first not understanding what we were about to do.

'Dad, are we going out?' I eventually asked. 'Really?'

'Don't pull a face, my boy,' he replied. 'We won't mess up that mop of yours. Not too much, I hope.'

Years later, I came to understand that acts like this weren't from ignorance or cruelty. My father believed in experiencing first-hand the adversity of any and all oceanic conditions. 'Learning through the school of hard knocks,' he liked to call it. Seaside adventures were to be tackled head on, embraced regardless how bad the weather was. I grew to realise only too well what 'for your own good' really meant.

Did it help? Well, that's a different question.

'Take your gumboots off, Jase,' my father instructed. 'Fall over the side in those and you'll be sucked under quicker than going down a plughole. Soon be feeding the sharks.'

'What?' I replied, looking up at him and momentarily horrified at that prospect. Either my father didn't notice my surge of fear or he chose to ignore it.

'Yep, socks too,' he added. 'And your jacket. Go on, you'll be right as rain. It's not that cold. The actual water temperature doesn't change much from day to day.'

Usually, I treasured the feeling of going barefoot outside. The tickling sensation of grass or sand or even thick mud oozing between my toes. I liked to do the shuffle dance that the gulls performed near the water's edge, the one where they paddled their webbed feet back and forth until the sand became like wet cement and slowly started to swallow them.

Standing there, I tried as hard as I could to show my father that I wasn't afraid. I reached out and placed one hand on the bulwark of the dinghy. It felt solid, reliable. I bent to roll my shorts a little higher so they wouldn't get too wet.

For a few moments I remained in the same spot, wriggling my toes, and attempting to go to my happy place. But then a knee-high wash of shore break almost knocked me over because my feet had become stuck in the wet sand. The cold was like a slap to my face. The water withdrew, but within seconds my legs had become clumps of deadwood. I dashed awkwardly up the beach towards the hopeful security that our car would provide.

I could hear my father calling out after me, but I didn't stop running until I reached the first sand dune. A single karoro squawked like it was laughing at me. Then came the heavy thud of approaching footsteps.

'Jase? Are you okay?'

I shook my head. The throb of numbing and thawing extremities made me shiver. I was close to crying.

'Come on now,' my father said. 'You know you have to do this. It'll be fun in the end. You'll see.'

Even though this was still early in my years spent learning the ways of the world, I already understood that the more gently my father spoke, the less likely it was that I could get out of whatever he wanted me to do. Despite feeling like a possum caught in the headlights of an oncoming car, I knew there was nowhere else to run to. My mother, who often bailed me out of these situations, was far away by now and no help at all.

Did my father think he was protecting me from myself? Even now, I don't understand. It just seems daft. He placed a firm hand on my shoulder and led me back towards the dinghy. I paused again at the water's edge, a last half-hearted attempt at avoidance.

'Why would he make you do it if you didn't want to?' Zoe asks in a quiet, concerned voice.

I shrug my shoulders. 'To be honest, I'm not really sure. Some notion of parental tough love perhaps. The ideals of a different generation. Proving that his love was as important as my mother's. Your guess is as good as mine.'

'Come on, boy,' my father said to me, the exasperation becoming obvious in his voice. 'Don't mess about, Jase. Jump on in and I'll get us out beyond the shore break. That's it. Up to the bow. Now, crouch down for the first bit so you don't get too drenched by the surf.'

The bow of the dinghy jerked violently skywards and then crashed down again with a thud. One wave and then another rolled by underneath. My father laughed loudly as a counter to the force of each impact. He grabbed both oars which were already threatening to slip from their rowlocks and stabbed a few short strokes to get us out beyond the reach of the breakers.

When I think about it now, I wonder why he did not get me to put my life jacket on before we left the shore. I certainly would have if it had been me and Zoe. I imagine any safety conscious person would consider this the right order to do things in.

Maybe my father just forgot about the life jacket. Perhaps he was trying to instill a feeling of surrendered helplessness in me, one that comes from committing unprepared to some unknown thing that is feared. And then the perceived safety - or perhaps more the resetting of our own reality - upon eventually adding that extra layer of protection.

Whatever the reason, once beyond the shore break, my father took my jacket out from under the seat and slid it over my head. He was careful to ensure each strap fitted snugly around me.

'How does that feel? Okay?'

I nodded slowly, admitting to myself that perhaps this wasn't going to be too bad. Sure, the dinghy was rocking like a cork in a bathtub and the motion made me feel a bit seasick. But at least I wasn't likely to fall out of the boat. And, anyway, now I had a life jacket on if things came to the worst. Which they wouldn't, I reasoned to myself. My father must know what he was doing. He had wanted to come out here after all, and he was always one hundred percent confident in the sea.

My father picked me up. It seemed as if he was about to hug me. He gently but firmly removed my arms from around his neck, and then he threw me headfirst into the water.

'He didn't!' Zoe gasps.

'You should see the look on your face,' I reply, trying not to laugh at her too much.

'Well, what a horrible thing to do to you,' she says. 'You must have been terrified.'

I nod, and then explain to Zoe how the impact of hitting the water knocked the air from my lungs. And the feeling of the cold. The intensity of it that crushed my chest like a vice. My whole body was submerged for what seemed like an eternity before the buoyancy of the life jacket finally bounced me back to the surface. I screamed at the same time as trying to breathe, also managing to swallow a mouthful of seawater in the process and which burned all the way down my throat. Another wave broke over me. I was dunked under again. I had my eyes open under the water the second time, and I could see the dark blue void that was doing its best to claim me. Struggling back to the surface, this time I realised the first thing I needed to do was to keep my mouth shut.

Amongst the cacophony of noise and the shock of the cold, from the confusion of the whining wind and the water slopping in every direction, I thought I could hear a voice.

'Swim Jase! Swim for shore!'

I floundered in the same spot for a few more seconds, resorting to doggy paddle rather than overarm before my brain managed to process what was going on. By now I was starting to shiver. Yes, I realised, my father had actually thrown me over the side and into the sea. Yes, it was on purpose. No, he was not going to help me.

My father was careful to keep the dinghy close by as an incentive, but just far enough off to one side so that I couldn't reach out and grab it for the reassuring protection I so desperately needed.

My father pointed towards the shore. 'Come on!' he yelled again, a huge grin on his face like this was the best thing in the world for any child to experience. In his mind, it probably was.

Even though I was young and there was so much I didn't understand about what my father was trying to get me to experience - whatever the hell his life lesson for this particular day was - I found that my fear turned to anger and my anger turned to action. When so desperately needed, I realised that at least I had something inside me that I could rely on.

I started to kick my legs as hard as possible, propelling myself away from the dinghy and my wildly grinning father. Using whatever means I could, I began to flounder back to shore.

III

Love or the lack of it has the tendency to make us do things we would not otherwise. We are faced with tough choices. We take risks. Maybe we become irrational in our actions. Or, maybe, we find that we can make the right decision even under pressure. My mother's love for her children - her need to protect us - no doubt influenced her decision to leave my father. To escape. To create an opportunity to start over.

As a youngster, I couldn't appreciate much more than what was in front of me. The sudden changes that were forced upon my day to day routines. The tearing apart of my family. The feeling of loneliness.

I can see that Zoe is mature enough to perceive other less obvious influences, and then want to understand them more. Her need to know is something I realise I can no longer deny her.

We had moved to what seemed like the end of the world. Despite there being a small town only half an hour's drive away, I still felt isolated. Lost. Alone.

There were barely a handful of cribs and other rundown buildings spread along the coastline and the rutted gravel road that headed inland. As I describe my first impression of the place to Zoe, I remember only too well the presence of sandflies and a near constant damp. The next outburst of rain felt like it was never far away.

'It's the most cleansing place in the country,' my mother had said, probably only half-jokingly, over breakfast after I returned from my walk along the beach and where I had met Kate for the first time.

'The rainfall here is measured in metres,' she added, 'Not centimetres like most parts of the country.'

'Yeah, like normal places,' Duncan added sarcastically.

Years later, someone told me that this part of the Coast was where people came if they were either running away or in search of something. And so, it was for us. Certainly, most who lived here seemed content to keep to themselves. Not unfriendly in any way, just accustomed to their own personal space and only choosing to make contact with any outsiders once they felt like it rather than because it was the expected thing to do. When I think about it now, I guess they were merely protecting their own right to privacy. And at least my family had a history here.

None of my concerns bothered my mother, of course. In her mind she was coming home. And it was an opportunity for her - for us - to start afresh. She made a point of explaining to Duncan and me during breakfast what the locals might be like. But my brother hardly seemed to be paying attention. He was too busy wolfing his cereal down, no doubt peeved that I had already beaten him to exploring outside. Being the oldest, he always wanted to be the first of either of us to discover anything new.

My mother sat between us with her cup of black, unsweetened coffee. She explained how our crib and the one next door, where my Uncle Francis and Aunt Nancy still lived, had been with her side of the family for almost a century.

'This area used to be a focus for gold mining,' she said. 'Thousands of people lived here during the rush.'

Apparently, her grandfather won both properties in an alcohol fuelled game of poker with another young miner. Duncan and I glanced at each other. Neither of us had heard this story before.

'They were drunk as skunks the pair of them, so the tale goes,' she said. 'Neither man realised what they had won or lost until waking up the next morning still half cut. For a change, Lenny Pops managed to make the right calls. By the sounds of it the other chap was lucky to get away with keeping his pants.'

We had a week before starting classes at the local school. Days disappeared in a blur of newness. Thinking back on it, and trying to work out which bits are worth telling Zoe, I can't remember much of what we did those first few days. Mostly, we explored our new surrounds, especially the beach and the estuary that stretched inland for miles. What stuck in my mind was seeing the mountains up close. And, of course, meeting Kate.

On one of the afternoons my mother took Duncan and me for a drive further inland, to a carpark where we could hike up to a local glacier that slid down from the mountains. The place where she had been able to get work guiding some of the busloads of tourists who traveled to the area every day to see it. The glacier, and especially its accessibility, was what this part of the Coast was most known for.

To me, the glacier looked like an icy serpent slithering out from its rocky lair, and the piles of rocks on top of it were its scales. Duncan reckoned it was more like a huge, glass staircase leading to the sky. As soon as he saw it he stated that one day he wanted to be able to climb up it to the snowy peaks that were waiting for him above. Before then, I had never really thought about climbing anything. For some reason, while standing there and looking at the glacier, the idea of trying to pick a way up it stuck in my mind. It was a jigsaw puzzle waiting to be put together.

Despite the weather being drizzly that day, we still walked partway up a stony riverbed until we could see the terminal face of the ice. At its base, the glacier had a dark, curving mouth where a river flowed out from. Every now and then blocks of ice would

31

break off the edge of the glacier and tumble into the river. Big bits falling and thudding earthward were enough to make the ground shake around us.

Groups of visitors passed us by, heading up and down valley and only pausing long enough to take photographs of each other or some scene that captivated them before hurrying on again. My mother explained to Duncan and me that the glacier had long been the main local tourist attraction, and how important it was to the town and the people living here.

'Most local income relies on it one way or another,' she said. 'Back in the day both my parents used to work up here. Cutting steps in the ice for all the tourists to follow. And I did too, when I was younger. Before I met your father. Did I ever tell you that?'

'Yes, Mum,' Duncan and I replied in unison. It was a story we had heard before, many times in fact, whenever our father was away with work and she had felt the urge to reminisce over a bottle of wine.

The local town was gathered along a single, main street. Surrounded by a dense forest that seemed more black than green, the town had a petrol station, three hotels for the tourists, the glacier guiding office with a helicopter pad out the back, an area school, a small grocery store and two pubs.

Later that same afternoon, while in town, we bumped into Kate and her father. It was the first time I had seen her since the beach, and I recall my heart doing a somersault or two. Kate's father and my mother recognised each other straight away. They hugged rather awkwardly, and Duncan sniggered until my mother told him to hush.

'These are my sons,' she said, turning to each of us. 'Boys, this is Dave…Mr Thompson.'

'How do you do?' Mr Thompson said in an obviously over-polite voice, almost in a way that suggested he was on our side, and which made Duncan and I grin. He stuck out his hand.

'This is Duncan,' my mother said. 'He's sixteen.'

'A big sixteen,' Mr Thompson said, pumping my brother's hand up and down with a vigorous handshake that Duncan had trouble matching.

'And, this is Jase. Wait…. You turn fifteen next December, don't you?'

'This February, Mum,' I replied quietly, glancing towards Kate and feeling myself blush.

'Oh,' my mother replied. Then she tried to cover her mistake by making a joke. 'Are you sure about that?'

I was too embarrassed to reply.

'Ah, so this is the famous Jase. I believe you two have already met,' Mr Thompson said when he turned to me. 'Lurking on the beach the other morning, wasn't it? If my daughter tells me correctly.'

My mother had an odd look on her face. 'Really? You've met Kate? You never told me that.'

'Oh, yeah,' I replied, trying to make myself appear relaxed about the whole thing. 'It just happened. No big deal, Mum.'

I glanced towards Kate for confirmation, like it was our secret and only to be shared if we wanted. But she was hardly bothering to make eye contact with me. In fact, I found it strange the way she was acting, so offhand towards me, and especially after she had been talkative and friendly when we bumped into each other on the beach.

Kate shrugged her shoulders. And then she looked away as if she was becoming bored with the whole interaction. She didn't appear to be interested in my company in the slightest, or even polite enough to say hello to Duncan.

It was then that I noticed my brother was also staring intently across to the other side of the road. He was looking anywhere that was not in the vicinity of Kate.

33

Our new school was a renovated farmhouse on the northern outskirts of town. It had a square of asphalt for padder-tennis and a single hoop for netball practice, and next door was the neighbour's house cow paddock which doubled as a rugby field. Warm cowpats added an extra element during ruck and maul time or during lunchtime games of bullrush.

There were around 30 students enrolled at the school, two classrooms, one full time teacher Mr Tupuna, one part time teacher Mrs Shaw who was the wife of the petrol station owner, and a couple of parents who came to help during Tuesday and Thursday afternoon sport.

Duncan had been placed in the other, older classroom. The same class as Kate. I don't know how they worked the student separation out as I was the oldest in my class by quite a bit. At the time, it grated on me that I hadn't also been put in the senior class. I was sure in my mind that it must have been a conspiracy to keep me from spending any more time in the presence of Kate.

Not that it would likely have made any difference, not at the beginning anyway. Depending on the day or who she was hanging out with, I quickly realised that Kate could be hot or cold around me at school. Sometimes she would take the time to say 'hi', but other times she would act like either she didn't know who I was or didn't particularly care.

Once I got used to her attitude, I guess it wasn't such a big deal. Not really. Kate had this way about her that meant I couldn't take my eyes off her whenever she was around or however she acted towards me. Sometimes I might lose sight of her, but then I would hear her voice, or the sound of her laughter and I would recognise it straight away. I could sit quietly and watch from a distance whatever she was doing, happy for the time being just to observe.

Watching Kate whenever I could, as well as starting a new school and learning its routines, was enough to keep my mind off the separation of my parents and the upheaval of our lives. Life might never be the same again but, for the time being, I found myself preoccupied.

For the first few days and then weeks on the Coast, I still thought about my father a bit. To be honest, it was probably more so than when he was a major part in my life back in the city. It wasn't that I missed him - being around him was sometimes like walking over broken glass - but more that I needed to find someone, or something, to fill his absence.

As more and more time drifted by, I came to think less about him or be influenced by how he had acted towards me. It was six months before he made an effort to come and visit us on the Coast. After only one night he blurted out an excuse about having to leave again. He stayed at a hotel in town, and he and my mother barely spoke five words to each other the whole time.

My father was happy enough to go his own way. I could be mistaken, but I reckon that Duncan and I didn't count in his plans. My mother said that he had found work on a fishing boat and was away from land sometimes for months without a break. Thinking about how much he connected with the water, I reckon it was probably the best job he could have hoped for. The time at sea might have been an excuse for him not making much of an effort with us.

After a while, I came not to care either way. The mountains and the ocean had grown to separate us. The huge expanse that they covered seemed appropriate.

IV

We were invited to Uncle Francis and Aunt Nancy's place for dinner the first night they returned home from a trip up north. Before Duncan and I were allowed to head over, my mother made us wash our faces, put on clean and ironed shirts, and brush our hair.

She said there was much we could learn from our uncle and aunt, especially if we wanted to fit in around here. 'They know how to get by on the smell of an oily rag. Living off the land. Most things they grow or catch or shoot. Frank especially is an institution round these parts. You would do well to pay attention to what he has to say. Own little and spend less is his motto. The way things were done back in the day and the way they should still be done.'

Duncan and I looked at each other. It seemed quite a speech, and I wondered what was motivating it. No doubt my mother was feeling nervous about the family get-together, and she wanted us to make a good impression with our relations. I was more than a little curious myself, as I had never met either of them. I recalled my mother talking about having a brother back when we were living in the city, but that had been pretty much it.

No sooner had we walked in the door before Aunt Nancy was trying to envelop us in a bear hug.

'I have been looking forward to this day for so long,' she said.

Duncan pulled a face as she squeezed him to her ample chest. I tried not to snigger at his obvious discomfort, but then it was my turn. After she had finished smothering me, she held me at arm's length.

'Let me get a good look at you. Ooooh, don't you take after your mother? Don't you reckon, Francis? Stop whatever it is you're doing and come take a look, will you.'

Aunt Nancy was kind and bubbly from the get-go. She took every opportunity to spoil my brother and I, handing us sweets and winking and nodding if we tried to sneak small sips of alcohol from the adult's glasses or when we asked to go back for another helping of dessert.

My uncle on the other hand, well he seemed like a man who had little he wanted to talk about or at least to us youngsters. And it wasn't until I met him then, for the first time, that I suddenly realised he must be the same 'Old' Frank that Kate had mentioned on the beach. I also understood how she was confused that I didn't know him.

Uncle Frank had grey hair and a beard with grey, brown and ginger flecks through it, and what seemed like a permanent frown. He sat quietly at the head of the dinner table as my mother and aunt chatted about how things were progressing on the Coast, taking his time to savour his beer and his meal.

From time to time, I saw him peer at Duncan or me over the top of his reading glasses. I tried not to stare at the small bits of salad that were getting caught in his beard.

'What sport are you in to?' he asked Duncan suddenly as the dessert plates were being cleared.

Duncan shrugged his shoulders. 'I don't know. Anything, I guess. Everything. Don't mind really.'

'A layabout, eh?' Uncle Frank replied, but in a way that meant he could have been joking. Duncan looked towards our mother to see if she was going to say anything, to support Duncan's self-belief in his sporting prowess. When she did not say anything, it was surprising that my brother didn't come up with one of his smart replies.

Then my uncle turned towards me. 'What about you, Sawn Off?' he said.

I stared at him and he stared back. He had just enough of a glint in his eye that I took his question to be one of those tests. That he was purposefully being bolshy to see how I would respond.

'I'm up for whatever you have in mind, Old Frank,' I replied, offering the widest grin I could muster. At the same time, I had my fingers crossed under the table.

My uncle kept staring at me for a few, long seconds, and I wondered if I had blown it by pushing things too far. I glanced towards my mother to see her expression. She was looking down at the table. It took me a few moments to realise how hard she was trying to keep her emotions contained.

Aunt Nancy was the first to break. She started a high-pitched squealing, and which took a second for me to recognise as laughter. Then the whole table erupted. By the end of it my uncle had tears streaming down his face, and my mother looked like the weight of the world had just been lifted from her shoulders.

I understood what Kate meant when she described Old Frank as only pretending to be grumpy all the time. What I originally took as my uncle being unfriendly was probably more of an attempt at hiding his shyness, especially around young boys who might have endless questions about every awkward topic imaginable.

Old Frank was actually rather observant towards Duncan and, it especially seemed, towards me. He had a dry sense of humour. Through the evening we seemed to warm to each other's company. He could explain things in such a way so that I understood what he was on about. He especially liked to talk about the environment and how precious it was, not just here on the Coast but everywhere.

'Take the big cities,' he said. 'Where you all have been living for far too long. Shit's going to come up and bite them slickers on the arse soon enough. You just watch.'

Duncan and I looked at each other, as if to confirm what he'd just said. And then we laughed.

'Francis!' Aunt Nancy called out from the kitchen. 'Language in front of minors if you will!'

My uncle scratched his beard. 'Well it is. What else do you want me to call it. Shit? Poos? Faeces?'

'Jase, why don't you tell your uncle about your interest in birds,' my mother suggested, walking into the lounge with a hot drink for her brother and obviously trying to change the topic.

'I saw a kea the other day,' I said. 'Well, I reckon it was.'

My uncle nodded. 'Tough lives they have up there in the hills,' he replied. 'Go and introduce a bunch of mustelids, what do you think's going to happen? Poor blighters have no idea what they're supposed to do. Got the tools that's for sure. A beak this big. Take your nose off it could, clean as a whistle.'

He leaned towards me and made a sweeping motion with his hand, brushing the tip of my nose. Then he poked the end of his thumb between two fingers, imitating that he had, in fact, stolen my nose without me realizing.

I grinned. 'I'd love to see one,' I said, the excitement obvious in my voice. 'Up close I mean.'

'Sure, Sawn Off,' My uncle replied. 'We might be able to arrange that.'

It did not surprise me that Duncan wasn't interested in the discussion Old Frank and I were having. He didn't have the same interest in birds that I did. I guess, for him, any consideration about the environment should have been more focussed towards having adventures in it.

As Old Frank and I talked, my brother wandered around the living room. Clearly, he was getting bored. There was a big ginger cat sleeping on a cushion on the floor in the corner. It had long grey whiskers, scars on its face, and one ear was mostly missing. Old Frank and I watched as Duncan bent forward towards it, reaching out with his hand.

'I wouldn't do that if I were you,' Old Frank said. 'Take your arm clear off, it might.'

My brother made a scoffing sound. But he decided to give the cat a wide enough berth, just in case. Then his ears pricked up when Old Frank mentioned the possibility of taking us all on a hunting trip sometime. He came and sat down next to me.

'Really?' he asked. 'What for? Deer? Pigs?'

'What's this?' my mother said, walking back into the lounge with her drink and only catching a small part of the conversation.

'Old Frank's taking us hunting in the morning,' Duncan replied.

My uncle chuckled. 'Well, I guess we could. Only if your mother thinks it's a good idea.'

'I don't know,' my mother said.

Duncan gave his most convincing smile. 'Oh, go on Mum.'

Old Frank looked up towards his sister. 'It'll be fine, Helen. Bit of scrambling round in the bush will be good for these tackers, don't you reckon? For all of us.'

Then Old Frank turned to me. 'Have you ever had wild pork crackling?'

I shook my head.

'Oh, it's the best,' he said. 'You just wait, Sawn Off.

V

I can still clearly remember the racket of the rain on the roof the morning we planned to go pig hunting. It was the heaviest rain I'd ever heard up until that point, sounding more like a waterfall as it poured over the roofing iron of our crib. Old Frank admitted that, even by Coast standards, it was fair bucketing down.

But my uncle reckoned the weather should clear up soon enough, and we still decided to go. Leaving the crib in the dark, we drove through town in Old Frank's old Land Cruiser and then further inland along a gravel road that couldn't make up its mind which direction to take. The road got narrower and windier the further we went, and I felt carsick by the time we finally stopped.

Duncan and I sat and waited in the backseat of the Cruiser. Despite the weather, my mother and uncle were standing outside talking. The rain was not as heavy, but it persisted against the roof of the truck. Even inside, the air was cold.

My brother gave me a whack on the shoulder. 'It'll be your fault if we can't go,' he said.

'Why's it always my fault?'

'Because. That's what being younger is. Don't you know anything?'

Then my brother held a finger to his lips. 'Shhh. Listen to what they're talking about. Can you hear?'

I nodded. The voices were muffled, but I could make out just enough of the conversation. I wiped the fogged-up window so I could see them better.

'He's still quite small for his age,' my mother was saying quietly, holding her hand at shoulder height to accentuate the point.

Old Frank scratched the back of his head, mumbling something I didn't catch.

'...just hasn't filled out the same,' my mother continued. 'He doesn't have the same resilience as his brother. You must recognise it.'

'Told you,' Duncan said.

'Shut up, will you! I can't hear if you keep friggen talking.'

Old Frank said nothing for a bit. He leaned forward, his elbows resting on the back of the truck. When I turned to look out the back window I could see his hunting dogs Sarge and Patch and our pet Sugar on the back tray. The dogs were still on their short chains. Despite the rain, they sniffed the air and looked about as if to inquire what the holdup was for.

Old Frank reached forward to give Patch a scratch behind his ear. The dog's leg thumped noisily against the tray.

My mother looked at the sky, then at Old Frank.

My uncle smiled. 'Helen, I reckon this should still push through,' he said, glancing up again. 'It will be fine, or certainly by the time we get to the clearing.'

'I guess so. That wind has swung southwest already. It'll be cool on the tops, though.'

Old Frank said something else, but I couldn't hear the words because Duncan was shuffling around while retying his boot laces. Then my uncle ran his thumb and forefinger down his beard as if he was pondering some other issue.

My mother let out a sigh. 'All right,' she said. 'But if anything goes wrong, I'm telling the authorities you made me do this, bad parenting or no bad parenting.'

Old Frank laughed. He had a good laugh, loud and erratic like it had taken control of him rather than the other way around.

My mother shook her head, but then couldn't help grinning back at her brother.

'I'd better throw in a change of clothes for them just in case,' she said. 'You've got that tent fly?'

Old Frank nodded.

My mother must have known that Duncan and I were trying to listen to the conversation. Likely she struggled with when to protect us as children and when to let us find our own path towards becoming young adults. Especially when it came to heading into the back country for the first time and in average weather conditions.

My brother and I remained sitting inside the vehicle. We knew to wait until she tapped her knuckles against the window before opening the doors. It was one thing to eaves drop on their conversation, quite another to act on it without being told you could.

There was not much of a trail to follow. In places we had to force through thick scrub. It scratched the narrow strip of exposed flesh between my shorts and the gaiters that Old Frank had loaned me. The cuts stung, but if Duncan wasn't complaining then I wouldn't either.

In my mother's hand was an old lever action Winchester 44-40 rifle. She carried it unloaded, the bullets threaded in the belt at her waist. She had always been a stickler for what she thought was the right way of doing things. It was the first time I'd seen her with a rifle, and the sight of her holding it made me wonder what else there was about her that I didn't know or understand.

I also noticed that Old Frank didn't have a rifle. 'This is all I need for porkers,' he said, tapping at the long, bone handled Bowie knife tied to his waist, then making a few imaginary stabbing motions with his hand.

The rain got heavier again. It slapped the ground so hard we could hear each new downpour approaching across the river flats. The dogs barked from somewhere down on the flats. As we approached the river the roar of rushing water killed the sound of our boots across its gravel banks. Old Frank was out in front. He shuffled efficiently across the boulders despite them being slippery with moss. He never seemed to falter. Thick in the body, and almost as short as I was back then, I noticed that he kept his boots close to the earth and made sure they were flat each time he stepped down. I kept watching his movement, trying to mimic him as best as I could.

'Been a while since I was last here,' my mother said to her brother when they paused to study the lay of the land ahead of us.

'How many years, you reckon?' he asked.

'Shit, I've lost count. Too many. Seems to have hardly changed though. Especially the wet stuff.'

'Just like riding a bike,' Old Frank said with a grin.

My mother turned to Duncan and me. 'You know the best thing about the rain?'

My brother and I looked at each other. After a while Duncan shrugged his shoulders.

'It makes the trees grow?' I answered.

'The sandflies hate it because they don't own raincoats.'

Duncan shook his head. 'You need some better jokes, Mum.'

'Or don't bother at all,' Old Frank added, before letting out a small chuckle. 'Spare us all the misery of hearing them, that would.'

Old Frank was first to reach the toe of a wooded spur. Through the mist I could see him up ahead, leaning against a tree stump like this was nothing more than a casual saunter across his backyard to the woodpile. At least the rain seemed to be easing to a stubborn drizzle.

'That coffee's kicked in,' My mother said when we all caught up. She passed the rifle to my uncle and lowered her pack to the ground.

Old Frank watched her walk off into the bush before he spoke. 'How're you boys doing?'

'Good,' Duncan replied.

I peered from under the brim of my jacket. 'Okay. Maybe. A little bit cold, I guess.'

'He's fine,' Duncan said. 'Don't be a sissy.'

Old Frank and Duncan stared at each other for a few, weighted seconds. Eventually my brother turned away.

My uncle stepped closer to me. 'Are you shivering?'

'No. Just my fingers are starting to get numb.'

'Here, slip your arms back inside your coat. That's it. Now put your hands under your armpits. Better?'

I nodded. Duncan had walked off a ways. He kicked at a stone to make it obvious how keen he was to get a move on.

'You let me know once you've had enough,' Old Frank said in a quiet voice so my brother couldn't hear. He placed his hand on my shoulder, and I remember feeling the strength of it and being reassured by that.

'We can come on back any other day,' he added. 'Those grumpy old tuskers ain't going nowhere.'

I sat on my mother's pack to rest. Sticking my tongue out, I tried to catch the raindrops.

My uncle kept watching me. 'You're not really bothered by this, are you Sawn Off?' he said.

I shrugged my shoulders. 'I'm okay. Just my fingers is all.'

'Resilient wee tacker, I'll give you that.'

I grinned. 'Where are we going from here?'

Old Frank pointed. 'See the spur up there? There's a trail that leads right on up through the forest, then to a pass near the top of the bush line, and down the other side into another valley. There's a clearing over that way where the pigs like to root about. We should hopefully find some good sign.'

The spur Old Frank was pointing to disappeared up into the

mist. After a time, my mother returned. She looked at Duncan pacing backwards and forwards and kicking at stuff, then at Old Frank and me. She nodded her head at the sleeves of my jacket.

'Who stole your arms?'

It took us two hours to reach the pass. In that time the rain stopped and sunlight seemed like it might actually filter through the cloud. My uncle pointed out how we must be nearing the top of the bush line because most of the trees around us had grown stunted. I tilted my head to match the same, deformed angle of their branches.

'Flag form,' he explained. 'That's what they're called when they grow this way. It's to cope with the direction of the wind.'

'They look like they're crippled old men,' Duncan said, stealing a glance at Old Frank.

'Easy on the crippled,' my uncle replied, elbowing Duncan in the ribs and pretending to scowl.

Over another short rise, and the earth dropped away sharply. The rough track we were following kinked to the left but it seemed as if the four of us had suddenly become detached from the land. Clouds shifted beneath our feet. It felt like we were floating.

'Hey Zoe, have you ever stood on the edge of a high cliff face and peered over?'

'Not really,' she replies, looking embarrassed. 'I'm a bit scared of heights.'

'Nothing to be self-conscious about. Lots of people don't like heights. I'm terrified of flying.'

My admission makes her smile.

'You? Mum reckons you're the only person she knows who's not afraid of anything.'

'Oh, there's plenty enough things that I'm scared of. Your mother's one of them too!'

As Zoe laughs at my joke, I am trying to work out how to explain to her the feeling of being perched on top of an abyss like the one I was experiencing as a youngster. Right at those moments when life is held on a knife edge. A shuffle forwards and everything must surely end. Even at that age I could feel the darkness, wonder at its elusiveness, at what might exist there just out of reach. Looking over the ledge felt hypnotic, until it almost seemed that I had to jump to find out.

There have been other instances since then when I have been overcome with the same urge, perhaps not quite as strong as that first time. I think my mother understood all of this. She may have gone through similar experiences. The intensity that comes with the emotional weightlessness of such an extreme exposure. That was why she stood so close to me that day, her arms taunt and ready, just in case.

Maybe everyone has the potential to be seized by such a moment, I tell Zoe. Something that's random or planned. Maybe it causes us to teeter, either knowingly or not, on the edge of a really big drop like the one I was standing before. Or it could be a decision of some kind. Before us is a possibility – a goal, perhaps, or a dream – and it can be both exciting and terrifying at the same time.

And this idea that drives us forwards, pushing us towards dealing with whatever edge might exist hidden in the cloud, it has to be greater than the fear that holds us back.

'Look,' my mother said, finally choosing to break the moment by pointing across the valley. The sound of her voice made me realise how close she was standing to me. I had been so hypnotised by the space beneath my feet that I completely missed the huge mountain looming above the other ridge. There was one steep, dominant rock ridge - The Buttress, my mother called it - that we could see leading upwards like the blade of a huge knife. And the very summit stretched so far above us that its sharpness seemed to stab at the sky.

'That is so neat!' Duncan exclaimed. My brother always had a need to speak whenever he experienced something different and exciting, as if he needed to make his mark on it straight away.

I was too stunned to say anything. Instead, I just stood there and stared. The summit appeared as perfectly shaped as a triangle. I had seen enough mountains since we'd moved to the Coast but not like this, not after having to work so hard against the altitude and the rain and cold, to finally reach a high viewing point just as the weather cleared and I was left giddy from exposure, and then to gaze over an untracked landscape, feeling that, perhaps, one could be approaching somewhere near the ends of the earth. I felt my heart beating quickly from the exertion of the climb but also because of the unexpected presence of this mountain before us.

'Isn't she something?' my mother said.

The clouds parted a little more, allowing even brighter light to spread over the summit and down to the valley beneath our feet. A veil had been lifted, perhaps just for us. For me.

'How high is it?' Duncan asked. 'Is it the highest?'

'No. Not the highest. But don't you worry, it's plenty big enough. And tough to climb too.'

'That'll be fresh snow on top,' Old Frank noted, a man of the backcountry but the first to admit he had never been drawn to climbing more than what was necessary.

My mother nodded. 'Just a wee skiffle from that last southerly by the looks.'

Duncan searched for a map in the top pocket of my mother's pack. He tried to work out which peak we were looking at.

'I think it's the biggest,' he finally said. 'Around here anyway. How do we get to it? I want to go there.'

'Well...,' my mother replied slowly. 'There's not an easy trail to follow to the top. That's for sure.'

I sat next to one of the stunted trees, holding my hand up to shield the sunlight from my view. Nothing could have prepared me for this, of such a sight that in the coming years I would come to treasure and then hate, that would dictate moods and decisions and encourage in me a more reckless desire like the one that Duncan was already beginning to exhibit, as well as an outlet for a growing competitiveness between the two of us. I felt lightheaded by the prospect, and more than a little overwhelmed.

To be honest, and I don't mind sharing this with Zoe, there are times when I wish I had never laid eyes on that bloody mountain.

Duncan stepped right in front of me to give himself a better angle of the peak, partially blocking my view in the process.

'I'm going to climb it,' he announced, completely unaware of what saying those words meant or the cost that might be associated with them. He only knew that, one day, he would dare himself to stand at the highest point possible. He had seen a worthy goal that he wanted to attain.

My mother looked at each of us in turn.

'Perhaps you'll get up it one day,' she said. 'Or at least try. But only if you train really hard. Both of you. Working together as a team. And if you're more than a bit lucky. There's always luck involved in mountaineering.'

'Have you climbed it?' I asked, suddenly wondering because her knowledge of it seemed so personal.

She made a clucking sound with her tongue. 'Got close once or twice a while back. Still time though, eh? Or do you reckon I'm getting past it?'

It took me a moment to realise that she must be joking.

'We could do it together,' I said.

'Maybe we could.'

'You'll have to train really hard first though,' I added, trying not to grin.

Old Frank burst out laughing, and my mother reached over to

tussle my hair.

'Cheeky whippersnapper,' she said. 'It'll be a wee while yet before you can think about heading up a mountain like that.'

Old Frank looked at the position of the sun and then at his sister. My mother nodded, picking up her pack and the rifle.

'Come on you lot,' she said. 'We've about wasted enough of the day gas bagging. Enough resting on your laurels. Let's go find some fat sow to take home for dinner.'

We dropped off the ridge, following another slippery, muddy track down past more stunted trees, eventually reaching the forest-filled valley I had been looking at from the pass. I kept glancing up to try to see the mountain again. But the forest was now blocking my view.

Down in the valley, Old Frank took a dog whistle from the pocket of his raincoat. No sound emitted to my ears but clearly the dogs heard it just fine. Scrub rustled nearby and they burst from it. Racing to be first, Patch and Sarge were well ahead of Sugar.

'Get away out will you,' Old Frank said. 'Go on now.'

The dogs milled around for a few seconds, Patch sniffing the ground and the first to head back upcountry, and with the others following along closely behind.

It must have been around the middle of the afternoon when the dogs finally got on to the scent of a pig. All of a sudden, they took off barking, disappearing from our view again and everyone chasing along behind. I had trouble keeping up with the others and, after a few minutes I thought I was alone. Voices called from dark places in the forest. I followed them as well as I could. I rushed past trees and fought tangles of undergrowth. I tripped and fell when supplejack captured my legs. Frantic to free myself, I rose from a mat of dead and dying leaves.

The voices came again. 'Come on. Where are you? What are you doing?' They felt directionless. Anonymous. Possibly threatening.

I thought I could see movement through the forest, but it was darkened and blurry and without the definition that comes with colour. Bellbirds questioned my slowness from branches overhead. I pulled against the wet sucking of mud at my boots. My heart pounded from the exertion and because I was suddenly afraid of being left behind.

Finally, I caught sight of my brother. He was waving at me from behind a fern. 'Hurry up, Jase. Can't you go any faster?'

'I couldn't find you. I'm trying.'

'Well, try harder.'

'Thanks for waiting,' I said.

'Mum told me to go back for you. Come on. I think we've almost got something.'

We reached Old Frank and my mother in a small, grassy clearing close to a stream bed, and to the shock and gore of shouting, thrashing, snarling bodies. At first it was the din that confused me. The noises were sudden and sharp and seeming to come from all directions.

My mother rarely if ever raised her voice, and I had never heard any dogs make noises such as what I was hearing then. But there was something else, something that sounded so unearthly.

The best way I can explain the sound to Zoe is for her to imagine a baby's crying somehow mixed with a deep-toned grunting. She is frowning at my description, but I do not know how else to describe it.

In the middle of the clearing was the lunging massif of a huge boar. A hulk of coarse hair and muscle fighting for survival, protecting itself at all costs. Protruding from its jaw were two long tusks, and they were gleaming red. It took me a moment to realise where most of the blood had come from. A crumpled, spasming form off to one side was Old Frank's dog Patch. My uncle was trying to reach in to drag his dog out of harm's way.

I wanted to cry out but couldn't get my mouth to work. My body no longer seemed my own.

My mother was shouting. 'Get up a tree you two! Get the hell out of the way and stay there!'

It seemed like my mind had become detached from my ability to react. I saw myself jumping for a low branch. But, with arms that were suddenly too heavy, I slipped back to the earth. There was another snarl behind me. For an instant I panicked at the unimaginable terror that must be approaching. The sound that it made was enough to freeze me to the spot.

I tried to swing up again but still couldn't. Then, for a moment, there was a feeling of hands pushing against my back. Duncan bumped into me again as he clambered up onto the same, low branch. My brother's eyes were wide, but with excitement rather than the absolute fear I was experiencing. I wrapped my arms tightly against the branch. More than anything I knew that I wouldn't want to watch what was happening below. I also knew that I couldn't help myself.

Sarge and Sugar barked and growled as they circled the boar. I really worried about Sugar. I didn't want her to end up like Patch. The dogs took turns darting in to nip at the pig's haunches, to try to get a firm grip, before drawing back each time it spun to face them.

Old Frank crouched behind the dogs, his knife in his hand.

'Get out of it you mongrels. Heel. Bloody well heel!'

Suddenly the boar charged. It caught Sugar in the shoulder, and the dog was flung around from the force of the blow. But she was okay. It was Patch who was still collapsed to the ground. Blood seeped from his neck and ears. He tried to stand up, but his front legs would not work properly. Old Frank swore again.

Sarge growled from the other side of the clearing. The boar pivoted to face him, allowing a brief opportunity for Old Frank to step forward to try to stab it in the neck. But the pig was still fresh, moving too quickly to be taken. My uncle had to stumble out of the way again.

'Now,' my mother shouted, still fumbling with a bullet from her belt and then cursing when she dropped it. Old Frank surged forward once more, this time grabbing at Patch by the scruff of his neck. But the rotten trunk my uncle had stepped on collapsed. He slipped over. The boar lurched towards him. I flinched when Old Frank cried out in pain.

Somehow my mother managed to force herself between her brother and the boar. She shouted and waved her arms, distracting the pig long enough for Old Frank to rise unsteadily to his feet. With blood seeping from his leg, this time he managed to drag Patch out of the way.

The boar spun around in another circle, trying to work out what to attack next or if there was an opportunity to run again. This gave my mother a brief chance to load her rifle. Two loud retorts from the Winchester finally echoed through the forest. The pig slumped to the ground, dead. Then came silence, like the releasing of a breath after it has been held for far too long. There was a pungent smell in the air from the rifle shots. My mother looked back up towards Duncan and me in the tree.

'You two okay?'

'Yep,' Duncan replied. I couldn't get my voice to work but managed a slight nod.

For a few moments I remained stuck to the branch, gripping it for all I was worth. Duncan had dropped to the ground, and I could see him walking slowly forward. He didn't even cast a glance over towards where Patch and Old Frank lay. He was more interested in the corpse of the pig.

I don't tell Zoe this, but I think that was the first time I saw my brother's rather matter of fact or some might even consider callous attitude towards life and death. He kicked the pig with his boot, and bent forward to touch the blood on its tusks. Then he sniffed his hands, smelling the redness. I half expected to see him taste it.

Even now, I haven't the foggiest idea what thoughts were going through his mind.

Finally, my limbs started to respond. I managed to slide from the branch. The earth felt unsteady and I couldn't decide whether to stand or sit. Old Frank was crouching over Patch. His dog was making wheezing noises while trying to breathe. My uncle gently stroked Patch's neck.

My mother stood close to Old Frank and she said something that I couldn't hear. I saw Old Frank shake his head, but my mother kept talking and nodding slowly. She put her arm around him for a few seconds.

Realising what my mother was about to do, I squeezed my eyes shut rather than watch her hold the barrel towards Patch's head. Despite being clearly in pain, the dog still managed to thump his tail gently on the ground in response to the added attention. Just before my mother levered another, final round into the chamber of the rifle, I heard a strange noise that I thought must have come from my uncle's dog. Then I realised it was from Old Frank.

VI

I look at Zoe, trying to gauge her reaction to what I have been talking about. About how Old Frank's dog died and how Duncan had reacted. Other than the smallest of frowns, her facial expression hasn't changed. It does not seem that my description of the incident has made her upset or squeamish.

'Were you scared?' she asks.

'Terrified,' I reply. 'Especially once I had time to think and take it all in. Things were happening so fast that it was more of a panicked rush at first.'

Zoe nods.

'It was much worse for Old Frank,' I add. 'After all, he was the one injured. And he lost Patch too.'

I explain how my mother bent to look at the wound in Old Frank's calf. It was puckered at the edges like the petals of a small, red flower, a bit like one of the flowers from that rātā tree, I say to Zoe, pointing at the window.

Finally, Zoe pulls a face. 'Ouch! That must have hurt.'

My mother poured water over Old Frank's wound before wiping away the grime and then dousing it with whiskey from a hipflask which was in my uncle's pack. She passed the flask to Old Frank. Fresh blood trickled from the wound. My mother placed a dressing over it and held her hand firmly on top. Blood oozed through the fabric. After a time the bleeding eased. She removed the dressing and studied the wound again.

'How's it feel?'

Old Frank grimaced. 'Ha! As you'd expect.'

My uncle had scrunched up against a log. He closed his eyes, and he draped one arm over Sarge when his dog came up for a pat. Duncan was leaning over my mother's shoulder to watch how she treated the wound. He flinched at the depth of the gash but didn't turn away. My mother finally realised he was there, and she handed him a drink bottle.

'Can you go and fill this down in the river? Make sure the water is clean, okay?'

'Yes. Mum.'

I sat a short distance from the others and Sugar came and lay down beside me. She put her head on my lap and I scratched her behind her ears. I was so happy that she was okay, but then I felt guilty for thinking that. My head still felt dizzy. Everything seemed like it was from a bad dream. Through a mental haze, I half-watched my mother use narrow strips of tape to try and close Old Frank's wound. Then she replaced the dressing and started to wind a compression bandage around his calf. My uncle winced as she pulled the bandage tight. The adults looked at each other. My mother sighed.

'What a cluster fuck,' she said quietly, hoping that I wouldn't hear.

Old Frank nodded.

Now, I can imagine only too well the feeling the two of them must have carried, something cold and hard in their guts, a foreign object forced into their emotions that they had to come to terms with. The suddenness of the injury and death, but also a realization of how much worse things could have been.

For me, the shock of the situation was still too much to comprehend at the time. Not surprisingly, my mind felt drained of emotion. My limbs were dead-tired. Not my own. All my energy had been evaporated in the post-rush of a fight, freeze or flight response. But, in situations like this, there's nothing else that can be done afterwards. No other outcome can eventuate other than the one where the lives that remain somehow find the strength to carry on. I did not realise it at the time, but this was a lesson I certainly needed to learn from.

Old Frank glanced over towards me. 'How're the lads?' he asked in a low voice.

I followed my mother's gaze towards the river. Duncan was still out of sight. He must have needed to clamber down a bank to get to it.

'They'll be alright.'

Old Frank offered my mother the hipflask, but she shook her head.

'I'll bury Patch as best I can,' she said, glancing over at Old Frank's finder lying next to the corpse of the pig.

'No. I want to take him home.'

'Okay. We can do that.'

My mother peered through the trees to a square of sky. By now, it must have been quite late in the afternoon.

'Well, I guess we'd better think about getting out of here,' Old Frank said, trying to stand.

My mother placed a firm hand on her brother's shoulder. 'Hang on. I don't think you should be going anywhere.'

'I'll be fine.'

'You won't and you know it. The bleeding has mostly stopped, but if you try and walk a distance on it. Especially back up there. I can't tell. The artery could be damaged. If it ruptures....'

Old Frank took another sip from the flask.

'I can go now and be out maybe before midnight if I keep at it,' my mother continued. 'They should be able to come in by chopper first thing. Mid-morning at the latest. Just hope that next system stays away long enough is all.'

'And?' Old Frank asked, making a point of not looking in my

direction.

My mother frowned. 'What do you think?'

Old Frank stared at the sky. 'Looks like the weather will hold well enough,' he replied. 'I'm sure Duncan will be able to keep up with you.'

They both glanced at me.

'We'll be fine,' Old Frank said. He gave a wry smile. 'Good thing we grabbed that tarp and the extra clothes, eh?'

Thinking back, I cannot remember much of what my mother said to me next. No doubt it was something comforting about how well I had coped and that everything would work out okay in the end. I recall her patting me on the shoulder, but also the worried look that she couldn't quite manage to hide.

A kererū flew overhead. We all watched as it struggled to gain enough height to reach the next treetop. In the end the native wood pigeon crash-landed partway up the tree, sitting on a branch that bowed under the weight. Its head moved back and forth, as if it was trying to work out what had just happened. Old Frank mumbled about getting dinner on the wing.

'Make sure you stick close to your uncle,' my mother said, turning back to me. 'Do whatever he says, okay?'

Suddenly I understood. 'What? Are you leaving?'

She sat down next to me. 'You know I have to. If we all stay here help is that much further away. Frank won't get out of this on his own.'

'You always tell us to stay together in the outdoors. The most important thing, you say. Never get separated. Everyone is stronger if they work together.'

My mother wiped her face, leaving a smear of blood and grime across her forehead. 'I know,' she replied. 'I understand how you must be feeling, really I do. I wish there was some other option. But this has to be the way.'

I could tell from the tone in her voice that it was no use arguing any further. 'Yes, Mum.'

'Good,' she said, standing. 'Now, I'll see you both bright and early in the morning.'

It felt important that I fight back the tears, and I nodded through clenched teeth. I stood up beside her.

'Good lad,' my mother said, giving me a long hug.

Duncan looked like he wanted to say something to me.

'Come on Duncan,' my mother said.

My brother nodded at Old Frank, and he gave me a small wave before turning to follow our mother into the bush. Sugar came up for a pat, as if unsure where her loyalties should lie. Then she trotted after the others.

Old Frank made sure to keep me busy, making the most of the remaining daylight. Passing his knife over, he said to cut enough tree-fern leaves so they could be used as both a bed and blanket.

'Be sure you cut away from yourself,' he explained, and then demonstrating with both hands. 'That's right. Keep your other mitt clear. Wouldn't want you slipping and going home with one or two fingers missing now, would we? What would your mother be saying about that?'

I could tell my uncle was trying to cheer me up, and I tried to smile back. He pointed out which branches the tent fly should be tied to. I gathered enough dead wood and brush for a fire. Then I made a small circle of stones from the river. Cutting into the pig wasn't as bad as I imagined it to be. Old Frank explained where to strip away the hide and how to avoid puncturing the guts of the animal.

We cooked wedges of wild pork skewered onto thin branches of kānuka for dinner. The chunks of meat were tough and had a feral smell that made me queasy. It was odd feeling hungry and sick at the same time, but part of me took pleasure in feeding on the enemy.

'Be better with a dab of apple sauce, don't you reckon?' Old Frank said from the other side of the fire, pointing at the meat in my hands. His face glowed orange from the flames like he was badly sunburned. Or his was the face of a bearded spirit man hiding in the forest.

'You didn't bring some by any chance?' He added, grinning. I tried to summon enough energy to smile back.

'Oh, look at that,' he said, pointing up.

With everything else that had happened, I hadn't noticed that the mountain could be seen from our clearing. From this angle it appeared quite close. But it was the evening light against its summit that Old Frank wanted me to see. The snow had taken on a warm glow, not too dissimilar to the fire I had built.

'That light makes them look like the spirits the old people think they represent,' he said. 'Don't you reckon?'

I nodded, not really sure what my uncle was referring to about the old people and making a mental note to try to find out more about them when we got home. But it did look like the mountain had taken on a different personality to what we had seen from the pass.

The evening closed in. We stayed near the fire, its warmth a cocoon against the chill of the coming night. I put on the extra clothes that Old Frank had been carrying and now passed over to me. And then I kept watching the mountain as the light drained from its highest ridges. Finally, it too faded into the surrounding darkness.

Old Frank gave a quiet groan, and I looked over towards him.

'Is your leg real sore?'

'It's alright. Throbs a bit if I move about too much. Don't imagine I'll be running a marathon any time soon.'

I leaned forward to place another log on to the fire. It crackled and spat, and I held my hands to the renewed warmth.

'Quite a day eh,' Old Frank said. 'How are you feeling, Sawn Off?'

'I don't know. Tired. A bit weird.'

'That's okay. Nothing here that you need to make hide nor hair of. You understand?'

'Not really.'

Old Frank pushed himself up on one arm. He winced again. 'Sometimes things just happen. There's no reason to it or none that we can much fathom. We think we can, but that's not the same. There's good decision making and then sometime there's just plain bad luck.'

I did not know what to say so didn't say anything.

Old Frank looked like he was going to tell me something else, but then a whistle pierced the night. Rising in pitch, it sounded strange. Almost ghostlike. Sarge's ears pricked and he let out a low growl.

'Hush it, boy,' Old Frank said.

I turned my head, cupping hands to my ears like my mother had once shown me to work out where the sound had come from. There was a rustling of undergrowth not too far away.

'What is that?' I asked. 'Is it a kiwi?'

Old Frank nodded. 'Helen said you knew your birds. Fine skill to have that is.'

The kiwi called again. 'A Great Spotted by the sounds,' my uncle said, cocking his head so he could hear more clearly.

'I've never seen one.'

'You're not that likely to neither. But you sometimes get to hear them, especially this far into the back country. Make a racket don't they? You've got to be pretty lucky to actually spot one in the flesh. But they can be quite nosy when they've got a mind to it.'

'How big do they get?'

'About this.' Old Frank held his hand almost half a metre above the ground, and then made walking movements with his fingers while doing a side to side movement with his head.

We listened some more but did not hear the kiwi call out again. I leaned back from the fire so that I could see better. But the cold encouraged me to shuffle closer again to the flames. Later, we curled together for warmth. Sarge also pushed under the ferns. Old Frank fell asleep quickly like he was tucked up in bed at home. Then he farted, which made his dog sigh.

I did not think I would be able to sleep for a while. Too much had happened that my mind still needed to process. Lying there, I looked up through the canopy of trees to the stars. The mountain was now a black silhouette in the night sky. I tried to work out whether my mother and brother would have reached the truck yet, and I hoped that they were safe and warm wherever they had got to.

I wondered if another kiwi would call out again. Or even if the rare bird might decide to wander close enough to our camp that I could catch a glimpse of it. To see its tracks would be something to skite about later to Duncan. The elusiveness of the kiwi intrigued me. What did they look like in real life? I had seen photos in my bird book but they never did justice to the real thing. Their feathers were quite different from what I remembered reading and they had a long beak and really big, almost clown like feet.

If I was patient enough and spent more time in the forest, surely a kiwi would choose to show itself to me. Thinking these thoughts were enough to finally ease my worrying young mind towards sleep.

The time before dawn was the coldest. I woke up shivering, but Old Frank kept on snoring like a chainsaw. The cold was an ache that felt like it had reached deep into my bones, and I thought I should do something to warm up. Slipping from my uncle's grasp, I watched to see if he would waken. He twisted into a foetal position but still didn't stir. Sarge raised his head to acknowledge me but stayed curled up next to Old Frank.

Rising unsteadily, I looked about our clearing. A thin mist hugged the land. The light slowly lifted and I could see through gaps in the low cloud up to what looked like a clear sky. Part of me was disappointed that the mist still hid the mountain. It was being elusive, just like the kiwi from the previous night. Another shiver ran through my body. I figured that if I did some vigorous exercise that should warm me up. I star jumped until my breath quickened. I exhaled small vapours in the morning air. Warmed blood started rushing through my body, and my arms and my legs throbbed with the relief of pins-and-needles.

Once my breathing settled down, I noticed how thirsty I was. Small birds preceded me as I walked down to the river to refill both my and Old Frank's water bottles. Flitting from branch to branch, they peeped at me and each other – riflemen or brown creepers, I thought. They did seem quite chatty and pleased with themselves, which encouraged me to think that things weren't too bad after all. This was certainly turning out to be quite an adventure.

The water from the river was so cold that it made me cough. But it helped to jolt my brain awake. Looking around was like for the first time. The clearing seemed peaceful and still, so different to what we had experienced the day before. I sat on a grassy bank above the river, happy to watch the water flowing by and listen to its gurgle. I hoped the mist would part so I could get another glimpse of the mountain.

A while later what sounded like a mosquito started buzzing near my ear. I waved my hands about trying to shoo it away. But the sound remained. If anything, it got louder. I cupped my hands to my ears, eventually realising that the noise was actually the low thumping of an engine. I figured that it could only to be the rescue helicopter. As I listened more, I decided that it sounded like the wings of a bird, a really large bird that had been watching from some high crag somewhere on the mountain. And now it was coming to save us.

I scrambled back up the short rise to our makeshift camp. Old Frank was still sleeping like the dead, but I thought that tipping a bottle of cold water over him ought to do a half decent job of waking him up.

VII

I hope I can be present to help protect Zoe through her first, no doubt gut wrenching, experience of falling in love. That instant when it stabs her right in a place she doesn't even know she has. It will hurt but hopefully in a good way. For all I know, she may have already experienced it.

I can still remember the sheer joy of realising such a feeling existed, and that there was a possible source for replenishing everything wonderful in my life. I was uplifted. Bulletproofed against the loneliness of the world.

But then, and I certainly don't know how to explain this to someone Zoe's age, consider another memory. The one when you suddenly realise how vulnerable you have become upon recognising the existence of this feeling. What if things go wrong? If being with someone can make you feel so alive in the glow of their aura, what about the possibility of that being taken away from you? The control that person now has over your emotions seems so unfair.

As chance would have it, the pig hunting trip eventually led me to such a realisation. I learned about risk and consequence and how to protect ourselves from whatever the elements threw at us. But the bigger lesson was from what happened with Kate afterwards.

My mother, Duncan and I were having breakfast at the kitchen table when there was a knock at the door. It was Kate. She had brought a copy of the local newspaper over from their place to show us an article in it. I was surprised to see her, especially after that awkward meeting in town with her father and then later at school when she hardly seemed to acknowledge my existence. Yet here she was in our kitchen, enthusiastic and happy and smiling at me just like the first time we had met on the beach.

'You look like a scared rabbit,' she said, pointing at the photo on the front page of the newspaper.

'Gee, thanks.'

'No, silly. Rabbits are cute. Their fur smells really nice when you snuffle them.'

My cheeks reddened, and I almost choked on my cereal. Looking up, I could see that my mother was trying to keep from grinning.

'Jase, the bunny boy,' my brother said, jabbing me in the ribs.

'Duncan!' my mother scolded. 'That's enough. Clear the plates if you've finished.'

My mother let me read the article first. 'Mountain Rescue' was in bold letters across the top of the page. The story told how local climbing guide Helen Williamson had trekked half the night through rugged bush to save her injured brother and youngest son.

My mother read the article over my shoulder. She shook her head at the description, and even I realised that the reporter had gone a bit over the top with every detail. The story ran next to a photo of Old Frank being transferred from the rescue helicopter to a waiting ambulance. I could be seen still sitting inside the chopper, a rescuer leaning over me to undo my seatbelt.

'You were really brave, Jase,' Kate said. 'Spending the night in the bush like that and without a sleeping bag or a tent. I bet it was cold and scary out in the middle of nowhere.'

Too tongue tied to reply, I managed to nod my head and shrug my shoulders at the same time.

'What about me?' Duncan complained. 'I was the one who had

to walk out in the dark for help.'

Kate made a point of ignoring my brother. I sat there and watched the two of them. Up until then I hadn't really known what jealousy might feel like, the wedge that can be suddenly driven into your emotions. But I also realised it was me Kate was paying attention to. After all, she was the one who had made the decision to come over and show me the story.

'Old Frank was pretty warm,' I finally stammered, trying to draw attention back to what I had been through, and instantly regretting such a lame comment.

'Sissy,' Duncan muttered from beside the kitchen bench.

'I heard that,' my mother said.

'Well, he is.'

'Duncan! For that you can do the dishes as well. Wash and dry them.'

My brother looked like he was going to say something else, but my mother stared at him until he turned back to the sink. I could hear him muttering away in the background but didn't care. I had someone much more important to focus on.

'You were being smart,' Kate said, smiling at me again. And what a smile. Her face lit up like it was only me she was interested in. Her teeth were so white. Her eyes a shade of blue I couldn't quite pin down. It was all I could do to stay sitting there and be sure not to say anything else that might embarrass me further.

Not that there was much else to say. I didn't recall much of the helicopter rescue, the flight a noisy blur with colours flashing beyond the window. A glimpse of a mountain summit that I thought I recognised as we passed it by.

I certainly remember the feeling of relief after we landed in town behind the guiding office, and especially when I saw my mother next to the ambulance. She stood there, her arms folded and with that concerned frown I knew and loved, waiting impatiently until one of the rescue team had escorted me clear of the helicopter. I hugged her as hard as I could.

I wondered whether to tell Kate about any of this. But I didn't. If nothing else, I wasn't about to give Duncan ammunition to tease me with later. He already had more than enough.

'Not surprisingly,' I say to Zoe, 'it was a while before I wanted to go pig hunting again.'

Zoe grins and nods. 'Yeah, I can understand that,' she replies. 'It must have been a terrifying experience.'

I tell her how I didn't sleep very well the first few nights back at the crib. Any noise and I would wake suddenly, imagining I was still in the forest and the wild boar hiding somewhere nearby in the darkness. Lying there, I imagined hearing footsteps in my room. The thought of them made my heart race.

One day Duncan felt the need to clarify that the accident only happened because of me. He could have been jealous because Kate had been paying more attention to me rather than him. I reckon it was also his way of finding something or someone else to blame. Maybe he thought he was explaining it like it was not totally my fault. He was just being a protective big brother.

'You know I'm not pointing the finger,' he said. 'But if you had been able to keep up with the rest of us perhaps the accident wouldn't have occurred. Mum never drops anything. She was worrying too much about you.'

I started to say something, but then stopped. What was the point? When my brother had his mind set on a view like this, there was no way I was going to change it.

'Look,' he continued. 'I'm sure you'll be able to come again, but maybe not for a while. When you're taller. A bit stronger. That way you can keep up better.'

Those comments stung, and they stayed with me long after my brother had said them. Whenever I would be faced with an overwhelming challenge, I recalled his doubting my ability. His lack of belief added to my own. More often than not, I found myself choosing to turn and run away rather than take the risk of failure while trying.

On the other hand, I remember it was Kate who helped me the most. Maybe she realised how sensitive and insecure I was feeling. She made an effort to spend more time with me. During lunchtime at school we would sit together to eat our sandwiches, talking and looking up at the mountains. My mother had loaned me one of her maps so that I could show Kate all of the different summits. We worked out what each mountain was called, and what might be the best way to get to them. Even though we couldn't see it from school, I paid most attention to the particular mountain that had captured my attention at the pass. The one with such a symmetrical shape and the startling ridge line - 'The Buttress', my mother fondly referred to it as. I studied the contours of it on the map, where the river tributaries started, and the way the lay of the land sloped from the highest point. I still didn't understand what I was looking at, but every detail on the map inspired me.

I could not tell if Kate was interested in what I told her about the mountains, but she paid attention whenever I spoke. All of this probably helped me recover from the hunting trip. Especially my wondering whether the accident only happened because of me. She asked lots of questions about the trip, the accident, and the night after. Like how difficult it was looking after Old Frank in the forest.

Sometimes, I struggled to find the right words and I would end up looking helplessly at her.

'It's okay,' she said quietly. Then she put her arm around my shoulder. I tried not to cry.

Kate also got annoyed when I told her what Duncan had said to me about the accident being my fault.

'Don't be ridiculous,' she stated emphatically. 'Your brother doesn't have any idea what he's on about.'

Unsure what to say, I shrugged my shoulders. Kate took it that I was agreeing with her.

'I mean, these things can happen,' she added. 'People have gone into the bush and not come back at all. Disappeared without a trace, so Dad was telling me the other night. There are heaps of stories of that happening around here. I think you were really lucky and did everything that you could have. You should be proud of how you handled yourself in the wilderness.'

I looked at Kate and smiled. For the first time in a while, maybe since moving to the Coast, I felt happy. I enjoyed how much time we were spending together, and how she obviously cared for my feelings. It was not something I would have said to her, but part of me wondered if we might become more than friends. Not straight away of course, but maybe one day. I told myself that it didn't hurt to hope.

Kate called by on a particularly sunny Saturday afternoon to ask if I wanted to go for a walk with her along the beach. Just the two of us, she added. My mother said it would fine as long as I made sure to be back for dinner as Frank and Nancy were coming over.

'You can come too if you want, Kate,' my mother said. 'The more the merrier. It's only stew mind you, nothing fancy.'

'That would be lovely, thanks Mrs Williamson,' Kate replied. 'I'll just have to check with my parents first.'

Surprisingly, the beach was quite busy. There were groups of people spread along the sand enjoying themselves in the sun. As we walked, we could see two small boys – brothers perhaps because they looked similar – playing on one of the sand dunes. They had a plastic bucket and a spade and were partway through creating an impressive sandcastle.

'Shall we sit here a while?' Kate suggested, pointing at another dune not far from the boys. 'I want to see what they build.'

We watched the construction near its completion. But then the smaller of the two boys slipped over, accidentally standing on one of the turrets which had just been crowned with twigs and a stack of pipi shells. There was an angry shout and the larger child began chasing the smaller one, trying to hit him with the spade as they ran around in circles. Kate and I couldn't help but laugh. The smaller boy tripped over in the sand again, this time right into the middle of the sandcastle.

'Oh dear,' Kate said when the older boy started whacking the prone child on the backside.

'Serves him right for wrecking the castle,' I said, but not entirely convinced.

'No, it doesn't,' Kate replied. 'Not that much, anyway.'

A woman who had been sitting and reading on a towel nearby rushed down the beach to the commotion. There was a flurry of words and a quick slap across the bottom of the taller boy. Now both children were crying, and the woman continued scolding them as she dragged them towards the carpark.

Watching the two boys made me think about having Duncan as an older brother. How sometimes things between us seemed simple and natural, and yet other times everything became so complicated that I didn't know how to make him happy. I wondered if his brashness and self-confidence had nothing to do with needing to compete and be better than me. Rather - and I didn't realise this until years later - he was overcompensating because he felt so insecure.

Kate stood up, breaking my train of thought. 'Let's walk a bit more,' she said. 'There are way too many people here.'

Later, we sat on another sand dune further down the beach. There was no one else about. We looked out over the sea. Kate began talking about her classmates at school.

'I hate it, really,' she said. 'You do one thing wrong or say something that you haven't properly considered, and someone won't be your friend again. You might not even know what it was you did or said. But that doesn't matter because it's too late anyway. It's all so confusing.'

I nodded without really understanding. Kate was happy to talk about what was worrying her, and me just sitting there and listening was the best thing I could do.

'You know, Jase. It's like you and Duncan.'

The change in direction of the topic unsettled me. I picked up a stick and started drawing squiggly lines in the sand.

'What do you mean?' I replied, suddenly feeling self-conscious again.

'Well,' Kate replied, watching what I was drawing. 'Duncan likes to be the centre of everything. He has heaps of friends at school. Everyone is drawn to him. For his sportiness and over confidence as much as anything. His bravado. He's so cocky, don't you reckon?'

'I don't know. I guess so.'

'He's so mouthy about everything he's good at. Full of himself.'

'He's alright.'

'All right? He struts around like he owns the place.'

I wondered about Duncan but only for a short while. 'He doesn't do it as much as Rudolph,' I say, trying to change the focus of the conversation.

Kate frowned. 'Who?'

'Rudolph. Old Frank's cat. You know, the big ginger one.'

'Oh that. He's a bit scary. What happened to his ear?'

'I know. He's like the local bodyguard or something. No one messes with him. Not even that Rottweiler from down the road.'

Kate giggled nervously. 'I hate that dog. I just hear a single bark and I'm running. Don't even turn around now to check if it's loose or not. I'm just out of there.'

I grinned, remembering my own recent experiences with it. 'Duncan and I have been daring each other to see who can walk for the longest when we hear him barking behind us.'

'That must be horrible. Does Duncan always make you do stuff like that?'

'It's my choice,' I replied, shaking my head a little bit, but then stopping. 'Usually it is, anyways.'

Kate had picked up a shell, and she was cupping it in the palm of her hand.

'I remember this one time,' she said. 'Running so hard to get away from that Rotty. After I got through our gate, I finally looked back, and realised it was a totally different dog chasing me. Hardly a dog at all. Not much bigger than a rat. I'm serious. I know. I should have realised way sooner. The bark did sound a bit different when I thought about it afterwards.'

The image of Kate being chased by a rat-dog made me grin. Then we both started laughing uncontrollably. Sitting there together in the sand, I felt myself relaxing. Kate was easy to talk to, and she paid attention to what I had to say. She was interested in me and not just waiting for another opportunity to talk about herself.

'We should go for a swim,' she said.

'What?'

'Come on. It'll be warm enough.'

'I don't have any togs.'

Kate peered at me. 'We could skinny dip,' she suggested with a grin that I took to be somewhere between shy and mischievous.

'Really?' I tried to keep my sense of a rising panic under control. 'Look. I'm not big on going in the ocean.'

'Oh. Why not?'

'It's a bit of a long story. Something happened when I was really young. It kind of scared me.'

'That's okay,' Kate said, accepting my lack of further explanation and smiling to show she didn't mind either way. She leaned back on her arms. 'It's nice just sitting here too.'

I looked north up the beach. Just along from us a small flock of tara were discarding their clown-like antics on land and taking to the air. With their swallowed lope, the terns rode the airwaves over the sea's waves with such grace. I wished I could transform myself away from my own fears that easily.

'What are you thinking about?' Kate asked.

'What?' Suddenly, I felt aware how close she was sitting. I didn't know what to say, and then she giggled.

'You should see your expression.'

Embarrassed, I glanced sideways at her. There was a light breeze coming off the sea, and it made her hair swirl around her face. She pushed some of it back as she peered at me and smiled. I kept trying to sneak glances without her noticing. Then I looked at the sea and the sky, trying to work out if either of the colours matched her eyes. But they didn't. Her eyes were a slightly different shade that I could not pinpoint.

'Don't worry,' she said. 'I won't bite.'

'It's not that,' I replied, embarrassed and finding that I could not hold her gaze for very long without getting confused. Instead, I looked down at my feet and then hers. Kate's skin was naturally tanned. I found myself focusing on her bare ankles for a few moments.

'Well,' she continued. 'What is it then?'

'Why me? This? Why aren't you, I don't know, hanging out with Duncan? Or another popular boy.'

Kate giggled again. I decided right then that I was totally in love with the sound of her laughter.

'What, and compete with everyone else,' Kate said. 'No thanks.'

We both stared at the ocean. A surfer had walked down the beach in our direction and then started paddling out past the breakers. He sat on his board, beyond the whitewater, looking like he was content living a completely different life to the one he had back on land. Perhaps, this was a place that occupied his mind far too much when he wasn't there. It felt good having that longing in his mind. Never being completely satisfied.

I wondered if it was like what I had experienced in the forest, way off a track, some place where everything was wild and untouched. And, what I hoped it could be like high up in the mountains. Especially that mountain I saw when we were pig hunting. It had been occupying my mind lately. Even by reaching the base of it, I would be so far away from everything else that bothered me in my life. I could be free. The thought of having a focus like that seemed simple. Sitting with Kate made my emotions feel the opposite. I was totally confused.

'Tell you what,' Kate said. 'I'll make you a deal. And hopefully this will convince you.'

I turned towards her. She had a funny, half smile. And her eyebrows narrowed, just a bit, like they did when she was concentrating.

'Okay. What?'

'You can kiss me. If you like.'

My heart started racing, maybe faster than when I saw the wild boar but with a totally different feeling attached to it. It was going so quick I wondered if it might explode. I started to speak. But then I stopped. I had no idea what I wanted to say, maybe seek reassurance that this wasn't just a dream or, worse yet, somehow one of Duncan's cruel pranks.

'Just this once,' Kate said, brushing her hair back again. 'Well, maybe. We'll see.'

The wind was getting up a bit more, but I only noticed because Kate had goosebumps on her skin.

'You had better not go skiting about it to anyone,' she added. 'Or it will definitely be the first and last time this happens. Especially not to your brother, okay? Don't tell him or else.'

I was stunned. My hands were shaking. I slipped them under my thighs so Kate couldn't see how nervous I'd become.

'Deal?' she asked.

Kate looked directly at me, intently, as if this was important to her. For a moment I became lost in her eyes, swimming in the not-quite-sea-blue. I took a deep breath. Finally, I got myself under enough control to be able to nod in reply.

'Deal,' I said, my voice not really sounding my own.

Kate reached out and touched my face with her fingers. Now, I had goosebumps. I closed my eyes. Held my breath. Waited. Sometime during the kissing, I realised that we were holding hands.

VIII

I stop talking for a few moments. The memory of kissing Kate for the first time has transported me back to other memories. I need to focus, returning myself to the present so that I say the right things to Zoe.

It is no surprise that finding the photograph has ignited so much interest from Zoe. And, it's only natural that she wants to know as much as possible about our family's past. I guess a part of the knowing is also about her finding her own place in a fast approaching adult world. Understanding the complications of love and trying to learn from others about what might go right and wrong.

I wonder how much to explain. Hindsight is only any good if we can learn from it and have the opportunity to apply it. Love, or at least the various complications surrounding it, tends not to be so forgiving.

Old Frank started playing chess with me at the beginning of the new school year. Now, at last, I was in the same class as Duncan and Kate and I didn't feel so left out anymore. It had been a dry summer so far, well by Coast standards, and our family managed to get back into the hills for lots of adventures. I was starting to enjoy myself again, the trauma of the pig hunting accident a distant memory.

My mother had been teaching me the rules of chess, but it was not a game I naturally took to. I kept at it and could play reasonably well, although I didn't make a big deal from it, especially to Duncan and his new friend Brian who couldn't be bothered with board games anymore because they had started climbing on the glacier.

Brian lived in town. He was from a sporting family. Both of his parents worked for the glacier guiding company. His father used to play representative hockey for the Coast a few years back and his mother had made the national swimming squad in her teens. Unfortunately for Brian he didn't inherit any of their genes. Like Duncan, he was big for his age. Whereas my brother was fit and agile for his size, Brian could be downright clumsy.

'An accident waiting to happen,' I overheard my mother once describe him as to Old Frank.

Thinking back, it's a mystery to me why she even let Brian start climbing with my brother. Maybe she felt sorry for him. Or, more likely, she thought Brian's incompetence might slow Duncan down. Cause him to take pause and realise not all things were a cakewalk for everybody. Regardless, Duncan and Brian still liked to compete. This meant that my mother would often sidle up to me as the older boys argued over who had been the first to finish something or was doing it better. She rarely intervened unless things deteriorated to shouting and pushing. We sat there and watched, mother and youngest son enjoying the entertainment of our ongoing private joke.

Although we had been on lots of trips in the bush, and I had always managed to keep up with the others, my mother said I had to wait a bit more before I could go climbing on the glacier with the three of them.

'I know you're keen as mustard,' she explained one morning at the crib after Duncan and Brian had been told to go out and wait in the car. 'But it's not like the bush, Jason. You slip over in the wrong place and you're gone, swallowed by a crevasse without a second's warning.'

I sat on the couch by the fire, staring straight ahead with my arms folded. My mother put her climbing pack and ice axe down. She sat beside me.

'It's not that I don't trust you to make the right decisions,' she said. 'Just, maybe you're not quite strong enough to carry them out yet.'

'Duncan hurts himself more than me when we go bush.'

She nodded. 'He can be a bit of a bull at a gate.'

'And Brian's a doofus all of the time.'

'Yes. Yes, he is.'

My mother sighed. She put a hand on my shoulder.

'Look, I can't watch the three of you up there.'

'It's still not fair.'

'You're probably right,' she said, standing up again. 'That's just the way of it sometimes. Don't worry. You will get your turn.'

My mother needed to slam the front door twice to get the lock to engage. I remained on the couch, refusing to look out the window and wave goodbye. I was so angry. This was just another of those times that I felt I was not measuring up. It was almost my fifteenth birthday, but I didn't believe that being excluded had anything to do with my age. More that no one else thought I was capable enough, especially when it mattered.

Wood crackled and hissed in the fire. I got up to add another log, but the basket was empty. The wood pile was a good place for taking out my frustration, sinking the splitting axe into the skull of a log, the force of each strike reverberating through my arms with a jolt of satisfaction. Despite the coolness of the morning, I was soon sweating from the exertion.

But I must not have been paying enough attention. Next thing, the axe winged off a knot in a stump and nicked my shin. I felt a stab of pain. Blood began oozing from the gash, nothing like the wound to Old Frank's leg but enough to give me a reality check. I dabbed the wound with a handkerchief from my pocket. I was damn lucky. Another whisker or so to the left and I could have nearly cut my calf in half.

Not going climbing wasn't the only thing making me angry. Other things hadn't been working out so well lately, or not the way I would have hoped.

'Think of chess as being a bit like life,' Old Frank explained when he came over later that morning. 'Or a bit like a woman in your life anyways. A complete bloody mystery.'

I must have had an odd look on my face because he burst out laughing. 'Don't worry, Sawn Off. You'll get it one day. I promise.'

The look wasn't because I didn't understand. It was because I had been busy puzzling over Kate the last few weeks. Old Frank's words were making perfect sense to me.

Most of the time I didn't have any idea what moves to make with Kate, or even what to say to her. We had been going for lots of walks along the beach and in the forest, and even to the local movie theatre in town a few times. And we'd kissed again, more than once, and which left me feeling breathless and tingling all over afterwards.

But then I noticed a change in how Kate acted when Duncan was around. Sometimes she could become a bit distant towards me. Or different anyway. It was the same as being with Duncan and Brian and their other friends. They all tried to act like grown-ups as much as possible, or rebellious teenagers at any rate. Talk was of how to get some alcohol and cigarettes, and who planned to hook up with who if they got half a chance. I guess Kate's awkwardness when Duncan was around made me grumpy. It felt like the start of a downward spiral.

'What happened to your leg, Sawn Off?' Old Frank asked, pointing at my bandage and snapping me out of my morose thinking.

'Nothing.'

Old Frank looked at me, but he didn't inquire further. I got up to make him a cup of coffee. I could drink it if I wanted but I still didn't like the taste.

'You will one day lad, don't you worry about that,' my uncle said, sitting on the couch by the fire and then dragging a small table from the corner of the room to set it between us.

Old Frank hadn't yet got another finder to replace Patch, and I wondered if he ever would. Sarge was looking a bit grey in the whiskers. The dog mooched around the floor, sniffing under the kitchen table before getting settled by the fire next to Sugar who didn't seem to mind the company. My uncle began reminding me of the name and movement of each different chess piece as he laid it on the board.

I sat down heavily in the chair opposite. 'Duncan calls it an old person's game.'

Old Frank made a scoffing sound. 'I bet he does.'

'Why can't I go with them? Up to the glacier. I'm good enough to take care of myself.'

'Your mother knows what's best and you don't need me telling you that do you?' he replied, taking the pawn I had been worrying in my hands and replacing it on the board.

I half nodded, still trying to be sullen but knowing it was unlikely to get me anywhere. My uncle put his hands behind his back. I chose left which was white and moved my king's pawn two squares forward. Old Frank copied the move. I angled my bishop out.

Sarge and Sugar paid no attention to the game, as if they already knew the outcome. They may well have. When I lost my queen to a stupid decision I thought to concede early. But I persevered like my mother said was the right thing to do, especially when playing your elders. Old Frank mated my king six moves later. But he didn't make a big deal about it. He got up to empty the stove top for another coffee while I pivoted the board and reset the pieces to their starting positions.

'There's something I've been meaning to get out of the way for a while,' my uncle said after we had stopped playing to have some lunch. 'I suppose you can come and help me if you like. Only if you've got nothing better to do, that is.'

I looked sideways at him. The invite was framed in such an offhanded manner that it raised my interest. Anything was better than sitting around and moping. Afterwards, I realised only too well why he was being so cagey.

Old Frank got me to row his dinghy across the lagoon in the direction of a wooded cove that he pointed out on the far side of the shore. It was a place that I had never been to before. As we crossed the lagoon, for the briefest of moments I could not help but recall the time my father threw me overboard. I gave an involuntarily shudder.

'You alright, lad? Someone walk over your grave?'

'Something like that.'

But, unlike that day, the lagoon was calm. Ripples arcing away either side of the dinghy were the only disturbance across the surface of the water. Sarge and Sugar pushed against each other to be the one standing furthest ahead at the bow, both with their noses forward, sniffing the air and their tails wagging at a rapid cadence as they watched everything about us. Kōtuku posed silently over the shallows as we passed, some of them propped elegantly on only one leg. It seemed to me that their slender white bodies were cast in bone.

Every now and then their heads moved, just a fraction, their eyes scanning for swimming tidbits.

'Some think of them as ghost birds,' Old Frank said.

'The herons?'

'They say each one has a soul that's chosen to wait here on earth rather than pass to the spirit world.'

I looked at the nearest bird. It stood tall and watched me back, no doubt wondering if we were a threat it needed to escape from.

'Waiting for what?' I asked.

'Who knows? That's their decision and so it should be. Who are we to say what goes on once we pass?'

'Do you really believe that?'

My uncle shrugged his shoulders. Then he turned away, saying nothing more and staring out across the lagoon. The water around us was so smooth that it felt like we were traveling through a mirage. I stopped rowing. I studied each of the herons in turn as the boat glided past them. My thoughts drifted. I looked at one kōtuku for some time.

We landed on a strip of pebbles near the north-eastern corner of the lagoon, together dragging the dinghy up to the nearest tree where Old Frank tied the bow line to a fallen branch. Then I followed him through undergrowth until we came to a small clearing.

Sarge had already disappeared ahead as if he understood where to go, and I could hear Sugar chasing through the scrub after him. They were both at the clearing when we arrived, sitting on their hind legs. Waiting. As if they knew.

'This is where he's buried,' Old Frank finally said.

'Who?' I began to ask. Then I realised why my uncle had brought me here.

'He was a good old boy, that Patch.'

I did not say anything. There was nothing to say. Remembering back to the day of the accident, my body shuddered at the scenes suddenly playing out in my mind again. Stuff I'd managed to hide from my psyche.

Old Frank limped around the clearing to peer at different parts of it, like he was checking for something that he might have left there or lost. Then he looked up at the sky. Clouds drifted by in different shapes that could have resembled anything.

'That was damn near the biggest boar I've ever seen,' my uncle said. 'You remember those tusks on him. The size of bloody bananas, they were. You saw what damage he could do with them.'

I felt ashamed. As if I had somehow failed my family, or that I should have done something different to alter the outcome of that day. I felt my cheeks redden and I tried to hide my face by bending forward to pick at the biddy-bids stuck to my pants.

Sarge padded up to Old Frank. My uncle patted him on the head and scratched behind his ears. Sarge licked his hand.

'You rascals almost had that old tusker too didn't you. Maybe could have if I hadn't tripped over a tree stump. What a clumsy arse. A goddamn tree stump!'

I stood there, watching Old Frank as he stared into a space only he could see. There was not a breath of wind, and the trees stood still around us like they were paying their respects.

'There's not a day goes by that I don't wish I did things different then,' my uncle said. 'Your dogs become family, you know that. Sometimes more family than your real family.'

Old Frank spat at the ground. He sighed.

'Bloody idiot!' he added softly. Then he stopped talking. He leaned against a broken stump, shoving both hands into his pockets. His eyes lost their focus. He stood there, fixed to the spot, perhaps never to move again if he could have his way.

After a time, I thought it would be more polite to leave Old Frank. He did not seem to notice me moving away. Sugar and I headed back through the bush to the shoreline. I felt angry with myself. I had wanted to help my uncle. To comfort him. A branch slapped my face and I struck out at it. I could see a group of herons stalking through the slowly receding water of the lagoon. I picked up a stone and threw it in their direction. One of the birds flew off, but the others didn't seem to notice my act of petulance.

Old Frank and Sarge took a while to return. When they arrived back at the shore, Sarge nuzzled my leg and I scratched him under his chin. Old Frank didn't say anything. I started rowing back across the lagoon, glancing at my uncle who was sitting in the stern. But he would not meet my gaze. He kept looking off to one side or the other, at the water and the sky and then tracking a flock of low flying oyster catchers that were heading up the coast. The birds could be heard peeping on the wing.

Old Frank was first out once we reached the jetty. He helped drag the dinghy above the high tide mark and tied it off to one of the posts.

'Thanks for coming with me, Jase' he mumbled before turning to walk away. 'Sarge, heel!'

I went to say goodbye, but he had already started shuffling up the track with a limp that seemed more pronounced than usual. I stood there, my feet rooted to the spot and wondering if I should call out something. Anything. Then Old Frank paused and turned.

'I mean it,' he said, looking at me. Even from the distance, I could see that his eyes were bloodshot. 'I really appreciated having you with me today. It means a lot to me that you made the effort to come. I know you didn't feel like it, that you had other stuff on your mind.'

I felt a sudden urge to rush up and hug him. It seemed like something that would be the right thing to do given the circumstances. I could have acted. But I didn't. Instead, I remained standing in the same spot as an idiot who couldn't make a decision.

Old Frank gave me small wave. He looked up at the sky and took another deep breath, then he continued along the gravel path, Sarge loping ahead with his nose to the ground.

I had the fire going by the time the others had returned from the glacier. Duncan and Brian burst through the door to the crib almost together, their faces tinged with sunburn and both of them jabbering on about who was better at using their crampons and who could swing their ice axes further into the ice and how they were famished and could eat a horse after all the exercise.

My mother walked in behind them. She placed her pack on the floor and looked at me before saying anything. I could tell she was trying to read my emotions, and I wondered if she knew what Old Frank had been planning to do. Perhaps that was part of the reason she had left me behind.

'You two shut up,' she said to the others. 'You're just full of it the pair of you. Truth be told neither of you were much cop with your axes or your crampons.'

IX

'Teenage years are the worst I reckon,' Zoe says, changing the subject for a moment.

'Why is that?'

'Well, every single adult in your life thinks it's their duty to tell you what you can and can't do. But then no one lets you do anything. Or nothing that you want to do. It's all very confusing.'

I cannot help but smile. It's no surprise that she associates with my own lack of understanding during my teenage years. 'I think you're probably right with that observation,' I reply. 'Well, from what I remember of it anyway. Clearly that was some time ago.'

Zoe nods. 'You are ancient after all,' she adds with a cheeky grin. 'Don't you reckon it's like you're expected to grow up but then not grow up at the same time?'

'It can be tough, I'll give you that,' I concede, thinking back to my own experience. 'But those same limitations and disappointments combine to make you who you are. Sometimes you just don't realise it until afterwards.'

I was pretty much done with all the mountaineering books my mother kept getting me to read. She called them 'the essentials' in any young climber's apprenticeship towards understanding the risks ahead. Other than not being a replacement for the real thing, I became bored with them or at least most of the concepts that the words within them carried. There seemed too much of a practiced staunchness from the climbers, and it was happily regurgitated by the authors. It reminded me of the way that Duncan sometimes acted, as well as most of the rugby players at our school.

'They walk like they've pissed themselves or something,' my brother joked to his friends outside in the school yard one day, a little too loudly as two of the team's forwards were walking past.

I had been sitting close by and was quick to jump up next to my brother when the rugby players strode forwards to him. Afterwards, Duncan was the only student to be caned by Owl Face.

'You should be ashamed of yourself,' Mr Tupuna said, wiping the sweat from his brow.

The cane went back on a hook in the hallway. For part of my punishment I had been told to sit there and watch. I was impressed with how Duncan made a point of not flinching during any of the particularly loud thwacks. Not surprisingly, there was no sign of the rugby players.

'They started it,' Duncan had argued beforehand, but it didn't do him any good. 'I didn't hit anyone first.'

Mr Tupuna was still breathing heavily from the exercise of swinging his arm. 'You shouldn't have hit anyone at all,' he said. 'What kind of an example are you setting your brother?'

Instead of also being caned, I got a week of lunchtime detention. Later, Duncan told me that the parents of two of the rugby players were on the school board and friends with Owl Face.

'That was the only reason I got caned and not them,' he said. 'When was the last time you heard of a senior getting the cane? And they all got off scot free. Bloody unfair, I reckon.'

'You showed him though,' I replied.

'What?'

'Owl Face. By not flinching.'

Duncan grinned. Then he dropped his pants to show six red welts stretching across his backside.

'I can understand why they call him Rubber Arm,' my brother admitted with a grimace.

Later, I explained to my mother that it was a tennis ball that had bounced up and hit me in the eye while we were playing cricket.

'That's where the shiner came from,' I added quickly.

She looked at Duncan's bruise on his chin and then back at me. My brother had his best poker face on, but I was pretty sure she didn't believe my concoction of the story even for a second. She kept staring at me for a few moments, as if expecting that I'd be the one to fess up. Then she shrugged her shoulders and turned back to preparing dinner in the kitchen.

'Make sure you both do your chores before dinner,' she said. 'We need more wood for the fire.'

I am also sure my mother wasn't referring to fighting when she said, 'Hit anything between the eyes and it'll drop like a sack of spuds'.

The wooden stock of the old Winchester 44-40 was nicked in places and oiled dark. She taught Duncan and me to shoot and hunt with it, along with a Remington 22 for possums and rabbits and a long barrelled 38 which was better for deer out in the open country.

While Duncan liked the 38 – he preferred killing from a distance – I was drawn to the weight and feel of the 44. I liked its balance when I drew down the sight and slowly exhaled. But the hair trigger caught me out more than once, especially if I got too nervous or excited.

'Keep your finger clear until you're ready,' my mother whispered in my ear whenever I lined up a target. 'That's right. Flick off the safety. Are you sighted? Don't pull at the trigger. Just breathe out, slowly. Now, gently squeeze with your whole hand.'

Over time I learned to separate the act of shooting from what I was shooting at. It didn't matter if I was hunting a pig, a nanny thar or my first deer. I could concentrate on being accurate with the shot, talking myself quietly through the process, and trying to keep my heart rate steady. And I seemed to have a knack for it. A kind of blankness came over me. If anything, the hunting taught me to be able to focus on what needed to be done.

'There is no consequence,' I would say to myself, repeating a line I once heard in a movie I had watched with Kate. More than once I thought to myself that if we were ever in another situation like the one when the pig killed Patch and hurt Old Frank, I was better prepared to deal with it. And I reckon my mother's lessons about self-control helped later with my own decision-making during climbing.

I guess my mother was trying to school Duncan and me on the outdoors as she had been schooled by her parents.

'The land is precious beyond understanding,' she explained to us. 'All creatures are to be respected, even if they are food. The connection is in everything, and everything's connection has its place.'

While Duncan seemed to get bored quickly, or acted like he was, I enjoyed it when she told us stuff like that. Joining the dots between our actions and our understanding of the wider environment. It's a philosophy that I'm careful to explain to Zoe.

'Your time for responsibility will come,' my mother continued. 'It might look like chaos, but there's a reason to all things in nature.'

She raised her arms to the landscape, striving to instill in us what had been instilled in her.

'One day someone will want to control this. All of this. The earth, the trees, the water, even the air probably. Never underestimate the stupidity of some people. You'd think they would have more sense.'

Although my mother liked to explain things as if she was in control of them, I realise now that she must have worried just the same. Chance has its opportunity as much as skill and planning and good decision-making, maybe more so if the truth is told. I think my mother preferred decisions to be simple. Black and white. But it was important to her that we realised the environment wasn't just one big adventure playground. We also had a duty to respect it, and to protect it if we could.

These days, I understand the angst she must have felt when a choice was never obvious. And when it came to trying to share the same knowledge she had gathered over the years with those she cared about. While she liked to push Duncan and me that little bit further each time we explored the outdoors, she also helped me understand the need for a connection to what she referred to as 'an almost normal' life.

I liked it when she took the time to walk with me in the hills close to home, following faint, narrow trails through the darkness of the forest behind the beach. She knew all the different flora and fauna that we saw, and she liked to keep increasing my knowledge of birds.

One time, near the top of a small, rocky mountain that we had scrambled up together, we watched a native falcon flying above us. The old people called it kārearea. My mother pointed out a distant rock outcrop where she guessed the falcon's nest might be.

'Watch you don't get between it and its young,' she advised me. 'Falcon are very protective. They don't care what the cost of that protection might be. Defending their territory, their offspring. Even if what they are fighting against is much bigger than they are. Even if it means death.'

It was obvious how much my mother loved the outdoors. Her values centred around clean air and water and trying to leave the land as you found it.

'The extravagance of money teaches you nothing,' she said when we started to descend another track. The falcon was still above us, gliding effortlessly on the thermals. 'Money only leads you to distraction from what's important.'

'So, what's really important then?' I asked.

'That's for you to find out for yourself,' my mother replied. 'And I'm sure you will, in your own time.'

The surface of the sea began to ruffle below us. There was a forecast southerly wind change supposedly approaching from down the coast, and we could see that the chop across the sea was being pursued by a dark mass of cloud.

In the time it took for the falcon to glide from view, the air temperature dropped almost ten degrees. We slipped our jackets and woollen hats on, before continuing the long walk back home.

X

The mountain we saw on the pig hunting trip and that made such an impression on Duncan and me was called Maunga ō Hine. Girl Mountain.

'Have you still got a map of it somewhere?' Zoe asks.

I manage to find a copy among the pile on my bookshelf and spread it on the floor between us.

'This is where we stood on the pass and looked across that first time,' I say, pointing. 'And this is where Old Frank and I spent the night.'

Zoe leans forward to study the contours of the landscape. 'It looks like a long way from anywhere,' she says. 'And steep too. Especially on this side.'

'It sure is,' I reply. 'That was part of the attraction. If it was easy everyone would do it.'

I stare at the map for a few more seconds, remembering. I point at another spot. 'Here's the clearing where the helicopter landed to get Frank and me. See, above it, how the valley continues, closing in as it gets closer to Hine. Notice the contours? They aren't as steep here, especially compared to the other sides.'

Zoe follows where I'm indicating. She nods.

'It is the only way into the mountain,' I continue. 'To climb it. All the other approaches are cut off or too broken. If you want to get there this is how you're going to do it.'

There's only so much an old man can keep track of in his final years. But I can't help thinking 'if only', especially when it comes to seeing that bloody mountain for the first time. If it hadn't been Maunga ō Hine doubtless it would have been another summit just as alluring. Just as toxic.

The mountain that I wanted so desperately to climb. The moment when I understood I was losing Kate to Duncan. I guess I had been expecting it. I finally realised how much my brother liked her. How he tried to show off more when she was around, and how she responded to the attention. For my brother, it probably wasn't so much about competing with me anymore as much as trying to impress her. The bigger surprise was how quickly Kate changed her mind from wanting to be with me to not. And then to being with Duncan. Thinking about it now, maybe our difference in age was a factor. She was growing up and maturing much more quickly than I was.

Of course, when you are in love, and especially in teenage love, none of this makes any sense. All you focus on is the shock and the hurt and the dark, cold void that follows. Insistent voices in the bottomless depths reminding you that you are not good enough. That you were never good enough. That you will never be good enough.

My mother made Duncan and me wear collared shirts and ties to the school dance at the end of the year. She got us to stand together in front of the fireplace so she could take a photograph. Part of me didn't want to go, as if I had a premonition of what was coming.

'Don't you look so handsome,' she said. 'What a catch, the pair of you.'

Then she turned to Duncan. 'Now I know you think you're old enough to drink alcohol,' she said. 'But I've told you enough times about drinking and driving, haven't I?'

My brother put on his solemn face for the lecture. 'Yes, Mum. Many times.'

'Good. Now drive safely Duncan. Be sure and wear your seat belts. I'll see you back here, before eleven mind you.'

As soon as we got into the car, my brother passed me a hipflask that he had already stashed under the seat.

'Go on,' he said. 'Don't worry, I've got breath mints in case we get checked at the door.'

The first swallow burned all the way down.

'Have another,' my brother encouraged. 'Dutch courage, if nothing else.'

The town hall was decorated in streamers and balloons. It looked ridiculous.

'What is it, a bloody kindergarten party?' Duncan said with a scowl.

Just as my brother had predicted, Owl Face was standing at the door to check everyone's breath.

'Hello Mr Tupuna,' my brother said in an obviously obnoxious voice. 'Are you planning to get lucky tonight?'

'Always a smart arse, Williamson. Stop setting a bad example for your sibling.'

'My one and only goal in life,' my brother replied, grinning widely and whacking me on the shoulder as we walked past.

My mother had made a corsage, and I gave it to Kate. I tried to pin it to her dress once we were inside the hall.

'Ouch, clumsy!' she said after I accidentally stabbed her with the pin.

'Shit, sorry.'

'Never mind. Here, I'll do it.'

I was not a very confident dancer. Kate had to cajole me off my seat when a song from her new favourite band A-ha started playing. Duncan and his date were already on the dance floor, and Kate led us to a space right next to them.

My brother said something, but I couldn't hear because the music was so loud. He gave me a wink. Then he made a deal of looking over my shoulder, which caused me to turn around. When I turned back, we had somehow swapped sides. I was now dancing with his date, a farmer's daughter whose name I wasn't even sure of. She was buxom and seemed quite chatty, but I was not in a mood for small talk with someone else.

Duncan and Kate were dancing to A-ha, and I was stuck with a girl who smelled of silage.

'My name's Jody,' she said, leaning close enough that I could feel her hot breath on my ear.

I smiled back to be polite, and then looked over at Duncan and Kate again. As luck would have it, the next song had a slow beat. Everyone moved closer to their dance partner. I saw Duncan put his hands on Kate's shoulders, and it looked to me like she didn't seem to mind. Then Jody obstructed my view. She had both of her hands around my waist and she pulled me so close to her that our hips were touching.

'You're nowhere near as big as your brother, are you?' she said. Then one of her hands slipped lower. She leaned closer to whisper into my ear.

'Quite cute though.'

I reckon the final straw was the time we went to the old gold mining ruins. It was a week or two after the school dance. I do not think it was anything Duncan or Kate had planned for. Like Kate and I meeting on the beach that first time, it just happened. But I could always be wrong about that.

It was late in the evening when Duncan shook me awake. He clamped his hand over my mouth.

'It's on,' he whispered. 'Tonight. Do you still want to come?'

A nighttime mission to the old ruins was something my brother and I had talked about for ages. As a final year school dare some of the older kids planned to do it, well the brave ones anyway. Someone said the place must surely be haunted.

'A kid was killed there even,' Duncan told me.

'Really?'

'I don't know. That's what Brian reckons. He said it happened ages ago. His mother told him about it to stop him from wanting to go. Probably it's just an old tale.'

The mining ruins were on private land, and there were lots of 'No Trespassing' signs. The landowner lived nearby. More stories had circulated at school. Some of the kids had apparently been shot with a slug gun by the owner.

Duncan reckoned he met one boy the previous year when we first arrived who definitely had. 'Got it right in his butt,' my brother said. 'But he's pretty fat so he probably didn't notice until later. They had to dig the slug out with a pocketknife. Serves him right for not being quick enough.'

It was one thing to sneak in to the ruins during the day, quite another doing it late at night.

'Less chance of getting shot, at least,' Duncan said as we biked in the dark to meet the others. In our excitement we hardly noticed the long slog up the hill to the end of the four-wheel-drive track.

A group of boys and girls had already gathered. Most were around Duncan's age. Bottles of alcohol had been taken from various parents' liquor collections. Someone lit up a cigarette and it glowed like a tiny beacon in the dark. Brian was there, and so was Kate. I wondered why she hadn't wanted to come with me. Everything seemed to be happening in a hurry, so I did not get the opportunity to ask her why.

Old macrocarpa and pine trees shielded the ruins, their outlines casting strange shadows beneath a half moon. The dare was for each of us to go down the rotted, wooden stairs into the entrance to the mine shaft on our own and without using a torch.

Duncan was the self-appointed leader. He made sure we stayed together and kept quiet so as not to alert the landowner. Of course, he wanted to be the one to go first.

By this stage of my life, I had grown well used to the aura that Duncan seemed to give out, especially when it came to the way other kids treated him. They all believed he was invincible. Whatever he tried to jump from, ride off or dive in to, it was always expected that he would come away unscathed. He never broke anything. Hardly even a fingernail. Now, I understand how much my brother needed others around him to reinforce how good he was at everything. He drew them in. Even Kate.

Some of the other kids chickened out that night when it was their turn to sneak into the base of the ruins. Duncan wouldn't give them much time to decide.

'Okay, who's next?' he said, shining his torch into their faces, and each person blinking against the invasion of the spotlight. My brother could be a harsh judge of others who did not measure up to his high expectations.

'Come on, no room for imitators here,' he said in a quiet yet surprisingly harsh voice. 'You're either game for it...or you're shamed forever.'

When no one else volunteered quickly enough for Duncan's liking he turned to me.

'Come on Jase,' he whispered. 'You can totally do it. Show them what a Williamson is made of. Don't think about anything else, Bro. That only makes it worse. Just focus on this and nothing else. No one can stop you if you put your mind to it.'

Whenever he made a speech like that, which wasn't very often I must admit, it really got me going. I would absorb every word. With his encouragement, I discovered I could be almost as driven as him to give stuff a go. Almost as stubborn.

Of course, I was scared. But I knew that I would never hear the end of it if I did not take up the challenge and go down those steps on my own. Besides, Kate was standing there with the others. No doubt she was watching what I would do. Really, I had no other choice.

My brother told me which steps were broken, and that there should be just enough moonlight shining through the slumped roof to see the safest areas to place my feet.

'There's a really big hole off to your right about halfway down,' he added. 'You don't want to go stepping into that.' Then he made a low, long whistling sound followed by a splat.

The old timber framed walls made an odd creaking noise as I descended. Water was dripping nearby. But it wasn't half as bad as I had imagined. By the time I got to the bottom I wondered what all the fuss was about. Climbing back to the surface, I figured that Kate should be impressed with my bravery.

Kate's turn came towards the end of the group. She made out that she did not want to go down on her own. Even then I thought it was a put on as she was usually game enough to give anything a go. I offered to head down again. She shook her head.

'Come on,' Duncan said, taking her hand. 'It's not so bad. I'll come with you if you want.'

'Okay,' Kate replied. She let him lead her down the stairs into the darkness.

They were down there for what seemed like a long time. One of the other kids thought that something had gone wrong. Someone called out my brother's name, but there was no reply.

'What should we do?' Somebody asked. 'We can't tell anybody. Shit, we'll all get in trouble.'

'Shhhh,' I said. 'Just wait a few more seconds, will you. I'm sure everything is fine.'

When Duncan and Kate finally came back up to the surface, they stood close to each other. Under the moonlight I could see that neither of them would look at me.

XI

Explaining all of this to Zoe in a way she will understand makes me realise more fully how one thing led to another. And, looking back, I can see how this was a key moment in everything that followed. Duncan and Kate getting together should not have been much of a surprise. Duncan was admired by everyone. He was confident and liked being the centre of attention. If he set his mind to anything he tended to succeed at it. In a way their relationship was probably inevitable.

I also recall thinking that if I couldn't be with Kate, I needed to replace the emptiness inside with something else. Something which felt every bit as consuming. Something which would take all my emotions and shake them into a jumbled mess and then make me sort them out again one by one.

Going climbing might not have been the panacea for everything that was wrong with my life at the time, but it was certainly a good enough place to start.

I rose early in the pale light. I could hear my mother grumbling and bumping into things in the other room. I set about getting breakfast ready for her, and even for Duncan.

My brother was still in bed. Mostly, we had been trying to avoid each other lately. Kate and he were pretty much going steady. But it was not easy for me to steer clear of him, especially when he slept in the bunk below mine. When we were forced to interact it was with a sense of reserved and somewhat distant politeness. Even his constant ribbing of me had eased. It certainly felt like there was a new wedge driven between us. Something that had divided us and, potentially, something that we would never be able to recover from.

But not on this day. This day, I knew I had something to look forward to.

'Bit keen aren't you,' my mother said when she finally walked into the kitchen. She made a point of scowling over the coffee I had already poured for her.

But I could tell she was pretending and tried not to ruin it by grinning too much.

She peered out the window. 'How's the weather look?'

'Clear,' I replied. 'A light sou'wester. No cloud.'

'What about higher up?'

'I've been out and checked. It looks fine.'

'No cirrus?'

'No, Mum. Nothing.'

She humpfed.

I sat on the couch, eating another round of toast for extra energy and concentrating on keeping my face set. Eventually my mother decided that she had held the tension for long enough. She walked out of the room. When she returned she handed me my birthday present.

'Figured you'd had one too many of your brother's hand-me-downs.'

I gripped the brand-new ice axe at the handle. It had a blue leash made from tubular webbing. I balanced it in the palm of my hand and gave a half swing into the air.

'Easy there, Tiger,' my mother said, stepping back. 'Now, it cost a few bob this one. It's supposed to be the latest fangdangle, so they told me in the shop anyway. I would be grateful if you tried not to fall down any crevasses with it.'

I grinned. 'No, Mum. I promise to be careful.'

Duncan walked into the kitchen a few minutes later. He was rubbing his eyes.

'Happy birthday, Bro,' he mumbled. 'Sorry, I forgot it was your birthday. I didn't get you anything.'

I pressed my face against the window of the helicopter. The flight into the mountains was a nice surprise. I figured my mother had been planning something for my sixteenth birthday - hopefully some kind of climbing adventure - but I didn't know what.

Duncan and Brian were sitting next to me in the backseat of the Squirrel, and my mother was in the front beside the pilot. She made sure I got the window seat. Looking out, I tried to gauge the size and the depth of the crevasses penetrating the glacier. I had seen the glacier many times beneath the terminal face, walking up the valley with Duncan, Brian and my mother, sometimes amidst the crowds of tourists who seemed more interested in capturing a photo of the view rather than actually taking in the experience for themselves.

From the valley, it usually appeared dirty with moraine. Sometimes it would collapse under its own weight as it melted more quickly than it grew. There would be a sudden crack when another tower of ice calved from the terminal face, then a low rumble and maybe a shudder of the earth as it exploded into giant ice cubes.

My mother would always stop us a short distance from the glacier, well before where the groups of tourists were putting their glacier boots on.

'See, the glacier is advancing because of all the snowfall up on the neve,' she had explained. 'Over decades and centuries, the snow is compressing from the weight of each new snowfall, squeezing out the air until what remains is icy and blue.'

She would point at the inside of one of the downward curving crevasses. 'That's the blueness you can see. The glacier is always moving, always sliding down the valley to a point where the melting rate catches up to its flow. And, as is the case now, passing it.'

I had known that this was probably the same speech my mother gave to all of the clients she guided on the ice, but I still enjoyed hearing it.

'So it's melting back then?' I had asked.

'Very slowly, but yes it is,' she continued. 'What you're seeing is unique in the world. Very few places do glaciers like this flow right down into the rain forests.'

We had stood there and watched the visitors traipse up a step line which was being chipped into the ice by their guide. The guide and my mother had recognised each other earlier, giving a wave as the group passed by. The tourists pulled on a hawser-rope. They swung their ice axes into the glacier with a thunk, like they were taking the final approach to the summit of some towering personal mountain. Despite the gurgle of the river flowing out from under the glacier's innards, the sound of the group chatting loudly and their laughter could be clearly heard. The guide called out to be sure to have a grip on the rope and to keep a move along.

My mother had also taken me up onto the ice plenty of times on her guided trips, and we had scrambled around in the bottom of melted crevasses with the clients. And I had been rock climbing on the local crags. But this was going to be way better. Finally, I was going climbing in the mountains.

Our helicopter landed on a knoll overlooking the main icefall. We clambered out with our packs and climbing gear, careful to keep our heads low while retreating clear of the helicopter's blades. When far enough away, my mother gave a thumbs up.

The pilot powered the machine back up, lifting off and swooping out of view over the fall of space below us, until it eventually appeared again as a speck much further down the valley.

The noise of the helicopter slowly retreated, until nothing could be heard. I stood there, listening for a sound - anything. The silence was so absolute that I found it unsettling. Eventually, I could make out a soft whooshing of wind as it escaped over a mountain ridge high above us.

The glare of snow against the sky was so intense that it hurt my eyes. I put my sunglasses on. We plugged steps down a short slope towards the hut, wading through calf-deep snow which had already started melting with the heat of the day. Then we knocked the snow from our boots before stepping inside.

I went back to a window to take in the view again. It was the sense of space that got me. In the bush or even on an exposed ridge, distances always had something to be measured by. I could estimate it by looking at the height of a tree and then working out how long it might take to get somewhere. But the hugeness of the neve and the scale of each mountain made me wonder whether I could judge anything up here.

Duncan and Brian were planning to climb further up the glacier and pitch their tent in the scoop of a crevasse. From there they would attempt a climb of Archer Peak the following morning. After a few words of advice from my mother, they trudged up the same snow slope behind the hut that we had descended, the weight of their packs across their shoulders and the sound of their voices carrying long after they had disappeared over a rise. I was happy when they left. It meant I was going to get my mother's undivided attention.

I was there to learn about mountaineering. How to crampon across the glacier without catching the sharp points attached to my boots against each other. How to practice sliding down the snow while gripping my ice axe so I could self-arrest and stop safely. How to travel between crevasses, using a length of rope tied between us that protected one against the other if either should fall.

'Traveling across glaciers can be tricky,' my mother said. 'You need to make progress as quickly as possible but also have enough protection if it is really exposed. Do you just keep the rope tight between you, like this, or do you need to stop and place a snow stake and start pitching? Sometimes the right decision isn't always obvious.'

'Why's that?'

My mother tapped the snow with her ice axe. 'Because you cannot see what's beneath you. There may a huge hole just under us here, hidden by a thin layer of snow. Or maybe the snow isn't stable and will slide, taking you with it. These things you will need to understand before you can stay safe in the mountains.'

All of the experiences and descriptions were new and completely different to what had been required in the forest. I had never feared heights. Anyway, there was so much to pay attention to while moving in the mountains that thoughts of falling never entered my mind.

I absorbed as much as I could. Realising that I did not know enough to have any proper questions yet. I thought about each new piece of information my mother told me and then how it built on the others. Slowly my thoughts expanded with the growing knowledge of how to keep safe. My mother made a point of explaining that respect for the mountains and always making good decisions about the risk that surrounded us and how to protect against it were the most important things to be aware of.

'This is the best place to be, Jase. But it can also be the worst. It'll test you like you've never experienced before.'

I stared up at the mountains, trying to imagine what the view might be like from the top of each of them. To be able to look down over everything. Then I studied the way the glacier flowed from the neve beneath them, sliding down the valley past us and towards the coast.

'The old people still call the glacier Kā Roimata ō Hine Hukatere,' my mother said. 'Tears of the Avalanche Girl.'

I looked at her. 'The tears of an avalanche girl,' I repeated to myself.

'The name describes how the glacier was formed,' my mother added. 'Hine used to live here. She was a great climber and liked to scramble around in the high country.'

I turned and studied the mountains again, listening to the story my mother was telling.

'One day Hine convinced her friend Wawe to accompany her. But Wawe wasn't very confident with heights. The tale goes that they were climbing together somewhere around here when Hine heard a shout behind her. She turned around in time to see Wawe tumbling and falling away from her into the valley.'

A kea called out from somewhere overhead. The sound was mournful, and it echoed around the peaks. My mother stopped talking, and we both tried to spot the mountain parrot.

'From Hine's vantage point, she could see that Wawe was certainly dead,' my mother continued. 'She started to cry. So strong was her suffering at the loss of her dearest friend that her tears flowed down into the valley, eventually all the way to where Wawe had fallen. It was so cold down in the shadows that her tears eventually froze, forming a layer of ice that covered Wawe. Burying him. That is why the glacier is before us today.'

Despite my mother's cautionary tale about Hine and Wawe, I was excited at the opportunity to finally be in the mountains. I had a chance to prove myself to her. To show that I was just as capable as Duncan. The very real goal of climbing to a summit would reinforce that. Here was something tangible that I could succeed on. A physical and a mental challenge. A risk to be managed. I had a long way to go to learn the necessary skills, but I was beginning the process.

In the evening we sat with our meals on a small rocky outcrop near the edge of the glacier. The sun began to slide past us and the mountains. We watched shadows slip across the long curve of ice beneath our feet and, finally, a blood-red sky merging into the ocean. My mother chose not to speak during this time.

I remained there, barely moving. Breathing as quietly as I could in case I disturbed the perfection of what was happening. It felt like I alone was bearing witness to one of nature's true wonders, the simple unobstructed view of a day's final breath. Sure, I had seen fiery sunsets on the coastline by our crib. But to be able to watch it from this altitude added something intangible, almost otherworldly, to the experience.

I explain to Zoe that, at the time, I could not work out what it was. Now, I realise it is because of the almost alien environment of the mountains. They are places not meant for humans. No one can survive up there all year round, not without a hut to shelter in and a constant supply of food and fuel. To be among them is to feel like an intruder. The luckiest of thieves, but a thief just the same.

It was mesmerising sitting there with my mother and watching what seemed nothing less than visual poetry. A seduction of light that melded the land with the sky. When the colours had all but gone and the air became chilled and the snow and the ice around us throbbed a blue-black, she suggested that it was time to head back inside the hut.

It came as a surprise to discover how much I was shivering. And, looking down, I realised that I had forgotten to eat most of my meal.

'Come on,' my mother said. 'It's time to hit the sack.'

I looked at her. 'It doesn't feel very late.'

'It's not. But you won't be thanking me when the alarm goes off at three.'

'Won't it still be dark then?'

'Yes, of course it will. But the moon is almost full tonight. You'd be surprised how light it stays at night. Especially up here. The moon reflects off the glacier. Sometimes, so much that it's almost like daylight.'

I followed my mother back into the hut, my mind filled with images of what the next day would bring.

XII

Thinking so much about the mountains has left me feeling melancholic. A bit tired, as if the reliving of each memory has made my body feel its age more than usual. I could probably do with a nap. But there is one more thing from my teenage years that I still need to explain to Zoe.

It was a few years after that first mountaineering trip above the glacier, and around the time when Kate and Duncan decided to get married. I guess their commitment to each other shouldn't have come as much of a shock to me. They had been going steady for a few years, and back then it wasn't unusual to tie the knot so young.

Duncan and I kept up with the climbing, heading into the mountains as often as we could. Our mother begrudgingly admitted that we were almost becoming competent mountaineers. I think she was chuffed with our improving abilities, proud that both of her sons were motivated to travel and challenge themselves in the high peaks.

My brother was twenty, and Kate had turned nineteen a few months before their planned wedding day. At the time Duncan was working with our mother as a glacier guide. Kate had been planning to study at the university over in the city, but it sounded like that was all done with once the marriage had been announced.

Tyler was born a few months after the wedding. Apparently, the baby bump showed under Kate's wedding dress, but everyone did their best not to make much of a deal out of it. Get the wedding out of the way first, and then celebrate the arrival of a new life as well as deal with the complications it would undoubtedly bring.

I had already left the country by then. I did not feel that I had much of a choice. The thing that sticks in my mind though is what happened one night around six months before the big wedding day.

At the time Duncan and my mother were away with clients on an overnight guiding trip on the neve above the glacier. They were staying at the same hut my mother had taken me to on my first mountaineering trip.

Since leaving school, I had been working at the pub, more out of having something different to do rather than just take the expected path of guiding on the glacier. Part of me had a purist if rather naive notion of wanting to keep climbing separate from becoming part of my work.

My shift at the pub on this day didn't start till six. I was mucking about at home in the crib when Kate turned up unannounced. It was around the middle of the afternoon. She looked like she had been crying.

'What's wrong?'

Kate didn't reply. She pushed past me and sat on the couch. Then she took a cushion, placing it in front of her stomach and holding it with both hands. She just sat there, hunching forward and hugging the cushion like it was a favourite pet. Or something she was trying to protect.

'I was going to make a drink,' I said, hopefully trying to ease her out of the state of mind she was in or at least break the silence. 'Do you want a coffee?'

'Something stronger,' she replied with a soft, broken voice.

I went to the kitchen and found what I was looking for, placing a bottle of port and two glasses on the table before sitting down beside her.

'Will this do?'

'Anything,' she said, taking the half-filled glass and emptying it in one go.

'Another?' I asked.

Kate wiped her mouth and nodded. She took more time with the second drink. I kept taking sideways glances towards her as I sipped from mine, trying to work out what was going on. I probably shouldn't have been drinking with my shift coming up but, at the time, it was the furthest thing from my mind.

I cleared my throat. 'So, are you going to tell me?'

Kate leaned back on the couch. She rested her head on the top cushion and stared at the ceiling.

'I don't know what I'm doing,' she finally said. 'I really don't.'

'Okay?'

'You know Dunc's gone and asked me to marry him.'

I tried to keep the quiver from my voice. 'No. I didn't know that. I guess congratulations are in order.'

Kate turned. She stared at me for a few seconds before replying. 'Are they? Really?'

It was my turn to take a long swig from my glass. Thinking back now, I remember having no idea where the conversation was going. Kate and Duncan had been together for years. Any feelings I might still have carried were long shoved into a locked corner of my heart and best forgotten about. But now this?

I chose my next words carefully.

'What are you talking about, Kate?'

'You tell me.'

'Don't you want to marry him?'

'That's not the point.'

I finished my glass and refilled it. 'Well, what do you mean?'

'All this time,' Kate said. 'I kept wondering if you would wake up. Grow up. Or something. Shit, I don't know. This probably isn't making any sense at all to you, is it?'

I could feel my heartbeat accelerating. Not sure what was the best way to broach the topic, I decided to jump right in. 'You chose him, Kate. You.'

Kate placed the glass down hard enough on the table that it made a loud clunk. She ran both hands through her hair.

'And you just let it happen,' she replied. 'Didn't even bother to say anything to me. Lift a finger against your brother.'

For some reason, when I should have been feeling nervous or confused, I started to get angry. Angry at Kate. My brother. The situation I suddenly found myself in. Everything.

'You're holding me responsible,' I said, probably too forcefully but now struggling to contain my emotions. 'For this? Because you didn't have any gumption to change your mind.'

Kate sighed. 'It's not that simple.'

'Of course it is. A choice is a choice. It's exactly that simple.'

'You can be such a dick, you know that?' Kate said. 'Why am I here then, eh? What do you think I'm trying to bloody well tell you? Why do you reckon I've chosen this particular time to come over? When Dunc and your mother are away.'

Just like that, Kate's words evaporated my anger. We both sat there in silence for a few minutes. I stared into space. Kate leaned her head on my shoulder, and then I gently ran my hand through her hair.

'Are you sure about this?' I said barely above a whisper, not entirely convinced what it was I was referring to but realising that it felt like my world had suddenly become complicated again. Out of control. And, if I am honest with myself, a small part of me also probably realised that I was about to screw everything up. Everything.

'I think so,' Kate replied. Then she nodded. 'Why? Don't you want to?'

'I do. I've always wanted to. You know I have. Just. What about Duncan?'

Kate took my hand in hers and she looked straight at me. 'Stop talking will you. Don't say anything.'

Port got spilt on the couch. I tore my T-shirt trying to get it off in a hurry, and Kate giggled at the sight of me doing an octopus dance after getting tangled in my pants. The sound of her laughter helped calm my nerves. I made sure I was more careful with her clothes.

Afterwards, Kate reckoned that I looked funny standing in the kitchen making coffee, naked apart from my socks.

'You'd better hope Old Frank doesn't suddenly pop over or there's going to be hell to pay,' I replied. 'I'm going to hide in the bedroom, and you can do all of the explaining.'

Kate came with me into town.

'It's alright,' she said. 'I'll be happy enough hanging out.'

I had a clear sight of her sitting in a corner of the pub drinking rum and coke as I worked the bar. It was a busy night. I was still feeling a bit tipsy from the earlier alcohol, not to mention flushed from our rushed lovemaking. There were plenty of people Kate and I knew who were there, and we both tried to act like nothing unusual had happened between us. Like everything was normal, whatever that meant. All I remember is my insides doing somersaults.

There were so many thoughts running through my head. Stuff that I needed to say to Kate. Ask her. I wanted to explain how deeply I cared for her. How complete she made me feel. How lost I had been without her all of this time.

And it seemed that she might still feel the same way. Why else would she have made the effort to come and see me? What then happened between us only confirmed it in my mind. Thinking back on it now, I realise how naive I had been. Love might be simple in its conception. Pure. But everything that comes with it only tends to complicate matters.

I snuck glances in Kate's direction, trying to catch her eye as well as work out what might be going through her mind. Part of me needed to keep confirming that this was actually real. That I hadn't imagined the whole thing.

Kate kept drinking. She appeared happy to chat with whoever recognised her. It seemed like she was getting steadily inebriated.

I waved her over to the bar. 'How are you doing?' I asked. 'Are you still okay? About. You know. Everything.'

Kate laughed loudly enough for people either side of us to turn and stare. 'I'm great,' she replied. 'Bloody great.'

I couldn't get the grin off my face. Admittedly, it was stupid of me to not consider that someone might have noticed us leaning across the bar and briefly holding hands.

Not long before closing, I needed to go to the back room to change over one of the beer kegs. When I returned to the bar I noticed that Kate had left. I rushed out onto the street. But I couldn't see her anywhere. Back inside, I asked everyone I knew, but no one realised that she had gone. She seemed to have just vanished.

After closing I walked every street in the town. Eventually I found Kate. She had fallen asleep in long grass next to the helicopter landing pad and was so drunk that she couldn't make much sense of anything as I gently helped her up.

'Leave me,' she mumbled. 'Let me sleep. I'm fine here.'

After more persuasion, I finally managed to get her into the car, and then I drove her back to the coast. Kate kept saying stuff, but I couldn't tell if it was to me or just talking to herself.

'We'll chat when you are ready,' I said. 'Just come and find me. Anytime. Okay?'

Kate did not say anything in reply. But she nodded like she understood what I was talking about. I walked her up to her parent's place, opening the door and making sure that she got inside safely.

It still surprises me how easily I hid what had happened with Kate from Duncan and my mother. At the time, part of me felt almost vindicated. Like it was payback for all the hurt I had been exposed to when Duncan took Kate from me. It had been a competition between us that he absolutely had to win. But he wasn't going to, not this time.

I do not know how to explain all of this to Zoe, so I don't mention about Kate coming to see me. It was two days later when Duncan told my mother and I to sit down in the lounge at home because he had something important to tell us.

It was early evening. We had all just returned from work. Duncan paced backwards and forwards, looking expectantly from one of us to the other as if we might be able to guess whatever was on his mind.

'Look at you,' my mother said. 'Like a bloody cat on a tin roof.'

Duncan nodded like this was a good thing. 'I've got great news,' he finally blurted, not able to keep the huge smile from his face.

I suddenly realised what my brother was about to say. This was why Kate had not been to see me. I felt faint, and then a sudden urge to throw up.

'Get on with it,' my mother said, neither of them noticing my growing discomfort.

'Well, I went and asked Kate to marry me,' he said.

'And…?' my mother replied in a tone that left me wondering whether she had known beforehand. I glanced towards her but she was keeping a straight face.

Duncan stopped pacing. His eyes were wide with excitement. I noticed that his hands were shaking.

'And, she has said yes! Just this morning she came up to me and gave me the longest hug. Then she looked in my eyes but did not say anything. It was like she was making me wait or wanted me to say something first. I don't know. She had a strange look on her face for a while there. But then she went and said bloody yes.'

It is early afternoon by the time I finish telling this part of the story to Zoe. I sit and wait for her to say something. She is clearly still deep in thought, trying to process everything that I have been explaining.

'So, you loved Nanna Kate,' Zoe finally says. 'Back then, I mean.'

'Yes, I did. Very much.'

'And did Granddad Duncan know?'

I shrug my shoulders. 'I don't think so. It didn't really matter after they got married, did it? That was that.'

Zoe looks at me, and she gives a thin smile. I can tell that she is not entirely convinced.

'How about I make us some lunch,' I say, getting up to break the sudden awkwardness. 'Don't know about you, but I'm starving.'

'Yes please,' Zoe replies.

'What about coffee? Do you want one?'

Zoe grimaces. 'You know I don't drink coffee.'

'Are you sure? It'll put hairs on your chest.'

She laughs and shakes her head.

After lunch, we sit outside in the sun and listen to the birdsong. It is warm and the air is still. I run my mind over what we've been talking about, thinking about what I've said so far and checking that there are no fishhooks. I also wonder about any new insight that Zoe might have provided me.

'So, where did you find the photo again?' I ask. 'Which one of your grandmother's books was it hidden in?

Zoe looks up.

'I'm just interested,' I add.

'It wasn't in one of Nanna Kate's books. I found it in one of Granddad Duncan's.'

'What's that?'

Zoe nods. 'The box we found was of his old stuff. Nanna must have kept it all this time. It looked like it hadn't been touched for years.'

I am only half listening to what else Zoe might be saying right now. Inside one of Duncan's books? How in hell did he get hold of that photo? Not that the how really matters. What sticks in my mind is when did he get the photo? Had he known all along?

PART
TWO

I

When I was seven years old, I saved twenty cents and ran away from home. Four week's pocket money could buy a decent bag of lollies from the dairy at the end of the road. Milk Bottles. Airplanes. Bananas. Eskimos, which were my favourite. But that wasn't why I had saved up. The money was for the wishing well.

I couldn't have explained where the idea came from. Maybe Tom made me do it. Tom and his best friend Huck snuck off to hide on an island. But we already lived on an island. Perhaps it wasn't so much about the running away, more that I was trying to get somewhere. I just needed the wishing well to help.

Friday was to be my last night at home. My mother sat on the edge of my bed to read another chapter from 'The Adventures of Tom Sawyer'. Duncan lay in his bed on the other side of the room, rustling blankets, and pretending to listen to his Walkman rather than the story telling.

My mother looked tired. She had shadows under her eyes and her hair was all over the place. There was a faint smell of alcohol that I had become used to. I guess we all had our own means for escape.

She stopped reading for a moment. Taking a deep breath, she let out a sigh before leaning back with her eyes closed. Eventually she took up the book again.

I could read well enough, but I preferred it when my mother did. Her voice was soothing and warm. With my eyes closed I could see more clearly the scenes she described. For a while it took my mind off what I was planning to do.

She tried different voices for each character, and she did Indian Joe especially well. I liked that the main character Tom was smart and tough, like Duncan.

'Mum?'

'Yes, Jase?'

'I think I should be Huck rather than Tom.'

'Mmmmm?' my mother replied in that non-committal tone which meant she was only half listening, and finally peering over her reading glasses when I shuffled my pillow to get more comfortable.

'Yeah,' I added. 'Don't you think he's more daring than Tom? He seems to get them into trouble all of the time. I like the idea of that better.'

My mother lowered the book and looked at me. Her eyes squinted the way they did when she had something serious to say.

'Now Jase, getting into trouble all the time isn't necessarily a good thing.'

I didn't reply. It wasn't because I disagreed with what she was telling me, but more that I wanted to show support for Huck. I reckoned he got blamed for lots of things that weren't his fault or not entirely.

'Jason?'

'Yes, Mum?'

'Don't make out you don't know what I'm on about.'

'I know.'

'Good.'

I reckon it was the tone in my mother's voice that did it. Without warning, the nerves and the guilt I had been holding back surged inside me. My palms started to sweat. I clasped them against the sheet. So close to blurting out what I was planning, it took all of my willpower not to. I must have looked guilty too because my mother kept staring at me.

'Do you feel sick?'

Not trusting myself to speak, I nodded and then shook my head as enthusiastically as I could. For some reason, maybe it was tiredness or the alcohol she had consumed, but she chose not to press me further.

'I think that's enough about Tom and Huckleberry for tonight,' she said, closing the book and placing it on the bedside table. She reached for the lamp.

'Night Dunc,' she said. My brother mumbled something unintelligible.

'Love you too,' she replied, and I couldn't help but giggle at her gentle teasing.

It didn't take long, but then it didn't tend to. The door closing to the lounge and the sound of the television being turned up. Never quite enough to hide their raised voices, one then the other and sometimes both at the same time, increasing in intensity until, finally, the door opened again and slammed shut and then one set of footsteps headed down the hall to either their bedroom or the spare room.

Duncan said something from his bed which sounded a lot like 'fucking dick whackers'. He possessed an impressive collection of swear words for a nine-year-old.

'What?'

'Nothing. Go to sleep, will you.'

Then came the sickness again, the one that twisted my gut and played tricks with my mind. Part of what drove me to want to escape, I guess. Thoughts and feelings getting all screwy. Anger. Fear. Frustration. Even loneliness. But, most of all, determination.

If Tom and Huck could do risky things. Adventurous things. Exciting things. If they could get someplace to start again, then I reckoned I could too. Slowly, and with a focus that surprises me even now, I started counting to a hundred in my head.

When it was time, I tied up four five cent coins in a clean

handkerchief and placed them in the front pocket of my shorts. I took the jersey my mother had knitted the previous winter, and which was still a size too big. A torch and a hand drawn map had been stashed under my bed along with other things I thought I would need. Our bedroom window squeaked as I opened it.

I had figured that sneaking along the side of the house would be the hardest part, the lounge being the last room to get past. Normally the curtains were closed but, when I got there, for some reason they weren't.

Right then I almost chickened out. There was only a narrow strip of grass outside the lounge window and with no trees to hide behind. Surely, whoever was still in there would see me. I decided that things couldn't get much worse.

Then the clouds parted. What was visible of the moon shone like a spotlight over the whole of our section. My presence was now an even bigger blob-shadow stretched right across the lawn. I dropped to the ground and froze, trapped beneath the window and the moonlight, holding my breath, wishing like anything that I hadn't been so foolish.

There was no going back. Even if I wanted to, I couldn't reach the height of my bedroom window to climb back in. I figured the front and back doors would be locked and, anyway, one of my parents would surely hear me trying.

Lying there on the cold grass, I discovered some small part of me that didn't mind feeling trapped. There was a delicious edge to it. Danger might be close by, yet I had a slim chance of avoiding it if I made the right decisions and luck went my way.

I wondered what Tom and Huck might do if caught in a situation like this. There was no doubt in my mind they would still give it a go. While taking comfort from the thought, I also figured I had no other choice.

Time slowed like it tended to whenever I lacked enough patience. Just wait, I told myself, but for what I wasn't sure. The trees whispered around me. Eventually - thankfully - the clouds seeped back into the sky enough to make everything dim again. There was a noise inside, the groan of the couch as someone got off it and then the thud of their footsteps.

Had I been spotted?

Straining to hear what was happening, I couldn't tell. Every sound had a dullness to it like when I put my hands over my ears. More footsteps followed, and then the couch squeaked again. I risked raising my head. My father's hairy toes were poking over the top of a cushion.

I let out a deep sigh. Inching back across the grass, which was damp with dew and tickling my legs, I began to shiver. Mostly, I figured it was due to nervousness. My jersey had come untied from my waist and I had to crawl back to get it.

Our house in the city was only a few blocks from the ocean. It was my father who chose the location. My mother preferred to look west towards the distant mountains. As did I. That view must have affected me in some way because the mountains became a central part to my plan.

I wondered if twenty cents would be enough at the wishing well to turn me eighteen and lend me a motorbike so I could ride to the mountains. It was two wishes, I realised that, but I also hoped those who made the wishing decisions might let it slide.

I walked for what had seemed like ages in the dark, down our street and then other streets. If there was enough light coming from houses close to the road and the occasional streetlight, I turned my torch off to save batteries. Dogs barked at me from backyards.

I thought I had a fair idea where the park was, as well as the map I had drawn. At one stage I saw a police car go past in the opposite direction, its siren off but lights flashing. At the time I hadn't thought that the police car would be for me. By then I must have walked three or four miles, maybe further. I wasn't entirely sure I was going the right way anymore and started to get worried.

During the day I could orientate myself with the hills to the south. But everything was a lot different at night.

I looked at my map, but it didn't help. Instead of recording street names on it, I had written things like blue house with big tree in front. Without going up to each house and shining my torch I couldn't tell the colour. And I couldn't see any lights on the hills. The clouds must have been blocking them.

The sound of a vehicle slowing down made me turn around. There was a man on his own in the car. He turned the inside light on so I could see him properly and then leaned over to wind the window down on the passenger's side. He was wearing a collared shirt and a tie. His hair was neatly combed, and he had a round, friendly face when he smiled.

'What are you doing?' he asked.

'Nothing.'

'Nothing?'

The man studied his rear vision mirror. 'Are you going somewhere?'

'The dairy,' I replied, wiping at my eyes.

'The dairy? Don't think there will be any shops open this late.'

'Oh. Okay.'

'What's your name?'

'Jase.'

'Hi Jase. I'm Robert. You can call me Rob if you like. Do your parents know you're out, Jase?'

I didn't reply.

'I don't think they do. Do they? You reckon they'd be happy you being here all on your own?'

I thought about my parents, especially my mother. I figured that what I was doing was wrong, but I hadn't stopped to consider how it might make her feel.

'No,' I replied. 'I don't reckon so.'

'Are you really going to the dairy?'

I stared along the road to see if there might be something I had missed. Then I looked at the ground. Another vehicle went past, quite slowly. Mr Rob watched it turn a corner.

'Wherever you're going Jase,' he said, 'I'd be more than happy to give you a lift. You look like you're getting cold standing out there.'

Mr Rob pushed the passenger door open. I still didn't move. Something bit me on the arm, and I scratched the itchy spot.

'Do you think you could take me to the wishing well?'

'The what?'

'The wishing well. It's at the park.'

'What's that you're on about? A whooshing whale?'

I was unsure how to explain it further. 'A well. Not a whale. It's for wishing. I have twenty cents.'

Mr Rob scratched his head. 'Can't say I've heard of that, Jase. Tell you what. Maybe we could go ask the police. They might know about what you're after. What do you reckon? Would that be okay with you?'

I thought some more on it. Stepping closer, I nodded. 'Sure. We can go there. They might know.'

The next day my father and I sat side by side on the couch in the lounge. Duncan had wanted to stay too, but my father said no.

'Go play outside for a bit will you? You can come back later, and we'll have a good talk then if you still want to.'

My father shuffled beside me and then he stared into space for what seemed like a long time.

'Of all the stupid things to do,' he said, still not looking at me. 'What were you thinking?'

I shrugged my shoulders. At least he wasn't frowning, not like he did when he was about to get really angry. If anything, he looked sad, maybe a bit uncomfortable, as if this was something he felt he should be doing rather than something he wanted to do. Either that or he didn't have the energy to face it anymore.

He turned to me. 'You certainly gave us a fright.'

I knew there was nothing I could say that would explain what I did or why. So I didn't say anything.

'Your mother and I have had quite a talk over what to do. Argued a little, I guess, whether we need more defined boundaries for you both.'

I wasn't sure what more defined boundaries actually meant but figured it wasn't good. I hoped I wasn't getting Duncan into trouble too.

'And we're yet to decide on a punishment. You understand?'

I nodded, nervous about what was to come. Normally, by now, my father would have his belt off and I would be in for it. But this was different. I caught a glimpse of Duncan at the lounge window. He was peering in and he pulled a face when he saw me.

I was careful not to smile back, especially because my father kept looking in my direction to make sure I was paying attention to him. When I glanced again Duncan had gone.

'First things first,' my father continued. 'We have to make a phone call. You're going to apologise to that man for lying. You knew it was wrong, didn't you?'

'Yes.'

'Yes, what?'

'Yes Dad. I knew it was wrong.'

'And still you lied to him?'

'Yes Dad.'

'What are you going to say?'

'I'll say "sorry Mr Rob. For lying to you. And for you not knowing where I wanted to go. I'm sorry for you having to go to the police to ask for me. I hope I didn't get you into trouble with them".... Is that okay?'

'Yes, Jase. That's okay. For a start.'

My mother came in with a tray of drinks, coffee for her, black tea for my father and a hot chocolate for me.

'How's Duncan?' my father asked.

'He's fine. I sent him to the Murdoch's. Joan said he could stay over for as long as we needed.'

My father frowned. 'What did you tell them?'

'Nothing.'

'Good.'

My mother sat in a seat opposite. She kept wiping her eyes.

'Jason,' she said. 'You must promise me something.'

'Yes, Mum.'

'You'll never do anything like this again. Not ever. You promise?'

'I promise.'

She leaned forward and made a gesture over my chest with her finger.

'Yep. Cross my heart.'

My mother kept glancing at my father, as if she wanted him to say something more or was worried what he might say or do. He cleared his throat but did not speak.

'It's not that you can't go exploring,' she finally added. 'Just, you've got to tell us first. Get permission that it's okay. And, be careful around people you don't know.'

I nodded, trying to make out I was sorry as well as being enthusiastic about any suggestions my parents might make, all the time hoping they wouldn't fight again and especially if it was because of what I had done.

'Yes, that man was nice enough,' my mother continued. 'But others might not be. You've got to realise that we have to say no some of the time. Maybe most of the time. It's our job to keep you safe. You and Duncan. I know you both think it's fun to run off and do things.'

My father made a funny sound. He stood up suddenly and walked from the room. A few seconds later the door to my parent's bedroom slammed. It was one of those moments when you could drop a single pin to the floor and likely hear it.

I think my father became frustrated with my mother's tone. If I consider it now, I reckon he probably felt that she was undermining him in. I glanced at her to see how she would respond. Her expression didn't change. Then she made a face like a balloon, slowly letting the air out through her lips.

After a bit, she leaned in close.

'Can I tell you something?' She glanced towards the doorway to the hall. 'Just between us?'

I nodded again, unsure what I was agreeing to or where it might lead.

'When I was young. A bit older than you are, mind you, but still a wee 'un. I did the same thing. Well, almost the same. Except we had an old motorbike and I took that. Back then, I was never allowed to ride it. Only my brother could. And that used to annoy the bejesus out of me.'

My mother had a funny look on her face.

'I took that as more reason to do it,' she said. 'Rode that bike as far as I could, till it ran out of petrol. Got a fair way on it too. Then I kept right on walking, up to the nearest house to see if I could borrow some fuel. They asked what I was up to and how old I was. I said I was almost eighteen and could do what I pleased.'

She gave a half smile. 'Think that's what gave the game away. If only I'd picked a more believable age, I might have pulled it off too. Sometimes reckon I'd still be going.'

I didn't know what to say. I hadn't fully explained about the wishing well, just that I had wanted to visit the mountains.

'They called the local copper,' my mother continued. 'He tweaked my ear, then gave me a good kick up the backside before taking me home. Yep, they did that to girls back then, well the ones who misbehaved enough. I was grounded for two months. Had to do all the chores around the place, and at the neighbour's too.'

My mother stared blankly at the wall. 'The thing is, Jase, we get these ideas in our head. They seem like the best. The light is shining right into them.'

It seemed important that I should agree with what she was trying to explain.

'Where do they come from?' I asked.

She laughed, quite suddenly and a little too harshly. 'That's a good question. Who has any idea? They're the strangest things though. Aren't they? Like they have a life of their own. And they seize us up, right in their grip. Tight like this, till we can't escape.'

Then my mother sighed, leaning back, and closing her hands together over her nose and mouth.

'I don't know,' she finally added, shaking her head slowly. 'Sometimes they must work out. Your guess is as good as mine. Who's to say, really?'

❚❚

I explain to Zoe that running away overseas at the age of eighteen was not so different to the time with the wishing well. By then I realised that avoidance was something I was good at. I could try to tell myself - fool myself - that I was running towards something, in search of new challenges and adventures. But, deep down, I knew that was not the case.

Instead of twenty cents for the wishing well, this time I had managed to save enough money for a plane ticket to Europe.

'It must have made you feel pretty sad, being forced to leave like that,' Zoe says.

I shrug my shoulders. 'It was my own decision, no one else's.'

'How long were you overseas for?'

'Um, ten years or so, I think. No, hang on, more like fifteen actually.'

'Wow. So long, I never realised. What did you do all that time?'

'At first it was all new and exciting. There were exotic places to visit. And so many awesome mountains to climb. I totally threw myself into improving my climbing.'

'Sounds cool.'

'It was, for a while. But then, I guess, things started to drift. I was wandering from one place to another without any real purpose. I got work when I needed to. Tried all the new food. Learned different languages, countries eventually becoming a blur. I don't know. It's a bit like getting lost in the middle of a really large forest.'

Zoe has a confused look on her face, but I'm not sure how to explain it any better. Of course, for me, saying fifteen years is just reflecting on a small portion of a lifetime of memories. The length of it merges into other experiences before and after. Whereas, for Zoe, fifteen years is her whole life. I can understand how my time away must seem like forever to her.

'I guess I didn't really know which way to turn,' I say. 'To get out. Or even if I should try.'

Thinking back, there is not much else to tell her about my period overseas. Nothing that's central to the story of our family. I traveled from one place to another. I became as good a climber as I could. I met different people. I had intimate relationships, but nothing that lasted.

Time slipped by like it can if you're not paying attention, one year after another until it became just a number. A blur. Letters and phone calls home were snippets from a former life, like being on the highest summit and seeing a cluster of lights low in the valley. A different world, perhaps with a roof and a warm bed, with food and a flushing toilet. It was distantly familiar yet may as well have been on Mars.

When my brother's letters managed to find me, he always wanted to know what the mountains were like. He wrote that he was jealous I had the freedom to just focus on my climbing, hinting at decisions in his life that he was unsatisfied with.

When I read his words a part of me couldn't help but feel angry at the insinuation. As if I was the one who got what they wanted. Of course, I realise now - and I don't mind telling Zoe - my judgment of my brother was born from little more than petty jealousy. His attitude also reinforced my thinking about needing to stay away. There was nothing left for me at home.

Towards the end of my period overseas, Duncan stopped writing to me. At the time I wondered what was going on. Perhaps he was too busy, I reasoned. I made a point of phoning him one time to talk, but back then it was hard to have a proper connection over a long-distance telephone conversation. The delays between speaking and hearing the other person speak would become filled with questions. What was going on? Why the attitude? Was he being deliberately obtuse? In the pressure to communicate, we would end up talking over each other, followed by long, awkward silences.

One of my regrets is that I never took the opportunity to question my brother about what he thought had come between us. Now, I think I understand. But this detail is not something I can share with Zoe.

My mother, on the other hand, always made a point of inquiring when I was planning to return to New Zealand. 'Surely you've done enough scratching that itch of yours,' I think was a phrase she used on more than one occasion in her letter writing.

I received a few letters from Kate. She told me about Tyler and how much her daughter was growing up. Occasionally she would include a photograph.

'Your mother looked a lot like you when she was young,' I say to Zoe. 'And by all accounts she was almost as much of a troublemaker.'

Zoe smiles at the comparison. I am not entirely sure what she's looking for in my retelling of this part of my life, but it seems that everything I choose to share holds some resonance for her.

During the time I was overseas, everyone else in my family ended up moving back to the city. For Duncan and Kate, it was because of better work options and so Tyler could go to a school that would give her more opportunities than if they had remained on the West Coast.

My mother followed them a few years later. Mostly it was due to her health deteriorating to the point that she needed to be within easy reach of a decent hospital. I think loneliness was probably a part of it too, wanting to be closer to family, or more specifically her granddaughter. Our family crib had become empty again.

The whole time I was away, Kate remained in my thoughts. There were plenty of moments when I wondered about going home. I even imagined having the courage to confront Kate and Duncan, to tell them both how I felt and how unfair everything was. I tried to see myself standing in front of Kate, ignoring my brother as best I could, until everything was said.

'You should be with me, not Duncan' I imagined blurting out. 'And you know it.'

What was the point? That part of my life was done with. Overseas was probably the best place to remain, for all our sakes. Me remaining as far away as possible was a way to protect the sanctity of Duncan and Kate's marriage. Not to mention my own sanity.

More to the point, it was Duncan and Kate who were responsible for Tyler. She depended on them for a stable upbringing. A normal life. Recalling my own childhood, I knew that the best thing for Tyler was for them to remain together. The disruption that the separation of our parents caused me and Duncan convinced me that everything had probably worked out for the best.

III

'Did Granddad Duncan ever forgive you?'

This is the type of question that can throw an old man off his stride, even on a warm, sunny afternoon spent reminiscing and listening to birdsong.

I can't help but stare at Zoe. Does she know everything? Surely not. There is just no way.

'What do you mean?' I eventually reply, trying to stall long enough for my mind to catch up.

Zoe had been facing me as she asked the question. But now it's her turn to look away.

'You know,' she says in a non-committal tone which makes me think she is probably just fishing for more information. 'He must have known about you two for a long time.'

Did Duncan ever truly forgive me? He said he did. But that isn't necessarily the same thing, is it?

'It's not quite that simple,' I admit.

If leaving had been an act of desperation, then returning was an attempt to face up to that realisation. To finally accept what had happened and to try to move on with my life. To become an active member of my family again, but to also be my own person. At least that's what I kept telling myself on the plane flights back home.

Fairness aside, one pressure that family has always exerted

over me is conditional love. It's an expectation, even after all of our mistakes are added to the ledger. We protect those we love - those we have to love - regardless of how that might make us feel. How that might screw up our own lives.

'In all honesty, coming home made me as nervous as I'd ever been in my life,' I explain to Zoe. 'It was worse than the scariest crux of a climb. I had no idea how everyone would be. So much time had passed. What had I done with that time other than climbing? What had I achieved with my life? Nothing really.'

There is so much more I could say to her. How the fear I carried in my heart almost caused me to change my mind. How everyone else had gotten on with their lives while I had just run away. In Singapore I almost didn't board my flight back to New Zealand. I stood at the gate with my ticket in my hand and so many thoughts rushing through my head. Self-doubt became a weight against my legs. Somehow, I moved. Stepping on to that plane was like standing at the bottom of the mountain filled with unknowns, and then committing to the climb. My experiences with climbing was helping me face up to what I knew had to be done.

My head was filled with memories of why I had left in the first place, and my heart with the possibility of remaining broken. Fear and love. Fear of love. Fear of not being in love. Fear of love not being enough.

My mother was the only one to meet me at the airport. It was probably for the best, although I couldn't help but feel a little surprised, even hurt, that no one else had made the effort.

'Sorry, you must be disappointed,' she said, reading my mind. 'Duncan is stuck working, and Kate has a thing at school with Tyler. Only me, I'm afraid.'

I looked sideways at my mother, but her face didn't give anything away. Was she dropping a subtle hint, something about what had happened before I had left all those years ago? Did she even know?

'Let's get you settled in,' she said, rubbing my arm and then hooking hers through it as we walked to the carpark. 'Look at you. Far too skinny for your own good. Need to get some meat back on those bones.'

'Lean and mean for climbing,' I replied.

'Pah, there's no such thing,' she countered. Then she winked. 'How are you supposed to carry everything into the mountains if you don't have enough muscle.'

We both laughed. I appreciated how much of an effort she was making to break the ice between us. I kept trying to study her face without being obvious, noticing how much extra grey her hair had become and how she was walking with a bit of a stoop. But my mother looked well enough, despite a recent time in hospital that she didn't want to talk about.

When I questioned her about her recovery, she brushed it off as a small irritation.

'It's so good to have you back,' she said instead. 'Finally.'

'It has been a long time coming. Hasn't it?'

'Too long. But there you have it. You can't change the past.' It was another of those double-edged comments.

Then my mother smiled. 'You never were one to do things by halves,' she said. 'Boots and all or not at all. Even back as a wee tacker, you hated to miss out.'

I could tell she was making sure to reconnect, breaking through the remaining awkwardness. Anything that would help ease me back into the life that waited at home.

'Just wait till you meet Tyler,' she added as we were walking to the car. 'You'll love her to bits.'

'I can't wait.'

'Neither can she.'

'Really?'

'Her parents have been filling her head with talk of your great climbing feats overseas. She thinks you're superhuman or

138

something. Jase the famous climber returns home triumphant after conquering all the great walls of Europe. Something like that.'

'Ha! Well she is going to be sorely disappointed.'

'She is a smart girl,' my mother said, smiling. 'But let's not burst your bubble the first day eh. I'm sure we can leave it up to her to make that realization for herself.'

An evening breeze swirled the aroma of steak around Duncan and Kate's backyard. My brother stood next to the barbecue, tongs held at the ready and him with that same, intent look over his face that I remembered so well. Despite the time that had passed, I figured he would still manage to overcook the meat like he used to.

My mother had been right. It was a bit awkward seeing Duncan and Kate again. My brother remained his usual up front self, and at least he made an effort to be friendly. I tried not to stare at Kate too much. She appeared almost the same as I remembered her, aged in a way that only enhanced her beauty.

And then there was Tyler. Looking at her, my chest tightened. If I felt any regret at being away for so long, it was missing her growing up. She was tall and a bit gangly with her limbs, a capable body still to fill in to. With thin features that resembled her mother more than Duncan. Actually, I decided, she didn't look that much like my brother at all.

'Have you been doing much climbing?' I asked Duncan.

He took a sideways glance towards Kate before replying. 'Nah, not really. Other stuff seemed to get in the way.'

'Sounds like just an excuse to me,' I replied with a grin, but then wondering if it was something that had caused conflict between them.

'Yeah, well, hopefully we can change all that now you're finally back,' he added.

Duncan and Tyler asked a lot of questions about my time in

Europe and where the best places to climb were. I found Duncan's questioning a bit unusual, almost unsettling. In the past it had been my brother who led the way, focusing on what he wanted to do and how he would go about doing it. This seemed quite a change of style.

I answered as best I could. Then jet lag started to hit me, so I found somewhere comfortable to sit. I was happy watching everyone interact, absorbing the busyness of their conversation. The warmth of a family who was used to one another's foibles. I hoped they would accept me back with the same sincerity.

Duncan and my mother started arguing over when to put the mushrooms and asparagus on the barbecue.

'Are you waiting on that beer to warm up?' my brother said, looking over towards me.

I laughed at his teasing. 'Pacing myself,' I replied.

'Too much time in that other hemisphere if you ask me,' he continued, waving his tongs in the air. 'They don't even know what temperature to have their alcohol.'

Duncan was making a big deal out of flipping the steaks earlier than he thought was necessary, and only because it was a special occasion.

'Well done,' our mother said, patting him on the back. 'No. Not the steaks. You. How long has it taken to learn?'

Apart from Tyler, in many ways the others were much the same. Their mannerisms, attitudes, how they interacted with each other, the way they were quick to laugh even if the joke was at the expense of themselves. Of course, nothing was ever static. And what I was witnessing on the surface might be a long way from the truth that remained hidden.

I stood and waited beside Kate. We were in the kitchen, and she worked her way through the small stacks of dirty dishes. The tea towel in my hand had faded pictures of pavlova and kiwifruit on it. I was running out of energy and ready to sleep, but this was the first chance I had to be alone with Kate.

'It's all Duncan has been talking about,' she said, handing me another plate to dry.

'What's that?'

'You coming back. When we heard you had bought tickets, it was like a kick up the backside to him. He started training again, going to the indoor climbing wall after work, even running which you know he hates doing at the best of times.'

I tried not to laugh at the image of my brother forcing himself to go for a run. Even if it was just out of concern at not being able to keep up with me.

'I didn't realise he had stopped climbing entirely. He didn't really talk about it the few times we spoke on the phone.'

'He never would. You know that.'

'Why did he chuck it in?'

'I don't know. Lots of reasons, I guess. You're better off asking him about it. That world. It's not really something I choose to understand.'

'Neither do we sometimes,' I added.

Kate pulled the plug. She watched the dirty water and soapsuds spiral. For a moment I wondered what she wasn't saying, or if my intuition was misguided. Wiping her hands on her jeans, she reached for another tea towel.

'No, I've got this,' I said. 'I've nearly finished anyway.'

'But you won't know where all the dishes go.'

I grinned. 'It will give him something to think about in the morning, won't it? Trying to find his favourite cereal bowl. Which one is it? I know he'll have one.'

Kate turned to me. She had an odd look on her face.

'What? Is everything okay?'

Kate nodded, then she smiled. 'We should probably have a talk at some stage, don't you reckon? Just the two of us. Like this but somewhere else, somewhere more private.'

I kept my face neutral. 'Sure.'

'Yes,' she added, pushing her fringe back and then nodding. 'There are things we need to discuss. Most likely, things we needed to talk over a long time ago.'

I was about to ask what exactly, but then Kate gently placed her hand on my shoulder. She stepped on her toes. I felt the warm press of her lips on my cheek. Her perfume smelled of jasmine.

'I'm sure it can keep till some other time,' she said. 'It's just so good to have you back. We've all missed you.'

IV

'What was my mother like?' Zoe asks. 'When she was young, I mean. Like, my age. You know she won't give me the real truth.'

'The real truth. Gosh, I'm not sure.'

How do I tell Zoe that meeting Tyler was like having the best of dreams, and then waking from that dream and realising that it wasn't a dream at all? But at the same time, this realisation was a reminder of what I had missed out on. What I had run away from. Who I had left behind.

Tyler's bedroom was a mix of kitsch and tomboy. In one corner was a collection of cuddly toys, a dressing table with a mirror and a glory box. In another corner was a tramping pack and a pair of boots that needed cleaning. A brightly coloured rain jacket was hooked over the wardrobe door. Posters of rock groups I didn't recognise were interspersed with photos of mountains and even signed pictures of famous climbers.

Tyler was proud to tell me that she had been climbing for the last two years. Outdoor recreation was an elective at her high school. 'Anything is better than having to do netball,' she said. 'I got second in the South Island indoor competition this year.'

'That's awesome.'

'I reckon I might have won, but my hand slipped off a hold near the top. I should have stopped climbing and chalked up again. I wasn't even pumped. Not really.'

Tyler showed me a photo album of her last school trip to the mountains. The class had camped by an alpine tarn, and then hiked and climbed on rock faces in the local area.

'Dad's always been super keen on me climbing,' she said. 'But I don't reckon Mum is.'

'What makes you say that?'

Tyler was sitting on her bed. She shrugged her shoulders. I had been crouching beside her to look at the photos, but I moved to sit against the far wall so I could see her face better.

'Things she says to me. Sometimes. And then I catch them having conversations. You know, stuff I'm not supposed to hear when I'm packing for another trip or just returned home from one.'

I brought my knees together. 'I wouldn't worry about it. Your Mum is being protective. That's a good thing.'

Tyler frowned. 'Sometimes it makes me feel trapped. Or that she thinks I can't be trusted.'

'Doesn't Duncan… sorry, your Dad take you out climbing much?'

'Rock climbing at the local crags, a bit more now which has been great. I love it. Especially if there is bush at the start and then how you get to emerge above it. The way the view gets better the higher you go. I prefer it when there are no bolts on the climbs. It's better without bolts don't you reckon?'

I smiled. 'Yeah, I prefer that. But some people like the certainty of bolts. That's fine too. I never like to push myself all the time. That's when stuff is more likely to go wrong. It's a fine balance.'

'I guess so.'

I flicked through more pages of the photo album. 'Does your Dad take you into the mountains much?'

'Only once or twice last year. A few times before then, but nothing recently. He's not going mountaineering much. Not anymore.'

'Really?'

'He and Brian had a couple of close calls. One was pretty bad, I think. I'm not sure. Mum probably told him off or something. And then when Gran stopped climbing. I still wanted Dad to take me. I kept asking when we could go again.'

I didn't say anything for a bit, preferring to just sit there and study Tyler. She had an intent, somewhat familiar looking, frown which almost made me laugh.

'Well,' I finally said. 'I'm back now. If it's okay with both of your parents, you can come climbing with me any time.'

'That'd be great, Uncle Jase. When I heard you were returning, I was planning to ask you. Dad said you've been doing heaps of amazing stuff overseas. Some really hard climbs, he reckoned.'

'I don't know about that.'

'I enjoy rock climbing but I want to go further. Higher, into the mountains. Up as high as I can get.'

'Small steps Tyler. You can't rush it. It's taken me a long time to understand the mountains. And I'm still learning. Every trip there's bound to be another lesson. It never really ends, the knowing how to protect yourself up there.'

Tyler nodded. 'Gran keeps telling me that. She gives me these old books to read. I don't know. They're a bit boring. I cannot help the way I feel. You must understand.'

I laughed. 'Think of it as an apprenticeship, one that never ends. There is always something new to learn. But yes. I would love to help you. As much as I can, anyway.'

'I think Mum worries about me not knowing what to do up in the mountains. When something goes wrong. How do you know what to do? How do you stay safe?'

'I don't always know. But I try to make a decision, so that I'm being proactive rather than reactive. Does that make sense?'

Tyler nodded. 'I think so.'

'Let me put it this way. If I was in trouble in the mountains I wouldn't just sit and wait for help. Because help may never arrive right? Or it might arrive too late. If I wasn't injured too badly, I'd keep moving as much as I could. Of course, I'd try to work out which direction the rescuers might be coming from. It'd be pretty foolish to go the other way, away from help now wouldn't it.'

A few days later I was parked outside Tyler's school. I could see her standing at the gates with a group of friends, but I didn't want to disturb her. She came running over as she spotted my vehicle.

'I've been thinking about this all day,' she exclaimed, clambering into the car. 'I could hardly concentrate in any of my classes.'

'Best you don't go telling your Mum that,' I replied.

We stopped for fish and chips, and then carried on to a crag which was on a hill overlooking the harbour. There had not been any rain for weeks, but the bush track was still muddy in places. At one point I slipped over, dropping our dinner into a fern. Tyler laughed.

The rock outcrop was in the shade, but the air still warmed by a wind coming from the northwest.

'Another front by the looks,' I said, looking up. Tyler was too busy finishing her battered fish to take much notice. 'It's always a good idea to keep an eye on the weather.'

That comment made Tyler look up. 'Okay Uncle Jase,' she said, taking a moment to study the clouds on the horizon.

'See the shape of them? That tells you how windy it is up there and which way the wind's coming from. Clouds are a good early indicator. Especially in the mountains. They might let you know about bad weather long before it hits you.'

Tyler looked at the guidebook. I was impressed she chose a tricky looking crack rather than one of the bolted routes either side. She watched intently as I racked my climbing protection in a certain order.

'That way I know where everything is without having to really look,' I explained.

I guess it should not have been much of a surprise how much I enjoyed a growing connection with her. Understanding kids had never been one of my strong suits. But I realised I could get by as long as I treated her as a young adult and a friend. She had her own opinions yet wasn't afraid to admit when she was wrong. We could be equals on so many levels.

'Why use nuts?' Tyler asked at the top of the climb. 'They take so long to place and can be really fiddly. I thought that cams would have worked better there and been much quicker to place.'

I unclipped the pieces of protection from my harness and held them in front of her. 'It's a personal preference. I learned with nuts when I was young. From Gran, of course. I reckon they are more reliable in some situations. Sure, they can take longer and are harder to place. But once you get them set right, you know they aren't going anywhere.'

'Dad always says to use cams,' Tyler replied. 'He said to back them up in case they shift.'

'That's good advice, too,' I agreed. 'But in the mountains especially I can carry more nuts than cams because of the weight difference. It all depends. Despite my best planning, there are plenty of times I still don't have the right piece at the right time. Especially when it's needed most. Bloody ironic if you ask me.'

Tyler grinned. She sat there and listened as I described my philosophy on the different types of protection and when best to use them. Then we turned to watch the glow of the sun as it settled over the harbour. It was getting dark by the time we started descending in the bush, the light from our head torches flickering back and forth across the track and the various fern shapes making strange shadows on the ground in front of us. Despite being more careful than on the way up, I still managed to slip over in the mud again. Tyler laughed so much at my clown-like antics that she almost fell over too.

V

There is no absoluteness to safety in any living, no security against even the most mundane of daily activity, no certainty other than the ending of it all. Sooner or later. And that caused angst, yes even to someone who had spent decades making sound decisions around risk and adventure and the worth or what some would call the foolhardiness of such ideals. You would think I had more sense.

'Likelihood and consequence,' was a mantra I uttered under my breath, not every day but maybe every other. At the very least, it was a philosophy I stuck to more often than not. Especially when it mattered.

But that wasn't, and still isn't, enough. Even now, after all this time and experience, I still doubt myself. My decision making. My mantra.

If you handed it to me again, the whole fiasco heaped on a plate, I wouldn't have the faintest idea what to do. Probably baulk like I tended to, and then more than likely throw up. Would the knowledge have aged me? Years added just like that, in the blink of an eye the losing of something I couldn't fathom.

When does the knowledge of what's before you become too much? What's to come. The final act, the only option, being to turn away if you can. Turn inside yourself, find the strength to say no. No more. Aloud if possible, but at the very least in your mind, whatever. Just act. Pack things to create a semblance of order, and turn your brain off if you have to. Because you will have to.

I guess it was inevitable that Duncan and I returned to Maunga ō Hine. The mountain had been a continual if understated presence on both of our lives. A reminder of our shared childhood. A controlling bind. And now that I had returned home, an opportunity to finally face up to the past and the climb. But it reflected a story of lies. The lies my parents told to each other and the country that lies between the two coasts of our island.

The colour blue is a lie. Blue is a cold colour. You would reckon it shouldn't be. Think the blue of a warm, cloud free day. Or that blue woollen jersey my mother once knitted, the thick scratchy one with a turtleneck and the sleeves a little too long. A hand me down of course, like most of a second born's clothes tended to be. That's why the sleeves were too long. A handed down life. Following in someone else's shadows. The dark blue that represented death waiting inside a crevasse.

My mother always referred to Maunga ō Hine as a bit of a loner, a mountain remote and distant not just from its neighbouring peaks but far beyond the access of most people. Her description probably was not too far off how I felt about my own life when I returned to my home country. The not being sure if I would fit in again.

If I recall correctly, Hine was the mountain my mother most regretted not reaching the summit of. It was certainly one of the peaks that she had talked about a lot, like describing a relationship with a favoured old friend but one who she never got to spend enough time with.

Tyler was enthralled by her grandmother's tales of the mountain. Or any mountain for that matter. One evening, a few weeks after I had returned from overseas, it came up in conversation for some reason. Tyler rushed off to search for a map – probably the same map Duncan and I had studied decades earlier. She pushed the map under her grandmother's nose, getting her to point to all of the locations she had reached and where she had been forced to turn back each time.

'What's the easiest way up and down?' Tyler asked.

'Right here, up this glacier see?'

Tyler intently studied the map, following the contours as her grandmother pointed the way.

'And you have to approach it from this valley. The others get you nowhere. They are dead ends. But this one, this is how you get in and out. The only way.'

Duncan and I both listened to the conversation. I glanced towards my brother, but his face was impassive. I wondered what memories of our youth were being ignited by our mother's description of the mountain.

'If you tried so many times Nan, why couldn't you get up her then?' Tyler asked.

My mother winked. 'Ask your father, or Uncle Jase, if you want to know how hard it is to climb that mountain. They've seen it in the flesh. They know, the both of them.'

I can't remember how many times my mother tried to climb the buttress she was referring to on Maunga ō Hine. And I'm sure some part of her regretted the eventual loss of opportunity, a portion of her life that couldn't be realised. Instead, it had been replaced by responsibilities towards a growing family.

For me, the idea of finally attempting Maunga ō Hine was like returning to a boyhood dream, of finally being able to meet a fictional character from a book I had read long ago. A memory stored in the back of my mind for so many years. I also saw it as an opportunity to revisit and maybe put right a part of my life that still held troubling memories.

What about Duncan's motivations? I never thought to ask him, but perhaps my brother had some of those same thoughts as my mother. Certainly, in the earlier years after Tyler's birth and when Kate might have wanted him to step back from serious climbing. She would not have been wrong in pushing for a more careful attitude.

I am also sure Duncan would have felt a sense of entrapment with Kate's expectation. No doubt he made an effort to appease her, but what was the true cost he felt inside? Did it leave him disappointed? Bitter? Even resentful towards his wife and, ultimately, his life.

And when the opportunity finally arose? Maybe excuse is a better word, what with me returning from overseas. How could Kate still say no to him? Especially after his younger brother had been away climbing all of these years and proven himself on some challenging mountains. Now I was back and keen to climb a route that had influenced our family for many years.

But, most of all, I reckon it was a challenge where both Duncan and I could measure up to each other as much as to the mountain.

VI

It was early morning. The sky remained clear of cloud, a breeze lifting from down country. The great spine of the island gathered across the eastern horizon, and its highest points carried an unseasonal dusting of late summer snow.

We stopped at the end of the same road where my mother and Frank had taken us pig hunting some twenty odd years earlier. Twenty years! Thinking back, it just seems like a blip on my timeline. And just like that first time, the sound of the river was like a train rumbling past.

'Hey, I checked and both of your packs are way lighter than mine,' Brian grumbled a few minutes after we had left the vehicle.

'That's because you eat more than we do,' Duncan replied with a grin.

I looked over to Brian. To be honest, I hadn't been that keen when Duncan suggested that he join us.

'Don't worry. He's been doing enough climbing,' my brother reasoned with me. 'He'll keep up. I'll make sure of it.'

Brian might have now been managing the glacier guiding business in town, but he did not look particularly fit. During my time overseas, Duncan said his friend's appetite had become legendary, and was somewhat followed by his waistline. He jokingly warned me to keep an eye out that Brian didn't sneak some of my food during this or any other trip.

All of our packs were heavy. Seven days worth of food and supplies was almost the most we could carry, especially when combined with all of the technical climbing gear we might need for the buttress. I rolled my shoulders, trying to get the pack to settle more comfortably. Suck it up, I reminded myself. The first day was always the worst.

The others descended to the river flats just ahead of me. A pair of paradise ducks squawked at our approach and kept on squawking till we were well clear of their patrolled patch of wilderness.

'Noisy blighters,' Brian complained, picking up a stone and flinging it in their direction.

'Steady on,' I said. 'It's their backyard after all.'

Brian's throw was poorly judged and the stone fell well short. But it got the birds squawking even louder. Brian reached for another stone.

'Oi,' Duncan called back. 'Stop messing about.'

Brian turned and threw the stone into a pool of water like that was what he had meant to do all along. At least it looked like he would pay attention when Duncan asked him to.

The three of us followed the same route that Frank had led us when in search of wild pigs. Walking through the bush was like a trip through childhood memories, all of the good and the bad. Inadvertently, I couldn't help but recall some of my time together with Kate. I glanced over towards Duncan to see if this was having the same effect on him. But he was busy chatting to Brian, and I couldn't tell.

When we reached the pass, the next range was shrouded in cloud. We could not see the buttress on the mountain that we had come to climb.

'She's keeping us in suspense,' Duncan said. 'Playing hard to get, eh? I like that.'

We dropped down the other side, passing the clearing where Frank and I had spent a cold night and then to a point where the tributary river I had drunk from fed into another, larger river. From there we would need to follow the main river further up the valley until we could cross it and then ascend steeply up to where the real climbing began.

Eventually we came to a rock face that traversed along the edge of the river. I stopped to study its features and then the forested bank above as an alternative. But Duncan had already decided which route he wanted to take. Brian was struggling along behind, no doubt still trying to prove he could keep up. He did not pause to assess the face.

My brother was moving steadily across the rock, with Brian a few metres behind, by the time I reached the start of it. The rock was quite steep, but there were book-sized in-cuts spaced a few inches above the water. I shuffled my boots between each stance, making sure to keep the weight of the pack off my arms. The surface of the rock was water-worn and slippery. In places it was coated with slime.

'Tricky bit here,' Duncan called back. I looked up to see which section of the wall he was referring to. I could just make out a short bulge ahead of him, where the footholds petered out to thin slivers. My brother moved efficiently through the crux like it didn't exist.

Brian had just traversed to the start of the bulge. I wedged myself into an alcove for a brief rest and to see how he would attempt the hardest moves.

'That's the way, Brian,' Duncan encouraged. 'Yep, there's a jug just a bit further. You're almost there.'

Brian seemed to be rushing. Then he faltered. The slip of his boot was so slow as to be almost comical. His right hand hovered in space seemingly millimetres from the hold Duncan had been pointing to.

'Fnnggnn, come onnnn,' Brian grunted, making a last lunge for the rock but which only made his upper body twist in the air as the weight of the pack sucked him backwards. I caught a glimpse of his face, wide-eyed in the realisation of what was to come. Brian made quite a splash upon entering the water.

'Whoa,' Duncan called out, a huge grin spreading across his face. 'Man down, man down.'

Swept with the current, Brian was well beyond my outstretched hand by the time he spluttered to the surface.

'Can you swim?' Duncan shouted, knowing that Brian had been the better freestyler their senior year at high school.

'Like this, swing your arms and kick.' Duncan made exaggerated doggy-paddle movements with his hands.

Brian floundered into the shallows, before dragging himself to a gravel bank above the river. Dropping his pack to the ground, he slumped beside it. Water oozed from everywhere.

'It's bloody freezing,' he said.

He looked in a sorry state, his hair matted to his face and wet clothes clinging to his body.

I tried to keep from laughing too much. 'At least the sun's out,' I suggested with a smile.

The look Brian returned convinced me it was probably best not to tease him anymore. He took his boots off to tip the water out of them and then rung out his socks. He didn't look like he would be going anywhere in a hurry.

Duncan had dropped his pack, and he scrambled back across the wall to us. He crouched and placed a hand on his friend's shoulder. 'You alright?'

Brian nodded. 'Don't fancy kicking the bucket that way,' he said with a lopsided grin.

'Dead's dead, mate,' Duncan replied.

It was late in the day by the time we reached the junction of the main river and a steep gut that we figured would angle up towards the base of Maunga ō Hine. At least that's what it looked like from the features on the map, and it seemed to match the description of the turnoff point that our mother had provided.

'Reckon that'll be our turnoff,' Duncan said, but I asked to take a quick look at the map to confirm his route finding.

'Are you happy now?' he said sarcastically after I had returned it to him.

A jumble of boulders with water tumbling between them allowed us to cross the river without too much difficulty. High above towered the steep buttress that was the northwestern flank of Maunga ō Hine. From this angle, the buttress looked more like the prow of a massive ship cutting through the vastness of an oceanic sky.

This was what we had come for. A huge chunk of unclimbed rock that had proven too much of a challenge for our mother and for many others who had ventured here to try. Something so daunting that it might keep you awake at night if you thought about it too much.

From below, especially, the rock seemed devoid of weakness. Smooth like it had been cut that way on purpose. Like it wasn't meant to be climbed. The sunlight reflected off its blankness, the glare in our eyes adding to the challenge.

Here was the potential for continuing a family legacy if we were up for it.

Looks can be deceiving, and this is something I am keen to highlight to Zoe.

'The crux of a thing is not necessarily in its entirety,' I tell her. 'The key might be hidden in small details, features unseen from a distance but up close a puzzle that slowly reveals itself if you know where to look. If you understand which way to explore. It's all in the reading of the terrain. A bit like a book, I guess.'

Zoe nods as if she is understanding.

'Then again,' I add with a smile, 'perhaps a feature like the one we were attempting had remained unclimbed for just that reason.'

'That's why you wanted to climb it though, right?' Zoe asks. 'The reason why you trained so hard. And did all those other routes overseas.'

'What do you mean?'

'Well for an occasion when something like this might be placed in front of you. Something that makes you wonder if you're good enough. Something that might even make you fear it. And then take you beyond that fear.'

I nod. Zoe has always seemed perceptive for her age. Then I give what sounds like a nervous laugh. 'Being scared is no fun, I can tell you.'

'Isn't it the fear that drives you to climb, something like this at least?'

'Mmmmm, sometimes I just like to climb because it's fun.'

'Walk in the park,' Duncan announced confidently after he turned and stared at Brian and me. Brian mumbled something, but I couldn't tell what it was because he was still breathing heavily from the exertion of the height we had already gained. I doubted if he should be here. Whether he was even fit enough to attempt a climb as challenging as this.

'Your face looks like a beetroot,' Duncan said to his friend.

'You can go and piss yourself,' Brian gasped in reply.

I was glad that Duncan had also been keeping track of how slow Brian was moving. I wondered whether to question him on it further, but Brian was too close for us to speak in private.

We stashed our spare food and a spare gas canister beneath a pile of boulders at the river confluence. This was the point where we would hopefully reach after descending the glacier on the other flank of the Maunga ō Hine.

'That should keep those bloody kea from finding it,' Duncan said.

'Hope so,' I replied. 'Industrious little blighters when they set their minds to a task.'

'I reckon,' my brother added. 'One time I saw a pair of them fly up with a stick and then work together to lever a rock to get at what was underneath.'

'You're kidding.'

Duncan smiled. 'But it wouldn't be that much of a surprise though would it? They sure know the meaning of learning and teamwork.'

By evening we had found a broad shelf of scree to camp on, detritus from the mountain and others around it slowly making its way down country and centuries from now either reaching the ocean or pulverized to dust in the interim.

Above rose the rocky buttress, towering nearly a thousand metres from where we were tentatively unrolling our sleeping bags and preparing to cook dinner in the dusk. The three of us sat there for a period, just studying the various angles of the rock and trying to find any hint of a passage up it.

'A beauty, don't you reckon?' Duncan said.

Brian was frowning. 'Which way do you think we'll take?' he asked dubiously.

I turned to my brother to see what he would say. From what I could make out, there wasn't any obvious line to follow to the top, well not one that our mother had discovered, or which revealed itself in this light. I wasn't too concerned, not yet at least. There had been plenty of times over the years when a route that seemed impossible from below changed once I had started climbing it.

Duncan shrugged his shoulders. 'Don't worry about it,' he said. 'We'll find a way.'

Darkness crept up the valley towards our high perch. Warmth was sucked from the land. The rock buttress stretched into shadows and contorted above us. The features we so carefully studied in the hope of unlocking its secrets changing before our eyes, as if the mountain had been fooling us all along. Lying there in my sleeping bag, I absorbed the presence of Hine. This was a technique I had learned on many of my harder climbs overseas. Perhaps the aesthetics that I searched for on a mountain such as this reinforced my need for an external order to things. Maybe I was just seeking an attribute that would help create more balance in my life. Maybe I had no idea what I was even searching for.

A gust of wind washed over us, a wind that had rolled over the tips of the mountains, accelerating through the alcove we were camped in, then further down to the valley and onwards to the coast. Dark woodlands swayed below, branches rustling with each new gust.

Brian was now jabbering on about his close call slipping into the river. It had been a long day and I didn't begrudge him the small rant. But Duncan wasn't so forgiving.

'You were totally fine,' my brother said harshly.

'Well, yeah,' Brian replied, clearly a little taken aback at Duncan's testiness towards him. 'But I could have hit my head or wrenched a knee. Or something.'

'The extra padding on your stomach would have saved you,' Duncan added, and I had to keep from laughing at my brother's take on it.

'Whatever,' Brian replied. Then he turned over in his sleeping bag. A few minutes later he was snoring. I was jealous how quickly he had managed to turn his mind off to what happened through the day. And to what waited above.

Duncan and I lay there in silence. The country we had traveled so far faded beneath us. My limbs carried a half-pleasurable ache of a fatigue from having worked hard to get to this point, while my mind kept its measured resolve because of the anticipation of what was ahead.

'Brian eh? Duncan said, the tone in his voice illustrating that he knew how much of a doofus his friend could be sometimes.

'Yeah,' I replied. I figured nothing further needed to be said on the topic. Brian was here and, because of that, he was a part of the team. Decisions needed to be taken with him always in mind, even if he was the weakest link.

'There's no great mystery to it,' my brother added.

'What's that?'

'You know. Brian's really close call. With death. It's only the most defining moment of all those little quirks that life throws at us.'

'Um, okay?'

I settled back on my foam mat. With both hands clasped behind my head, I waited for the stars to appear. And I prepared to listen to another of my brother's philosophies on life. When he was younger, Duncan always had a habit of talking a lot before a climb, like it was his way of processing any pent-up energy. I guess not much had changed.

But I did not really mind. I wondered if Brian's wee outburst may have been an instigator. Anyway, whatever outlandish theory my brother might come up with this time would take my own thoughts off what we were faced with tomorrow, at least for a while.

'Take the perfect couple,' Duncan continued. 'She's a fashion designer, attractive and sensitive. He's a sporting hero, bronzed, surprisingly articulate. They strut around in their bikini and board shorts, knowing they would demolish Ken and Barbie in any beach volleyball tournament.'

'Ken and Barbie?'

'Yep. Everyone else is jealous, their eyes drawn like magnets and their minds confirming that the couple they idolise represent something they could never be.'

'Doesn't sound like anyone we would know!'

'Shut up, Dirtbag. I'm trying to make a point!'

'Oh, one of those.'

Something heavy whacked on top of my bivouac bag. 'Pay

attention, will you.'

I felt around, picking up the boot and throwing it back in Duncan's direction. 'Keep your shirt on.'

Duncan's bag rustled. His head torch flicked on for a second, and I could see his hands silhouetted in the beam of light. Reaching for the boot, he returned it to his pile of kit and flicked the light off again.

'For some inexplicably stupid reason, like someone leaving the toothpaste lid off or one too many mother-in-law jokes, the couple hit on the idea of a trial separation. Out of the blue. Everyone does it. Even perfect couples have days off, right?'

'I'm supposed to answer?'

'Will you shut up.'

'Right.'

'Or perhaps it's something bigger. Maybe one of them has had a love affair without someone else and that has been the real cause of their problems all along.'

I glanced at my brother. His description was beginning to make me feel uncomfortable. But I could not see his features in the dark to work out whether he was trying to be ironic. Or something else.

'All they need to do is find common ground again,' he continued. 'But no. Ken tries harder than Barbie does to reconcile. The more her indifference the harder he tries. One day he turns up at the house where she is staying. Her mother hears their murmured conversation in the next room and then sees her son-in-law walk out to his vehicle.'

I could hear some rustling, and just make Duncan's dark form as he sat up. He must really have been getting into the story.

'Returning to whatever she is doing, further movement catches her eye,' my brother continued. 'She thinks that he has forgotten his keys, or something else. The retort is deafening, like thunder at the exact same time as lightning or the television suddenly switched on too loud because someone has stepped on the remote.'

Duncan stopped talking, as if giving me time to absorb the situation he had been describing. And before delivering the punchline.

'The mother bursts through the door,' he said. 'Straight away she spots her daughter, bleeding to death right there on the carpet. She is just in time to see her son-in-law awkwardly turning the barrel of the rifle towards himself.'

'That's pretty depressing,' I said, wondering where the fuck this was all coming from. I wasn't entirely sure, but I didn't reckon my brother was hinting at anything further. Well, nothing personal at least.

'Think about it,' he added. 'Death for them was infinitely more defining than life. Relationships are all about trust. What else is there if you don't have trust for each other?'

'I don't know,' I replied. 'Protection is a form of trust isn't it? Or a duty to protect.'

'What, like climbing protection? Trusting that it won't fail. Is that what you're on about.'

I shook my head. My brother and I were on completely different wave lengths with this topic. Perhaps that had always been the case.

Zoe is shuffling around in the beanbag, and I stop talking. She sighs.

'What?'

'Granddad Duncan....'

'Yes?'

'The way you're telling it, he seems too hard. About the prospect of dying or something.'

I shrug my shoulders. Duncan always seemed to come up with some new theory on life, and on death which at least I could understand given where we were. This was my brother's way of keeping everything in perspective. He believed that any attempt at humour, however dark or misguided it might seem, was still better than avoiding the topic altogether.

Zoe is frowning. I don't think she agrees with how I am justifying his attitude.

'But you don't seem to be agreeing with it,' she finally says. 'The way you are telling the story anyway.'

I must admit that she has a point.

'Okay okay, one more,' my brother said to me, shuffling back down into his sleeping bag. 'This one'll get you. Another couple, newly connected lovers still in their honeymoon phase, their life plan a conveyor belt of sharing.

'A conveyor belt?'

Duncan ignored me. 'One last climb he pleads, I've always wanted to do this route. His body remains are like that of a rag doll after cartwheeling six hundred metres down an icy slope. From the distant hut where she waits for him, she suddenly sees a blur of movement on the distant mountain face. Then the faintest of smudges. Of red.'

'You've got a twisted mind, you know that?'

Duncan laughed. 'Or worse still, a slow death. Trapped somewhere. Maybe a bivouac up high on the side of a mountain and no way to get down. And the cold slowly eating away at you.'

I tried to think of some way to counter his angle. 'It'd be painless at least.'

'You know I'm right,' Duncan persisted. 'It's all around us. Especially up here.'

'Part of your Granddad Duncan's description about dying was just his way of dealing with the risk in the mountains,' I say to Zoe, hoping it might help explain his seemingly callous attitude better.

'How did it help at all?' she replies. 'If anything, it just reminded you what you were up against. Surely talking about all the good things in climbing would be better.'

I nod. 'Each person has their own method for justifying their reasons for climbing. Especially in the mountains where the risk is always present.'

'I guess.'

In an effort to change the topic, I tell Zoe how I remember scrunching into the warmth of my sleeping bag, and then looking up again at what now appeared to be charcoal etchings of Maunga ō Hine looming over us. The darkness heightened the weight of its presence. At least in my mind, it also softened the harshness of the mountain.

The stars twinkled like they always did, and I loved the way they stretched my mind beyond what it might normally comprehend. Orion was almost straight above Maunga ō Hine. And further off to one side, just above the horizon, the constellation of the Pleiades gathered in their introspective cluster.

As a youngster I always thought of the Pleiades was a rather odd gathering of stars. I reckoned their grouping was shaped almost like a tennis racquet that had been used too often. For some reason I felt a strong connection to them.

Frank had explained to me that they held significance to the Old People. The Pleiades was the star sign which marked the Matariki New Year, a special celebration to the tangata whenua, the people of the land.

'Those stars appear near the same time each year,' he had said. 'Later on, they disappear completely from our night, slipping beyond the boundary of the Great Southern Sky Father like they have some more important place to be.'

VII

The call of a kea woke me. I rubbed my eyes and looked about, but I couldn't see the little rascal in the early morning light. I wondered if it had already been pilfering through my kit.

'I love the way you describe the kea,' Zoe says. 'They sound like real characters. Troublemakers even, and despite the harsh environment that they are forced to live in.'

'Maybe it's their choice though,' I reply. 'To live in the mountains. To be up there. Not a bad place if you can handle it.'

The kea called again. I turned to look up at the mountain we had come to climb. It remained hidden in the morning shadows. Masked of its true nature.

Brian was sitting up. He was staring hard at our buttress on Maunga ō Hine.

'What do you reckon?' he said while still looking up, before glancing in my direction and then shrugging his shoulders to accentuate the uncertainty of it all.

From the look on his face, I could tell he found the sight of the route intimidating. He was probably only just keeping it together in his mind.

I was well used to the presence of early morning jitters before the start of a climb. I accepted them as a normal part of my preparation, and they tended to disappear soon after I began to climb.

'Big country, isn't it?' I said back to Brian. I figured that he needed to sort out his own head without any soft talk from me.

'Yeah,' he said without conviction.

Duncan was already up and about, crouching over the stove and boiling water for a brew.

'Christ, you two look like death warmed up,' he said with a grin.

'Well, having that thing hovering over us through the night certainly doesn't help,' Brian muttered.

Duncan laughed loudly. "Cheer up, it's not all bad. Got to kick the bucket of some random thing one day.'

I looked at Brian again, waiting for him to say something. But he remained silent, taking a drink from the coffee Duncan had just handed him. This was typical of Brian and one of the many aspects to his climbing and his character that had frustrated me when we were younger. I hoped his indecision, not to mention his dubious fitness, would not be too much of a hindrance during the climb. I hoped he wouldn't endanger us.

The already narrow ledge system we had chosen to follow was becoming even narrower. Grasping a horn of rock, I leaned back to search for more handholds and to try to gain a broader perspective of what was above. The three of us were soloing. Duncan was ahead - where he liked to be. He had just clambered up onto the next shelf.

I noticed that he wasn't talking much, which meant he must be feeling the need to focus on the terrain, not to mention the lack of a rope and protection.

Glancing down, I could see the look on Brian's face. He was muttering away, trying to encourage himself through the various moves.

'Rock! Rockfall! Watch out below!'

Duncan's warning echoed across the void. I quickly looked up. Through the air came a grate and whistle of rocks plunging from a great height. They whirred through the air, tumbling towards our exposed stance. Each impact was like a slap to my ears. I scrambled for somewhere to hide, hugging the rock, cowering beneath a too-tiny overhang and trying to hunch myself into as small a target as possible. The barrage got closer.

'Fuck. Fuck. Fuck,' Brian repeated as if in prayer. I glanced towards him. He had his eyes squeezed shut and his arms wrapped around himself. He wasn't even holding the rock anymore.

'Grab on!' I yelled across. 'Brian!'

Stones began pinging off my helmet, getting bigger until the impacting of them was all I could fathom.

Thwack…thwack…THWACK!

Something really big exploded close by. I flinched. Luck and not much more held the next few, precious seconds together. The largest of the falling rocks sounded like cannon fire, which they were in a way, bouncing and ricocheting randomly. Another one thudded against the buttress less than a metre to the left of me.

I heard a sound that could have been Brian moaning. Then something hit my arm, knocking me sideways. I was momentarily off balance and needed to clasp the rock to stop from falling. My breathing came in shallow gasps. I pulled myself back as tight as I could against the buttress.

Finally, the rockfall lessened and then stopped. It could have been seconds or minutes that passed - time does its own thing in these situations. Along with fading echoes, everything slowly receded to a weighted silence. The sun was still shining above us. A burnt smell and clouds of dust hung in the air.

I shook my arm. It was numb where the rock had struck me. Feeling slowly returned to my fingers. I had been watching Brian the whole time as if to detach myself from where I was trapped. He slowly opened his eyes, looking around as if surprised at where he found himself. Then he glanced in my direction.

'Having fun yet, mate?' I asked.

'Fuck off,' he replied with a lopsided grin.

'I think I might have shat myself,' I added, figuring humour was the best way to exert control over what had just happened. Brian gave a nervous laugh. I gingerly stood up, testing the rest of my body and to see how stable my legs were.

'Brian, you guys alright down there?' Duncan shouted, leaning out and looking back towards where we had, moments earlier, somehow managed to escape death.

'Fine,' Brian yelled back, an obvious warble still in his voice.

Duncan looked at me and gave a slight head nod of acknowledgment.

'Pretty good up here,' he said. 'I managed to find a decent sheltered spot.'

'Good for you,' I replied. 'Was a tad exposed down here.'

'Oh yeah? I wondered that. All good now by the looks.'

'Guess so.'

Duncan turned and studied the edge of rock rising before us as if nothing had changed. Or, if there was something, we couldn't allow it to inhibit us in any way.

'Maybe grab a bite to eat up here before continuing?' he said. 'There's room for all of us up on the ledge beneath this overhang.'

Just like that, my brother was back into decision-making mode. The nearness of death might not have happened at all given his casual manner. But I knew this was just a ruse. We all had our own way of dealing with the void that always waited.

'Duncan was right,' I explain to Zoe. 'The moment had passed. We were alive and for the most part unharmed. Our best option was to get moving again as soon as possible.'

Zoe is nodding, which I take as a good sign. It's important to me that she has a positive impression of my brother. I point out to her how there had been no time for a real build-up of fear. And the shock of what had suddenly happened washed over me in a giddy rush of adrenaline. Our best option was to keep climbing up. There was no reason not to.

I remember drinking some water to wash away the sour taste in my mouth. Then I mumbled a few quiet words of thanks.

'What was that?' Brian asked.

'Nothing,' I replied, turning away from him and looking towards my brother.

'Could be about time to put a rope on,' I suggested. 'What do you reckon?'

'Damn bloody straight it is,' Brian added in a low voice.

VIII

'How did you find that, Jase?'

It was a couple hours after the rockfall. Duncan was grinning broadly. I shuffled across the last section of a clean-cut slab of rock, angling towards the small ledge he had been belaying me and Brian from. The size of a coffee-table, the ledge sloped sharply on one side and ended in a drop pretty much straight down to where we had spent the previous night in the shadow of the mountain.

My brother stood there casually, as if he was resting on the curb outside a city cafe rather than anchored to the side of a rock face with various forms of metallic paraphernalia and everything held together in protection by a thin length of rope.

His pack was clipped to the anchor, and he was coiling the two ropes at his feet as Brian and I moved together, traversing the last few metres towards him.

'Great,' I replied, reaching the ledge well ahead of Brain. Duncan shuffled across so I had a small area to place my feet and rest. 'Those moves getting over the roof were brilliant.'

'Weren't they just. Did you find that jug in the back of the crack, just above where I placed that small cam?'

'Uh, eventually. I was scratching around a bit wondering how you did the move.'

'Bit of a reach wasn't it?'

'Yeah, you lanky bastard. Long arms make you appear more

Neanderthal. You realise that don't you?'

'Ha! Flattery gets you everywhere, Bro.'

'Tyler will hate you forever if you've given her your gangly arms.'

Duncan shook his head. 'Don't even think about mentioning it to her. Teenagers, eh? Her friends get so focussed on how they look to everyone else. It's scary to see.'

I pulled a face. 'Don't envy you one iota.'

'Like walking through a minefield when they come round, I can tell you.'

It was refreshing to talk so freely to my brother and especially about Tyler. His earlier reservation whenever I brought her up in conversation seemed to have vanished. For the first time since returning home I felt that we were really connecting again.

'That cam, the one you placed at the roof? It had moved though eh.'

'Yeah?'

'Yeah, walked in heaps. I reckon a wire might have been better.'

'Whatever,' Duncan said dismissively. 'Got me through the roof which was all I needed it for.'

We waited for Brian to join us. I had time to take in the view – the steep peaks across the other side of the valley, the jumble of ice cliffs off to one side of us and the bush choked West Coast spreading out beneath our feet. I could even make out the pass that we had crossed all those years ago on the pig hunting trip. Recognising it made me smile, and I felt the urge to point it out to Duncan.

'Remember that?'

'Oh, yeah,' he replied, squinting to make it out. 'That's the flag form pass right? Sweet.'

The low cloud had almost dissipated, and I could see through it to the upper terminus of the valley. Narrow glaciers from the range on the other side of the valley fed finger-like into the broad palm of the boulder-strewn basin. In turn, the river folded and twisted, losing altitude between our range and the other high country west of Maunga ō Hine. We might have been a long way from home, but for a few moments I imagined our family crib and the good times we had experienced growing up here and going on adventures. It gave me a warm feeling thinking of that time and seeing how everything connected below us from this point.

I placed a hand on Duncan's shoulder, just for a second. He turned to me, and he had an odd look on his face. Almost like he was angry at something. I wondered what he must be thinking about to feel that way up here. But then the look seemed to pass, and he smiled. It made me think that everything was going to work out just fine between us.

The sound of Brian's voice broke the moment.

'Bloody hell!' he yelled. 'Take the rope slack in, will you. I can't reach the hold under the overhang. This last bit is really hard. Could have done with some more protection here to stop my swing if I fall!'

Rope length after rope length measured off the climb. The passing sun and an arch of cloud gathering over the mountains to the west created shadows that stretched across the buttress. It seemed like everything was now conspiring to keep the three of us in the cold while, a few metres away, warm sunlight reflected off a narrow snowfield.

At the start of the climb we had chatted at belays almost as if this was little more than a sunny afternoon at our local crag. But that seemed ages ago. So did the near miss with the rock fall. Now, we exchanged the shoulder-sling of protection with barely more than a word of encouragement to the one whose turn it was to lead. We didn't talk about how far we had climbed or how close the summit of Maunga ō Hine might or might not be.

But it was on all of our minds. We were utterly committed.

It was Duncan's turn to lead again. He had just traversed across a huge scoop of rock in the shape of an apple cut in half and with a narrow split running through the middle of it. Even just the sight of such an unlikely feature seemed to defy gravity up here. The rock looked like it would be better placed in an art museum. Or a kid's playground.

Then my brother disappeared around yet another steep looking corner, and the two ropes slithering from my belay device did so with a hint of reluctance.

'Must be a hard bit,' Brian said beside me. He had tried to sit on our narrow ledge but managed only half a butt cheek. He looked utterly exhausted.

'Could be,' I replied in a noncommittal tone. My mind was set. Whatever the route threw at us had to be dealt with. There was no other choice.

Brian stared back down towards our starting point, and it wasn't hard to guess what he was thinking. Everything felt like it was conspiring against us. The route was more difficult and taking much longer than we had anticipated. And then there was the weather - the cloud and the increasing wind. But none of these things needed to be highlighted through conversation.

I followed Brian's line of sight down the buttress, back to where we had spent the previous night in relative comfort on that flattish scree shelf. Eating freeze-dried stew from the warmth of our sleeping bags and imagining the climb ahead. The unknown had felt so intoxicating. Everything - anything - seemed possible in our minds.

And now we were, quite literally, on the edge of things. To descend from this height and down this aspect of the mountain would be impossible, the number of abseils required to reach flat ground far greater than the amount of protection we had with us. Duncan and I could probably down-climb solo, at least big sections of the route, but not Brian. Continuing up was the only option.

Eventually, both ropes came tight. A muffled cry echoed across the void. I started to dismantle the belay, flicking two poorly placed wires from the flared crack that had been our pretense for security at this stance. Sometimes anything was better than nothing.

Brian took ages to get back to his feet. He tightened his pack straps and then turned in to the rock.

'See you on the other side,' he said.

I forced a smile, appreciating that despite his fatigue he was still attempting a bit of humour.

'I would quite like your four-wheel-drive. If you get to the other side before me can I have it?'

He laughed. 'Fuck off. Dunc's got first dibs.'

The tightness in my muscles took a few moments to lessen as I followed Brian across the scoop. The rope led the way, pulling against my harness, a small and insistent comfort that everything would work out all right. For a short time, the wind seemed to be easing.

I could hear a faint rasping as the rope drew across the roughness of the rock. The sound was hypnotic, causing me to notice other weird details, like the colour and shape of a small blob of lichen a few inches from my face. I reached out and gently brushed my fingertips against it.

Then a grasshopper with really long legs boinged from somewhere. Where the hell did that come from? But with it came the realisation that I was being consumed by trivia.

Shit I must be getting tired! Sort it out, Jase.

Somewhere ahead, but out of sight, Brian muttered like he did when tackling a harder section. The sound of his voice carried across the space between us, and it helped me to refocus on what needed to be done.

I wondered what he might be dealing with that was causing him to talk to himself so much. Shaking my head, I told myself it didn't matter. We - or more specifically Duncan and I as the strongest members of the team - could cope with whatever the mountain had left for us. There was no other choice.

Then Brian swore.

'You all right?' I yelled, but he didn't reply. My rope stopped moving for a few moments, and I waited for Duncan to take in the slack. The confidence I had felt only seconds earlier now evaporated. What was around the corner? What new challenge waited? Had we finally reached a section of rock that was impossible to climb? Fuck, what do we do now?

Moments later I was smiling. Brian's swearing had been due to surprise rather than fear. Finally, and quite suddenly, we had climbed to the top of the buttress. Hidden beyond the corner that Duncan and then Brian had passed before me was a platform of rock the size of a small house. The summit of Maunga ō Hine appeared to be only a short snow slope away.

It was late in the day and we wouldn't be getting far before nightfall but, for now, that didn't matter. Duncan was sitting on the coils of rope. He was huddled over a muesli bar and savouring the last of the water from his bottle. Despite his fatigue he still looked relatively relaxed. Almost at peace with himself and the situation. He managed to give me one of his goofy, lopsided grins.

'Never had a doubt,' he said confidently, a remark which showed how close to his limit the climb had pushed him.

Brian let out a tired 'whoop'. He tried to do a little dance, but it looked more like the steps of a drunk. I realised, again, that I really did not like the guy very much.

I walked a few metres away from the others, closer to the edge and where I could look back over the valley we had climbed up from. At the abyss. Part of me perhaps searching for its insistent pull. I noticed that the clouds to the west had gained bulk, swallowing the last of the sun. Another gust of wind could be heard approaching.

Whereas moments earlier I had felt invigorated at reaching this point, now I felt nothing. Despite the physical exertion and the mental satisfaction and even the relief that the risk of climbing up was over, I carried an empty feeling. Even now, all these years later, it is something I have never fully understood about myself. Perhaps a sign of weakness or inadequacy, or a dissatisfaction with what I think of as my so-called normal life. At the very least, a detached melancholy. What is wrong with me?

Climb the last few metres, I said to myself. To the actual summit. Perhaps there it would be better.

So, I untied from the rope and attached crampons to my boots. I took my ice axe from the back of my pack. Then I soloed the last snow slope to the summit of Maunga ō Hine. Momentarily alone, I stood there and looked around. The view dropped away on all sides. North, east and south, the mountain summits stretched as far as I could see. Some I recognised. Others remained a mystery, perhaps holding enough allure to entice me on another day. Westwards were more mountains, but they quickly tapered to the narrow strip of lowlands and then the sea.

I thought of my mother trying so many times to reach this place. I remembered some of my other climbs, ones that had gone like clockwork and others that had been equally as epic as this. I wondered where all of this was leading me, and why it tended to make me feel sad about myself.

I am trying to come up with a way to explain my feelings of reaching the summit to Zoe. How I've since interpreted this feeling as being because of the realisation that what I had experienced during the climb couldn't last. The memory of something that felt so critical and intimate at the time would always fade. All that's left is swallowed by a nothingness, as if reaching the actual summit is an anticlimax rather than enforcing any sense of achievement.

What I have set out to do means nothing. It holds no purpose. No outcome other than having to return.

Despite any angst I may have felt while in the act of doing it, the will to climb only ended because there was nothing more to climb. Inevitably I am left with an overwhelming sense of what do I do now?

Later, in the dark, the cold ice of the glacier penetrated my mat and sleeping bag. I scrunched onto my side to lessen contact with the ice. I tried to imagine myself going to sleep in a warm bed at home.

The three of us were bivouacked under the protective lip of a crevasse not far below the summit of Maunga ō Hine. Through a slit in the ice I could see stars twinkling like fool's gold and then disappearing when another dark blotch of cloud passed close by. The glacier beneath us groaned again, like it was complaining at our presence.

The approaching cloud indicated that the storm would likely be a doozy. Digging in was not a good option. But it was the only real choice we had once darkness caught up with us. Brian had been almost dead on his feet by the time we reached the summit. He would likely have been a liability if we had made the decision to descend any further in the dark.

The full force of the storm hit sometime in the early morning. I had been snoozing sporadically and was awakened by ice shards rattling against the fabric of my bivouac bag. Outside, the wind was the cacophony of an entire orchestra being strangled. Even inside the crevasse, my legs were lifted by the power of gusts rushing through gaps in the ice. Beyond the protection of our shelter it sounded like a full-scale war.

It looked like the others were also awake. I turned on my head torch and leaned towards Duncan.

'What's the time?' I shouted.

He removed a gloved hand from the depths of his sleeping bag and held it up with his fingers curled and his thumb extended. He was right. The time probably didn't really matter right now. Just suck it up and see what happens.

Nothing else needed to be said.

IX

Dawn arrived. If it could be called that. We were able to see the inside of our crevasse but not much else, the land and sky cloaked in a dirty grey cloud and mostly indistinguishable from each other. The sound and force of the wind was less sporadic than earlier. Now it was like standing next to a train rushing past at full speed.

At least, in the crevasse, we were sheltered from the worst of the weather. It must have snowed overnight because my bivvy bag was coated in spindrift. But we could wait out the storm as long as there wasn't too much fresh snowfall, remaining inside the crevasse in relative comfort for as long as was needed. No doubt we'd be hungry and thirsty by the end of the ordeal. But we would survive.

Brian got out of his bivvy and his sleeping bag to take a pee. In the process, he managed to lose his grip on both of them. They were torn from his grasp by the force of the wind, sucked up from inside the crevasse and swallowed in the maelstrom. Brian made a last second lunge, almost slipping out after them.

Duncan and I looked at each other. My brother shrugged his shoulders slightly. I wanted to swear at Brian. Berate him for being such a useless bloody idiot! And, more importantly, because of the increased risk he had now placed us all in.

Duncan and my bivvy bags were so small that there was no room for an extra person. I wondered if we could cut them in half and try to join them somehow. But we didn't have anything that could secure the bags together enough to keep the cold out. The best option – the only option now, thanks to Brian's incompetence – was to try to make our way off the mountain and down through the storm.

For breakfast, we each ate a third of our last muesli bar. The gas ran out while melting a second cup of ice chipped from the wall of the crevasse. Duncan and I made extra sure to get our own bags into our packs. We put on the rest of our clothes. We tied into one of the ropes, rigging it for glacial travel. Then we clambered cautiously out of the crevasse.

At first it wasn't too bad. Below us was the long glacier that descended off the other side of Maunga ō Hine. The angle of it meant that we could mostly walk facing downhill rather than having to descend on the front points of our crampons. But we knew it could have any number of crevasses hidden by the fresh snow.

I went first, mainly because I was lightest and probably the best at route finding in these conditions. Then Brian, tied in the middle of the rope, and Duncan at the uphill end. We had around thirty metres of rope stretched out between the three of us. I could only just see my brother's silhouette at the rear. When he saw me looking back, he stood to attention and gave a short salute, like this was an easy morning lark.

The wind buffeted us from side to side. I had to work hard to stay upright on my crampons. It felt like the temperature was dropping even more, and then it started sleeting horizontally. Afterwards came more snow. Everything that was wet froze. The snow slope we were on descended into the cloud-filled void, and I kept stopping to refer to the map and my compass.

Initially the crevasses I was trying to avoid loomed as darker blobs against the greyness of the snow and cloud. But the latest layering of fresh snow was beginning to settle over the openings, and hiding potentially huge slots beneath our feet, gaping holes that I figured would likely open to tens of metres of fall space.

Now, thinking back to the predicament, I can see how everything was tending towards a disaster in the making. Even at the time I realised it to a certain extent. That was why I was being so careful with my route finding. At one stage I wondered if we should try to find somewhere else to shelter. It would be a risk, but Brian would just have to make do. Waiting out the storm would be safer than trying to avoid the hidden danger of crevasses in these conditions as well as an increasing risk from the fresh snow. Then Brian started shouting. I looked back, raising both hands for him to stop moving, but he kept walking closer to me.

'Further left!' he yelled again. 'We need to go further left.'

'How the hell do you know that?' I shouted back. 'I can't see a goddamned thing.'

'A gap in the clouds. That way. I'm sure of it.'

I waved at Brian again to stay back and to keep the rope straight and tightened between us.

'Just hold your horses.' I shouted. 'I'll sort it out.'

We all shuffled further a few more metres. Stopped again. The rope arced through the air, taunt with the wind but not as tight between us as it should have been.

I leaned down and tried to judge the angle of the slope before me with my axe. My toes were numb from the cold. Bouts of shivering came and went. The snow swirled around my body so that I could hardly see anything. I might have been walking on cloud.

Duncan was getting impatient. He shouted that maybe he should go first for a bit. I shook my head. I didn't know how exposed we were to any crevasses that might be nearby, and to change positions in this situation could be too risky. I waved at my brother to stay back.

Maybe Duncan did not see my gesture. He kept walking forward, traversing past Brian and then me, until the three of us were parallel to the slope. The wind eased momentarily, and the rope dropped to the snow and was now slack between us. I realised that if someone slipped, the shock of the fall might take us all.

I retreated a few paces to try to get tension back onto the rope. But Brian wasn't paying any attention to the rope. He was too busy urging Duncan forwards, standing close to him and gesturing with his ice axe. His mind had become clouded with a drive to get down. He wasn't paying enough attention to the situation we were in.

I remember feeling a sudden, desperate urge to do something. Change something. But, by then it was too late. There came a shushing of snow beneath my boots. I saw the others slump forwards. And then I started to slide after them.

I stop talking for a few seconds. I glance at Zoe to see how she is taking this. She has the look of a person who knows something bad is coming but who has steeled themselves because they need to hear it anyway.

'We all fell into a crevasse,' I tell her. 'A really big one.'

Zoe gives a slight nod. There isn't really anything she can say. She has already heard the gist of this story from her mother, and I remind myself that I'm just filling in the extra details.

'I think it took me a while to regain consciousness,' I explain. 'And the first thing I heard was my own laboured breathing. Things seemed more peaceful with my eyes closed. I tried to move, but I barely managed anything before the pain in my chest hit me. Then I passed out again.'

X

In my dream I am falling. Letting go and falling into the silence. Frankly, it's a relief. No more suffering. No more telling myself all the reasons to keep fighting. Because that is what we're supposed to do, isn't it? At the very least kidding ourselves we can exert control.

The silence of an ending, but of not knowing when. Surely it should be weighing on me. Pinning my body. Crushing my chest, forcing me into shallower and shallower breaths until I'm gasping like a fish out of water. Only it doesn't. I feel like I am in the clouds, floating and with the brightness of unusual bluish light surrounding me, surrounding everything in a kind of pulsating opaqueness. Maybe I am spinning, my body at least because - again - that's what we do when we fall. Spiral out of control, pulled by gravity to that fateful impact.

Then everything stops. More silence.

Now I can't feel my body. My legs won't move. There's only stabbing pain, then the faintest of sounds that I finally recognise as my own breathing. Or not, it could be someone else's. It comes ragged and uncertain, as if I am listening to it from a distance. But there's nothing else for my senses. Nothing I can focus on, cling to in hope.

Should I accept this? Do I just let go, allow myself to slip a little and then a little further until I'm drifting away? Until there's only the prospect of exquisite oblivion.

Or do I possess enough of a spark? Can I convince myself that maybe it's not too late to fight? Drag myself back from the dead, like I'm only dreaming, or I have a choice. At least until the pain starts.

'Jase…. Jase!'

It was the sound of Brian's insistent voice that roused me the second time. But something in my eyes was blurring my sight. I wiped my face, and my gloved hand came away covered with blood.

'Jase. Help, Jase. Come on, wake up will you.'

Brian was lying on a narrow shelf of ice a metre or so from me. Straight away I could see that one of his legs was at an odd angle. I tried to move towards him. Every part of my body told its own story. Breathing was fire in my lungs. It took me two attempts to shuffle into a sitting position.

Brian was still calling to me. I could hear the desperation in his tone and see that he was in pain. He was reaching forward, trying to shift his leg.

'Hang on Brian,' I said. I just needed a few more seconds to take everything in. Assess where we had ended up.

The crevasse was about three metres wide. Dark blue-grey walls of the glacier rose either side. A few metres above us was a hole in the ice where we must have fallen through. Snow drifts swirled down towards us. A part of my mind wondered how we were going to get back up there.

Then I suddenly realised that I couldn't see my brother.

'Duncan. Where is he, Brian? DUNCAN!'

'I don't know. I tried to see where he fell. My leg. I think it's broken. Below the knee.'

Beyond Brian, the other end of the rope disappeared into a dark hole further inside the crevasse. I tried to call out, but my chest hurt too much.

'Duncan!' I croaked.

There was no reply. I leaned past Brian and pulled on the end of the rope. It was jammed tight.

'I've been calling to him too, Jase. A while now.'

'How long have I been out.'

'I'm not sure. A few minutes, maybe longer. Can you help me move my leg?'

I became angry with Brian. He was more interested in easing his own pain than worrying about how my brother was.

'Hang on,' I replied. 'You'll be fine. Let me check on Duncan first.'

Fighting waves of nausea, I shuffled my pack off to get to the other rope. 'Where's an ice screw?' I asked. 'Find a screw.'

Brian had one clipped to his harness, but he didn't seem to realise it was there.

I snatched at it, twisting the screw into hard ice beside me.

'I'm cold,' Brian said. His voice was taking on a whiny, almost petulant tone.

'Use this,' I said, handing him my sleeping bag from my pack. 'Don't bloody drop it.'

I prepared to abseil further into the crevasse. Sliding awkwardly off the shelf, the weight of my body pulled against the harness. The pain hit me like an electric shock. I closed my eyes and took deep breaths.

Stay awake, Jase.

The walls of blue narrowed, and I had to keep wriggling my body to make progress between them. They were less than a metre apart by the time I saw my brother.

'Duncan,' I called again as best I could. 'Can you hear me? Duncan!... Dunc?'

It seemed like an eternity. Finally, he moved his head in the direction my voice was coming from. He opened his eyes.

'Hey, Bro,' he said weakly, trying to smile. 'Where you been?' Then he tried to look around. 'Guess at least we're out of the wind now, eh?'

'Are you alright?'

'Seem to be, yep.'

I managed to abseil down to where the walls of the crevasse were pinching tight around me. I could feel the cold pressing against my clothes. Any further and I didn't know whether there would be enough arm space for me to prusik back up the rope.

But I still hadn't reached my brother. It was quite dark this far inside the crevasse, and my voice echoed when I spoke. The bottom still seemed like miles away.

'Can you move?' I asked. 'At all?'

'Nope.'

Duncan was wedged between the ice walls, and still another metre or so below me. His arms were raised straight above him, like he was reaching out for help. There was no sign of his pack. It must have been torn from his back during the fall.

My brother could twist his head from side to side. There was a trickle of blood escaping from under his helmet. Otherwise, or from what I could tell from my position, he appeared to be uninjured from the fall.

'At least down here we are well away from the storm,' he said with another thin smile.

I leaned forward as far as I could, trying to grasp my brother's hand. To even touch it. But I couldn't quite reach. I stared into his eyes. Was that already a look of resignation?

'Yep,' he said. 'Like a cork in a bottle.'

I look at Zoe again. 'Are you sure you want me to go on?'

She appears uncertain. 'Was Granddad Duncan in any pain?'

I shook my head. 'Just the cold was getting to him. And after a while you don't tend to notice it so much.'

'How far did you all fall?'

'I reckon about five metres, for Brian and me. We landed on that snow bridge partway inside the crevasse. But Duncan went much further. Where he had impacted, the bridge wasn't as solid, and he must have broken through it.'

Zoe runs both of her hands through her hair. Then she nods.

'What?' I ask. "What is it?'

'For years I've wondered about this. Mum would never tell me everything, or not everything she knew, I reckon. I want to know. Yes. I do want you to go on.'

I tried for hours. Everything I had learned about crevasse extraction and the different pull ratios, I attempted. Most of the time I needed to work with my head angling down. With the rush of blood and the pain in my chest making me dizzy, I tried to stay focussed enough to keep chipping a gap with my ice axe so I could at least get closer to my brother.

But it was no use. The ice was like concrete. It would have taken days to create enough width. I have since read about other times things like this have happened in the mountains. Stories of famous climbers becoming trapped this way. A trick of fate, alive and unharmed from the fall only to be wedged in an icy tomb. Facing a slow, cold, inevitability.

At the time, I refused to accept what had happened. I kept flailing at the ice. My legs went numb from hanging in the harness for so long. My hands blistered and then started to bleed. The constant throbbing in my chest acted like an incentive. I embraced the pain.

Initially, Duncan was quite talkative as I worked. He chatted about life back in the city and how part of him missed living on the Coast. He was just trying to keep both of our spirits up, I guess.

At one stage, I don't know what the time was or how long I had been trying, I had to prussic back up the rope to Brian. I needed to ease the pressure on my legs and waist from swinging about in my harness.

'I'll be back soon,' I said to Duncan.

'Take your time,' he replied with a weak smile. 'Don't think I'll be going anywhere.'

Brian was hunched against the ice, the sleeping bag still draped over him.

'You've got to have a go,' I said, showing him the state of my hands.

Brian stared at the walls of ice surrounding us. 'I can't. If I try to sit in my harness the pain in my leg is too much. The weight pulls it down.'

I grabbed Brian by the shoulders. 'I can't do this without you. You have to at least try.'

Brian met my gaze. The look on his face was of helplessness, like a drunk with no idea where they are. He was going to be no help.

'You can do it, Jase. I know you can. You have always been the strong one when it matters. Duncan told me that all the time. He looked up to you.'

The words weren't making any sense. They were hollow. They didn't matter. Brian was rambling now, losing control because of his own fear, and saying anything that came into his mind.

'You've got to get him out,' he pleaded. 'I know you, Jase. You always find some way. We can't leave him. Not here. Not in... this. Do something. Anything.'

I stopped listening. I tried to work out what other options there were. I looked around again. Beyond the bridge that Brian and I had fallen on, a ramp of ice appeared like it might almost lead to near the surface. I would need to pendulum across a gap to see if I could reach it. And, from there, maybe climb to the surface of the glacier. It was a chance.

But first, and the only thing that mattered at this stage, was that I needed to free my brother. I abseiled back down.

Duncan roused himself as I approached.

'How are you doing?'

'You know,' he said. 'A box of fluffies. Being hugged by Mother Nature eh?'

'This might take a while. I'll get it. Somehow. Don't worry.'

'I know you will.'

More time passed. My brother was starting to shiver uncontrollably. He slipped in and out of consciousness. Sometimes he was delirious, mumbling words I did not hear or want to hear. But most of the time he was lucid enough and continually encouraging of my efforts.

At one stage I must have passed out with exhaustion. I dreamed of the mountains. A field of snow stretched to the clouds. In my dream I remained in the rocky shadows. My fingers reached for a hold on the rock. My knuckles flexed against the bite of a keen southerly. And then I was moving upwards, pulling and stepping up the ridge, stair-cased and endless. Every nerve twitched. Muscles flexed on their own, as if my mind had detached and was floating, refusing to accept that I must climb. Hold on to the blackness or let go and slide down an ivory wall, spiraling slowly at first but then accelerating, knowing that this could never end. Every breath I took reverberated against the mountain. I punched first one hand and then the other through a freezing veneer that had formed in front of me. Ahead was a knife-edge of ice that carried rainbows. I looked down and was without ice axe or crampons. Still, there was promise of a summit, a reason so close if only I could reach it. My cries of anger shattered the world of mirrors.

I woke suddenly and didn't know where I was. Momentarily I panicked, before finally realising again what had happened. And what still needed to happen.

I looked down. Duncan was passed out again. I'd taken my sleeping bag from Brian and managed to drape it over my brother's shoulders. But, without getting him free of the ice, it was a pointless gesture. Eventually, hypothermia would still set in. The cold would become too much. In self-protection, Duncan's body had probably already stopped circulating warm blood to his fingers and toes. Next it would be his arms and legs. Eventually, his vital organs would begin to shut down. He would stop shivering and fall asleep one last time.

'You should go for help.' Duncan's voice was slurring.

I had worked through the night and was still half swinging my axe as light seeped down from the entrance to the crevasse. I didn't have the time to check, but in the back of my mind wondered if the weather might finally be clearing.

'What?' I replied. 'No way. I'm not going anywhere. By the time anyone gets back….'

'Who's to say,' Duncan replied. 'It's actually quite cosy in here. I still feel pretty good, all things considered.'

I said nothing, and then started to chip at the ice again.

'Look,' my brother continued. 'I bet the storm's gone through. Now's the time to go. There could be more bad weather on the way.'

'Brian can't walk.'

'But you can. Two days at most and you're out.'

I shook my head.

Duncan softened his voice. 'Jase. If you go, there's still a chance. If you stay, there's none. Not for any of us. You have to, and you know it. You should go now. While you still have enough energy.'

Emotions welled up. I was horrified at the prospect of leaving. It felt like I was running away again.

'What about Kate?' I replied, my resolve finally breaking. 'Tyler? What do I say to them? What the fuck do I say? That I left you? That you were still alive when I up and fucking left? No way. I'm not going anywhere. I can't give up. There's no way I'm leaving you here.'

Duncan moved his head. My brother winced but he tried to hide it.

'It's the only way. For once don't be so pig headed. Use your stubbornness in the right way.'

I tried to think of something else to say, another reason that would keep me there. This could be the last conversation I had with my brother. I wanted to know what the right words were to say. I tried to keep from crying.

'I can't. I am not leaving. I'm not strong enough for that.'

Duncan's voice was getting weaker. 'I would. If you were here. In my place. I would go. I would have gone already. You know this is the only option. Staying dooms us all. If you leave now, there is still a possibility. Please. Jase.'

I reached forward again. For all the effort over the last twenty hours, I still could not reach my brother's outstretched hand. I would have given anything to touch him just for a moment. A fucking second of contact.

'I'm so sorry,' I finally said.

'It's alright. I…I forgive you.' Duncan took a long, wheezing breath. 'For everything,' he added. 'I forgive you.'

I was confused. 'What?'

'It doesn't matter anyway. Not now. I need you to go. Tyler needs you. You can't wait any longer.'

My scream reverberated inside the crevasse, out its entrance and into the clearing sky. I screamed again. Kicked at the crevasse. Swore till I couldn't breathe. Until the pain in my chest threatened to make me pass out again. I wanted the darkness. Craved the finality of it. More than anything, I wished it was me trapped in the crevasse.

I wanted to die.

My emotional outburst was swallowed effortlessly by the crevasse, and by the mountain. Uncaring slivers of ice tinkled down from the surface. Then there was silence. The wind outside had eased. Looking up, I thought I could see a patch of blue sky.

I prusiked back up the rope one more time. I knew that I had failed. At the time when my skills and abilities were needed most, I wasn't worth a damn.

I sit still. I cannot speak for a few moments. I hardly have the energy to breathe.

Zoe gets out of the beanbag. She stands up, leans forward, and wraps her arms tightly around me. She is warm. I can feel her young heart beating strongly against my frail, old chest. It takes a while for me to stop crying. It was so long ago, and yet remembering affects me this much. I am still carrying so much guilt.

'I did everything I could to try and free him,' I finally say. 'Maybe if Brian had made an effort. I don't know. He probably couldn't have done anything. I just wish there was more.'

Zoe takes my face in her hands. She looks straight at me. 'There is no fault here,' she says. 'How can there be?'

I shake my head. 'No. I should have stayed. For when he died. I should have been there with him. No one should have to die alone.'

'But Brian was there.'

'That's not what I mean. It should have been me. It always should have been me.'

XI

When I was young, I figured I could control much of my life. But, really, the randomness of it seems to be the deciding factor in most things. All I wanted from the mountains was to have adventures and make good decisions, but these counted for nothing when faced with a series of mistakes and then a quirk of fate that took someone important from me.

There I was, struggling to walk out alone for help. Trying to keep the pain and exhaustion and occasional hallucinations at bay. Every heavy step filled with regret for not being able to somehow predict what had happened or do more. It felt like I was going in the wrong direction, forced to fight an emptiness and an anger that ate at my core and with nowhere to direct it but towards myself. I could not begin to imagine what words I would use to explain to Kate and Tyler.

The slowness of my brother's dying was probably what haunted me the most. Normally a death in the mountains would be sudden, violent – a foot slipping and a body falling through the air, bouncing to the earth, shattering itself and tumbling further from view. It would be over in an instant.

But not with Duncan. I hated myself for not having the strength to do more. Even if it had meant staying and facing up to the reality. Even if it cost me my own life.

Instead, in my mind, I felt that I had taken the coward's option.

I do not remember much about the walk out. 'Not that surprising really,' I say to Zoe in an attempt at dry humour.

I had to be careful descending the glacier on my own. I managed to get back to our extra stash of food. And, eventually, I reached the vehicle. It took me a while to remember where we had hidden the keys. I was exhausted during the drive back to town, but I knew the helicopter rescue guys would need me to point out where the crevasse was.

There was no way they could have left me behind anyway. I had to go back up. Just in case. The weather had cleared completely by the time we flew up the valley. I managed to spot the part of the glacier where I thought we had fallen without too much trouble. But the rescuers would easily have seen my steps in the snow leading downhill from the crevasse.

The mouth of the crevasse was wide enough that the easiest way to rescue Brian was for the helicopter to hover directly overhead. One rescuer lowered in and, a few minutes later Brian was winched up. He looked absolutely shattered. Barely conscious. For a time, he didn't have the energy to glance in my direction or even speak.

It appeared that another radio message had been received from the rescuer who remained inside the crevasse. I could not hear the full conversation but, shortly after, a pack was lowered down.

I leaned forward to look out the window. I could see that the rescuer was now on the surface of the glacier.

'What's going on?' I shouted above the noise of the engine, but another of the rescue staff next to me just shook his head.

The pilot glanced back over his shoulder. He gave a cutting motion with his hand across his throat. I went to ask another question, but there was a shudder as a gust of wind caught the machine, and the pilot had to turn away.

Even though, deep down, I knew this would be the outcome,

the realization took time to sink in. My mind refused to accept it.

'I want to stay too,' I said to the rescuer beside me. 'To make sure. I need to take my brother home. Put me down here. I don't care.'

'Can't do that,' he replied. 'Our job is to get you both out. Your friend needs medical help. You both do.'

Clearly the rescuer could see how distraught I was. He placed his hand on my shoulder. 'Don't worry,' he said. 'Our guy will stay to see if anything else can be done.'

The helicopter lifted away from the glacier, leaving one of the rescuers behind. I watched him and the entrance to the crevasse get smaller. Brian finally acknowledged me. Maybe it took a while for him to realise that I was in the helicopter. He leaned forwards and reached out a hand to touch me. The look on his face said more than any words could.

Zoe knows they never managed to recover Duncan's body. Conditions had become too dangerous to even attempt a recovery, I explain to her. He was wedged in so tightly that it would have taken too long to clear a wide enough space. And then, when another storm came through, it filled the crevasse with more fresh snow. The whole glacier had become avalanche prone and the rescuers would not go near it.

My brother would remain buried on Maunga ō Hine.

XII

It was my turn to speak at the memorial service. I stared at the words that I had tried to write the day before. Feelings I needed to portray. Grossly inadequate phrases that could never begin to encapsulate the essence of my brother.

Part of me refused to be present in that crowded room, the part wishing beyond anything that this still wasn't happening. Just one of those random what-if nightmares that might wake me in the middle of the night. I would lie there in the dark, blinking and trying to work out if what I had just experienced in my mind couldn't possibly be true.

At least the church was poorly lit. Each time I looked up from the page I managed to focus on a dim space that hung over those seated before me. Faces appeared and faded, but through the grey light I couldn't see enough to judge their expressions. I could just make out Kate's form in the front row, sitting next to Tyler, my mother, Frank and Nancy. I couldn't see Brian, but I knew he would be there somewhere.

Light flickered against stained glass window at the rear of the church, and the glare made me blink. I needed to stop speaking for a few moments. All I could do was stand there and grip both sides of the dais. I closed my eyes for a second, and then took a series of deep breaths. Opening my eyes again, I stared at the page in front of me until the words I had written came back into focus. I coughed and apologized for the interruption.

After the service we moved to the hall next door. People came up to me and said that the words I had chosen were kind and appropriate, and then they clasped their hands together and expressed how sorry they were for my loss. Everyone agreed that Duncan was a great guy and he didn't deserve this. No one did.

I remember hugging Kate. Then I kissed her on the cheek and said I would always be there for whatever she needed. She stared at me, blinking. At that moment I wondered if she even registered who I was. If she hadn't, it might actually have been for the best.

It was a surprise to see my father at the service. He was standing off on his own. Our eyes met, and then he walked slowly forward, extending his hand.

'You said all the right things.'

I nodded in reply, trying through the mental haze to work out how long it had been since we last saw each other. As we struggled with small talk, the gulf felt as big as ever.

Later, on the edge of the mourners, I caught a glimpse of Tyler. She was surrounded by a group of her school friends. For a moment I thought it would be better to not approach her. But she saw me looking in her direction, and she walked straight over. She hugged me tightly without saying anything. Then she turned away again.

I watched her walking slowly back to her friends, wondering what I could ever say that would be enough to console her. Or even just to explain how sorry I was that I had failed in my duty to protect her by bringing Duncan home.

There was alcohol and food on a table in the back corner of the hall. I reached for a bottle of beer. I opened it with a coin from my pocket. I thought for a moment and then picked up another bottle and carried them outside. The church and hall were set on a hill overlooking the city. The sky was cloudy inland over the distant mountains, and a cold breeze blew in from the sea. At least the forecasted rain had held off for the time being.

My mother walked outside a few minutes later. We sat on a park bench near the stone wall which separated the church and the hall from an old cemetery. Neither of us said anything. We just remained there, looking across the old gravestones towards a grove of oak trees. A lone blackbird was sitting in a branch and calling out.

Then I turned west, towards where the distant mountains would be. If anything, the cloud was thicker over them. I wondered how the pain that I felt, not just in my mind but physically also, could ever ease. Grief was a part of life, I understood that. But it's easier to recognise and understand the different stages when witnessing someone else going through them.

My mother must have seen the look on my face. She placed her wine glass carefully on the ground, and then she wrapped both of her arms around me. I felt as lonely then as I ever have in my entire life.

XIII

I wonder how much to tell Zoe about the days following my brother's death, and how they mostly passed in a gut wrenching and emotional blur. How time dragged like fingernails across a blackboard. How I struggled to muster enough energy to do simple things such as eating and washing. And then how specific moments would sneak up on me. Flashbacks from the crevasse and especially the look on Duncan's face as I prusiked up the rope that one last time. These mental images would take hold and cling so tightly until all I could do was shut myself in a dark room and try to think of nothing at all.

After the funeral, I remained at Kate and Duncan's house. Kate said she was keen for me to stay, and I thought it was the right thing to do. At least for the time being. Just being there for Kate and Tyler, and whatever they might need. Regardless of how much I was struggling inside, I knew it was my responsibility to support them any way I could. Duncan would have expected nothing less.

Sometimes Kate and I would sit on the couch in the evenings and drink wine and talk about Duncan. Remembering all of the good things he did with his life. What mannerisms made him unique and what we loved about his character. Tyler would often join us, sitting on the floor and listening to stories of our childhood. Eventually she drifted off to bed, but there were times Kate and I stayed up past midnight.

One night I remember well, we were both drunk. I don't think it is appropriate to tell Zoe this bit but, next thing, Kate had leaned close like she was going to confide something. She took my face in her hands and looked straight at me without saying anything for a few seconds. Then she began kissing me.

I understand now that Kate wasn't in control of her emotions. And the amount of alcohol both of us had consumed would not have helped. No doubt she felt a huge emptiness and she just wanted to fill it anyway she could. Of course, I still felt attracted to her. And, if I am entirely honest, I probably kissed her back for too long. It was a few moments of white bliss through an extended period of darkness.

But I had to fight the urge. There was no way I could desecrate the memory of Duncan. I had to protect Kate and Tyler and this was not how to do it. I had to do the right thing. Given the circumstances, the only right thing.

'Wait, please,' I said softly, and then gently pulling away from Kate. I held her hands in mine.

'Don't you want to?' she asked, the expression on her face a mix of uncertainty and hurt.

'You know that's not what it's about. We can't. Not now. Not like this.'

Kate leaned back. She took a deep breath, perhaps only then realising what we had done.

'Oh, I'm so sorry to do that to you Jase. It's just. I don't know. I need something good to cling to.'

'It's okay. I totally understand.'

'Will you? Will you please hold me? Is that okay?'

'Of course.'

We hugged for what seemed like forever. I leaned forward and smelled her hair.

I was unsure how long Tyler had been standing at the doorway. I think I noticed her before Kate did. From the look on her face, I presumed she must have seen us kissing.

'What are you doing?'

I began to get up. 'Tyler….'

Then Kate stood also. 'Tyler, Honey. Wait. It's not like that. It's not what you are thinking.'

Given that I don't believe Tyler heard any of Kate and my earlier conversation, now I can understand her responding the way that she did. I guess, to a teenager, emotions tend to be black or white. Right or wrong. The shades of grey and uncertainty won't come until more of the nuances of adulthood have been experienced.

For a moment, I wonder whether the inherent lesson in Tyler's misplaced anger is worth explaining to Zoe. But I decide it's better not to tell her about this. Even though she seems perceptive for her age, I don't think the risk is worth it.

Tyler pushed her mother away, but it was me she was staring at with a look of betrayal.

'Don't say anything,' she said. She started to walk away. Then she stopped and turned back towards me. 'How could you?'

'I know. I am so sorry, but I need to explain. Tyler, you have to listen.'

'No. There's just no way. After all that's happened, you do this to me? To your brother. My father.'

'Tyler, it's not about you. Or Duncan for that matter. It's about your mother. And me. The way we are feeling.' I glanced sideways at Kate who was standing beside me. 'It doesn't mean anything.'

Tyler stomped down the hall towards her bedroom. I made a movement to follow. To see if there was some way I could reason with her. Before everything was too late.

'I don't ever want to speak to you,' she said with her back turned. 'Or even see you. Not ever again.'

Then she slammed the door in my face.

A few days later I packed up my gear and started to drive back to the Coast. In the back seat of an old four-wheel-drive I had recently purchased was a pack and a duffel bag, my climbing gear and two filled cardboard boxes. One of my mother's old rifles lay across the seat beside them.

I was crossing the island, one coast to the other, following the sun as if its gravity was pulling me, as if my journey was meant to be. Away from the city with its morning sickness of smog, onwards past the suburbs and then the satellite towns that despite their struggles would still be overcome with commuters hoping for bigger backyards and a lane quiet enough to walk the dog.

Yes, I was escaping. Way, way across the plains, going like the clappers because I had my foot to the floor, and my truck shuddering like it was having a seizure. The window was down due to the heat, and the warmed air blew in against my skin. I could smell the hot dampness from overnight rain in the fields passing by and I could hear the hum of my truck's tyres against the seal.

The chest pocket of my jacket held the letter I had written to Tyler to try and explain things. She was still refusing to speak to me. I couldn't blame her. I had meant to place the letter on the chest of drawers in her room before I left. But it remained folded and forgotten in my pocket as I backed down the driveway. In time I would decide against posting it to her, instead holding it to a fire some months later and watching the sheets of paper I had agonized over tighten and cinder.

A few days before I left the city, Kate and I had talked about what was the right thing to do.

'Maybe it is better if you head away,' she said. 'For a while. Give her time to cool her heels.'

'If you think it's for the best.'

Kate shrugged her shoulders. 'I don't know what's for the best anymore. I just feel so tired of it all.'

I went to stand, but Kate placed a hand on my arm.

'Jase, we really need to talk. Not right now okay, but there are some things I need to tell you. Other…things. Stuff that I should maybe have told you a long time ago. I just don't know if I have the energy to deal with it.'

'Don't worry,' I replied. 'There is plenty of time. Everything will sort itself out. Between us, I mean.'

Kate frowned, as if what I was hinting at wasn't what she had in mind. I distinctly remember wondering what else she might be referring to. I leaned down and gave her a hug. But she didn't return the affection, which only confused me more. And this confusion stayed with me as I escaped back to the Coast.

PART
THREE

I

In my dreams - well, the ones that wrenched me awake in the middle of the night, covered in sweat and clutching the blanket to my chest - there was the sound of wind and rain, and a dark, pulsing blue light. The summit of a mountain rose from the others like an anvil. Cold air drew down from the steep, knifing through my clothing until it felt like I was standing naked and defenseless. The chill in my breathing obstructed my view. I couldn't properly see the feature upon the mountain that I needed to avoid. That I needed to help the others avoid.

Not surprisingly, telling this story to Zoe has transported me to my darkest past. It has me remembering how distraught I felt driving back to our crib on the Coast after Duncan's death and the mistake with Kate and the unfortunate mix up with Tyler. And then trying to find a way, any way, to resettle into a way of life at the same time as sort myself out. Watching the weeks and then months pass by, hoping to somehow rediscover what it was I might still want or care for.

I am not a religious person in the slightest, never have been. But maybe this retelling is my penance, my only chance to absolve the guilt I have carried for so long. Perhaps Zoe is my saviour. I must tell her everything to have any chance at redemption.

Then again, maybe this is just the rambling thoughts of an old man facing the prospect of death for the final time. Because I can't tell her everything. I just can't. That is my cross to bear, as well it should be. Not something to burden a fifteen-year-old with, even one with an inquisitive mind. She has her whole life ahead of her.

As was usual, I woke well before the dawn. I lay there in the dark, listening to the sound of the surf and the wind careering around the sides of the crib. I could hear Stags in the other room drinking from his water bowl and then pacing back and forth by the bedroom door to let me know he reckoned it was well past time.

'You'll be wanting outside?'

Stags whined in agreement and, despite me getting up, still gave a small bark just to be sure I understood my first job.

'Go on then. Watch you don't get your nose pecked off by a weka or something. Don't say I didn't warn you.'

I turned to the fire, took a cast iron poker, and stirred at the embers which still glowed faintly from the previous night. Re-stacking the fire with newspaper and kindling, I lit a match. The wood took quickly. I crisscrossed two thicker logs over the flames, held the palms of my hands up and then stood to warm my rear.

It was starting to get light. I walked outside again, looked to the east and peed off the deck. Breathing in the cold, briny air, I heard the call of a bellbird nearby.

Stags soon returned from his marauding by peeing against a flax.

'Oh, so now you want something to eat?'

I took a dog roll from the fridge, cut a chunk off it, and put the roll back. It was then that I noticed the fridge light had stayed off. Stags sat without being asked, looking on impatiently as I tried the light switch over by the table and then walked back to his bowl on the bench.

'Power must be down again, mate.'

Stags wagged his tail in agreement, probably just to speed things along. Then he did a full circle as I remembered to put his bowl on the floor.

'Don't choke yourself, you guts.'

I kicked at the mound of clothes still on the floor from where I had dropped them the night before. Ferreting through the mess, I found my favourite beanie and pulled it snug over my ears.

Cutting four thick slices from a loaf of wholemeal bread that Frank's wife Nancy baked every other day, I placed them on a wire rack and set it over the fire. I unscrewed the stove top, tapped out the dregs, rinsed and refilled it with fresh grinds and set it next to the bread. Soon the smell of coffee percolated the room.

With breakfast, I walked out to a wooden bench near the old rātā. Stags stuck his nose outside again, sniffed, and returned inside to his mat by the fire.

Hard country rose to the east and my memories floated ghostlike with them. They drifted over the promise of mountain summits. Over the translucence of swollen ice and the off-white cloud that smothered everything in one valley but not another. Over the hauntings from a darkened abyss, and then the prospect of another that cannot yet be imagined.

Or, perhaps, a particular memory - and one worth protecting - might journey along with a more lilted rhythm, climbing and falling to the wing beats of a kea. Coming from an entity that, like me, perhaps never understood how to remain in the same place for long enough. It was something to focus on. Hope for.

A rustle in the hedge that bordered our place with Frank and Nancy's disturbed my morose thinking. I looked up.

'Good drop of rain yesterday.'

'Morning Frank. Tucker.'

The old man's bailer loped up, sniffing at my crotch then the wooden seat before cocking his leg, scars across his shoulders still raw and puckered from a recent encounter with some wild boar.

'Get out of it you bloody mongrel.' Frank kicked at the spot where his dog had anticipated and swayed from less than a second earlier.

'Shit, sorry. Suttry's bitch is on heat again, and he's been pissing on everything tied down to mark his territory.'

I scratched Tucker behind his ears, before pushing him away and standing up.

'Power out at your place too?' I asked.

My uncle nodded. 'No surprises there,' he said. 'Bit of a blow last night, wasn't it? Line must be down somewhere between here and town.'

'You'll be sneaking over here for a brew then.'

Frank kicked at the ground. 'Sure. Why not? Since you've asked.'

'Nancy still got you on that no sugar diet?'

'Just one for me, eh. Heaped, mind.' Frank gave me a wink and a smile. 'What she doesn't know won't hurt her none. Right?'

I returned outside, followed by Stags who finally realised we had visitors. The two dogs circled each other, stiff-legged with their hackles raised. Tucker maneuvered in for a sniff of Stags' backside. Stags retaliated by peeing against flax and then sidling up for another go against Frank's gumboots. The old man didn't seem to notice as it trickled down his leg. I made sure to look in the other direction and tried not give it away by laughing.

Frank scratched his head. 'You were up on Reynolds' block again this last week?'

I nodded, taking a drink from my coffee.

'How'd it go?'

'Managed to cull a few of those wild cattle he's been grumbling about. But tracking down the old black bull that has been at his heifers is going to take more work. Crafty old beggar.'

Frank laughed, and then started coughing. 'Reynolds has had enough chances,' he finally said. 'Should have popped it himself years ago.'

'Don't mind while he's paying me eh?'

'Yeah, I bet. Did you get the note I left?'

'Thanks. You think she's still going to come over from the city?'

'Wouldn't surprise me. Has a mind like a gin trap that mother of yours, especially when she sets it on something.'

I said nothing. A sapling near the driveway dipped alarmingly when two hefty kererū landed on its branches. They bobbed their heads and pecked at the new growth.

'So, are you around for the rest of this week?'

I nodded. 'Far as I know. Probably got some days guiding on the ice.'

Frank took a sip from his drink, screwing up his face and nodding. 'Now, that's a brew. Nancy's been wanting me to cut back altogether. Doctor says it's not good for my heart.'

I grinned. 'Everything's bloody well bad for us, isn't it?'

'So they'd have us believe. Most of them wouldn't know what was right if it upped and bit them on the pecker.'

Frank leaned over, his coughing echoing off the house again. I tried not to be too obvious in checking to see that he was okay. It seemed he had aged more in the last year than any of the years before that, which probably shouldn't have come as much of a surprise, especially given everything that had happened recently to our family. I couldn't help but feel responsible.

'You been talking to Kate at all lately?' Frank asked.

I glanced towards my uncle to gauge how particular he was being with the questioning, but he made a point of staring off towards the mountains.

'Just the other night actually,' I replied.

He turned back. 'Oh yeah?'

'Yeah. Nah. Same same, eh.'

Frank shook his head. 'Women.'

'Well, to be fair this has been dumped on her,' I reasoned. 'The whole bloody mess. If it's anyone's fault, it's mine.'

Frank kicked at the ground. 'I don't know about that. No one's fault when stuff happens the wrong way like it tends to. Especially when we least expect it. Anyway, far as I understand things, Brian should be the one shouldering the largest portion.'

I didn't reply. Instead, I looked up to the same mountains my uncle had been studying so intently only moments earlier. Clouds curved their hogsbacks over the summits, blocking out the light from the highest points.

The rain came in again that evening. Torrential and persistent, it pooled across the footpaths and rushed along the roadside curbs of the town. Despite the weather, the local pub was still humping along to loud music. Most of the guiding crew I worked with appeared to be there along with a typically boisterous mix of tourists.

'That you JW?' Papps called out, shading his eyes from the lights as he saw me step inside. The other guides all turned around. Papps walked up and put an arm around me to lead me to their table.

'Where you been?' he asked. 'Get up here. Get the man a beer. Rally!'

'Not my round,' Rally replied. 'I got the last one. Jase you look like a drowned rat. Is it still bloody well raining?'

'Would seem that way.' I smiled, pulling a stool up.

'Troy!' said Papps, slapping his hand on the table. 'Must be your turn.'

'Nah, I'm off home. Leave you lads to it.'

'What?'

'Missus said I'm not home by seven, no point me going at all.'

'She got you by the short ones,' Papps commented, putting both hands in front of his groin and clenching them tight.

'At least I got a missus, mate.'

The guides all laughed.

Papps stood up. 'Bloke's got to do everything himself. JW, take my shot. Rally, shove over will you. Give the man some room.'

'You sure?' I replied dubiously, glancing over towards the pool table in the middle of the bar.

'Sure I'm sure.'

I took the pool cue and made my way to the table. 'What are we on?'

'Overs. Try to sink something for a change.'

'That'd be the day,' Rally said, smirking.

'Can't all be sharks,' I replied.

'A guppy would do, mate. A wee bloody tadpole even.'

'Yeah, yeah.' I stood at the table and studied the options. An English voice came from the dark on the other side of the bar. 'Hey! Where's the other fella?'

'What?'

'The other fella. The big guy. Blondie.'

'He's at the bar.'

'You can't swap.'

I squinted, trying to see past the low fluorescent light hanging over the table. 'What?'

'I said you can't swap partners. It's against the rules.'

'Rules?' I looked around. 'You're kidding right?'

'Does it sound like I'm kidding?'

I still couldn't see who I was talking to. Eventually someone stepped into the light. He had his hands raised. 'Sorry, pal. My buddy's a bit of a stickler. You take your shot.'

'Don't tell him that, you twat.'

The guy turned back to his mate who was still hidden in the dark. 'Pull your bloody head in.'

I looked at the bloke standing in front of me. He was unshaven, had slicked-back hair and wore a dark hoody. Then, I glanced towards the source of the first voice. Maybe they were construction workers from the new hotel being built in town. For some reason,

I felt a bit annoyed at the carry on. Must just be tired. Let it go, I reasoned to myself.

I turned to the guy in the hoody. 'You sure?' I said, trying not to sound too sarcastic. 'I don't want to go treading on anyone's toes if it's that important.'

He waved his arms around again. 'You're all right.'

I studied the pool table. The balls were mostly clustered together with no clear angles. I finally decided on the ten for the far left pocket. Hopefully, the white ball would kick back and break the pack. At least it seemed like a good plan.

'You going to shoot or what?' Rally called.

With my chin lined over the cue, I exhaled, and stabbed at the white. The balls bounced around the table, and nothing dropped apart from the white which eventually cannoned in off the ten ball.

'Great shot!' the English voice shouted. 'You can keep playing.'

'Bloody hell JW,' said Papps, returning with three pints and a bag of chips. 'My dog could shoot better than that.'

'Your dog can't even piss straight.'

I rested the cue against Rally's chair. Rally was emptying his glass. He smacked his lips and reached for a fresh pint. 'Good pickings tonight,' he said.

'That's what you say every night,' I replied.

'I'm telling you. Papps reckons he's well advanced.'

'Could be,' Papps agreed, nodding his head in the direction of another table. I did not turn around.

'Bloody young 'uns, always thinking with the smallest part of your body eh?'

'Use it or lose it JW.'

I leaned back on my bar stool, stretching my back, and feeling at the old scar on my head. 'Wouldn't want to cramp your style. I'll just have this and be off then.'

'You've only just got here,' Papps complained.

'Older you get the more shut eye you need. I'm on steps in the morning, as are you Papps. Aren't you?'

'Oh yeah. Can't you handle it, old timer? What are you now, must be mid 50s by the looks of that receding hair line?'

'Smart arse.'

I enjoyed Papps' company. While some of the other younger guides seemed too cocksure for their own good, Papps had a confident, friendly cheek to him that reminded me a bit of Duncan. By all accounts he could climb decently too. I slapped him on the back.

'Drink up mate,' I said. 'Dutch courage, that's what you need.'

I felt a hand on my shoulder. 'You're back then.'

I turned in my seat. 'Hi Brian. Yep, got out last night.'

'Hope you're not too tired to do your shift tomorrow. I've got you on steps first thing.'

To any observer, Brian's comment might have seemed innocent enough. But I could tell that he was having a dig. Despite his own incompetence, I figured he still held some resentment. Maybe having a go at me helped ease his own guilt.

'Don't you worry, Jase'll be fine,' said Papps beside me. 'Fitter than the most of us by a fair margin. You especially,' he added, giving Brian's stomach a cheeky pat.

I must admit I enjoyed seeing Brian cringe a little at the jibe. I had never really liked him much, but since the accident his presence tended to irk me even more.

'Right then,' he said. 'I've got some more office stuff to sort out. See you all later.'

'Not if we see you first,' Papps mumbled under his breath.

'Amen to that,' I added, before draining the rest of my beer in one long swig.

'Don't let him needle you,' Papps said quietly so the others couldn't hear. 'He's full of it at the best of times. You know that. We all know it.'

'Yeah,' I replied, the anger obvious in my voice. 'Anyway. Must be my round, isn't it?'

'There you go,' Papps said with a wide grin. 'Drown your sorrows mate. That's the mature way of dealing with stress.'

A loud voice came from the other side of the bar. 'Have you lovebirds finished over there or what? Been waiting for you to take your bloody shot.'

I recognised the voice as being one of the English guys again.

'Better go take your turn,' I said to Papps.

'Yep. Wouldn't want to go and offend their fragile senses now, would we?'

I was standing at the bar, waiting to order, when there was a shout from near the pool table. I turned around to see someone holding Papps by the front of his jersey. A chair tipped over. Papps' head jolted forward after getting struck from behind by someone else. I quickly realised it must have been the same two English blokes. Something in me snapped. Next thing, I grabbed hold of the closest guy and started hitting him as hard as I could. He put his hands up to protect his face and I kneed him in the groin. The guy slumped forward, and I kept kicking him until someone grabbed me from behind. I was about to sock them one too, before realising it was Rally.

'Jase. JASE! Ease up, mate. It's all done with.'

My rage settled enough for me to see what was going on. And just before Geoff the manager strode in from the kitchen. Geoff was probably the only guy in the pub bigger than Papps.

'What the fuck's going on here?' he yelled as he filled the door frame, standing there with an old cricket bat in his hand which he claimed was once personally signed by the cricketing legend Lance Cairns. 'The Master Blaster' he called it. It had many dents and the handle had been replaced more than once. Geoff was a third generation Coaster. He liked to brawl as much as the next local, just not when it was his own pub getting beat up in the process.

Papps had the taller of the two English blokes in a headlock and looked to be almost enjoying himself now. Reluctantly, he let go.

'These two needed a bit of explaining to,' he said to Geoff. 'You know, about the local table rules.'

'Okay gentlemen,' Geoff replied, pointing towards the door with his bat. 'Think you've outstayed your welcome. You too Papps.'

Papps started to protest then shrugged his shoulders. 'Can I finish my beer first?'

Geoff looked at me but didn't say anything. He nodded towards the English guys. 'You two, off you go then, go on.'

They glanced at each other. The one with a split lip bent down to pick up his jacket, and then they walked slowly from the bar.

Papps picked up a chair which was now broken and handed the various pieces of it to Geoff. He smiled sheepishly. 'Sorry mate. I don't know what they were on about.'

'Like a fly to a fresh pile of horse shit, Papps,' Geoff said, shaking his head. 'Just tidy up will you. You too Jase. Best let those two cool off in the rain before you head out.'

'Sure, Geoff,' Papps said. Then he smiled cheekily. 'Hey, can we order some chips while we're waiting?'

Geoff shook his head again as he walked back to the kitchen.

Papps settled in by me and brushed at his hair.

'You just can't keep out of it can you?' I said.

'Me? You went off like a double happy. Talk about flicking a switch.'

I didn't say anything in reply. My hands were still shaking, but Papps seemed hardly ruffled by the experience.

'So JW,' he said, choosing to change the topic. 'When are you coming out for a climb? Rally and I are keen for a mission sometime if you're keen.'

I felt a spot on my jaw where one of the English guys had clipped it with his elbow. 'No, no I don't think so. Thanks anyway.'

'Are you sure?'

'Yeah I'm sure.'

Rally wandered off to the toilet. Papps watched him go and then cleared his throat. 'So... when are you going to get back on the horse?'

'What's that?'

'Climb again. You know you've got to at some stage.'

I looked at my workmate and friend. Usually Papps was a bit of a joker, but his face appeared serious for a change.

'Hadn't really thought about it, to be honest.'

'You should. Doesn't matter what it is. Even just being up there will be enough. Don't you reckon?'

'I guess.'

Papps' voice softened. 'Just the two of us if you want. Next fine day off we could chopper up to one of the high huts and go do a decent route. On Crowter even. Whatever you feel like. How about that?'

'I don't know, Papps.'

'You don't have to know. Just about time you did it is all.'

There was nothing to say. I stared at the window. The rain plopped against it and water droplets slid down the pane. Of course, it was one of the many mountains I had climbed with Duncan, just the two of us tackling the steep and icy South Face. I had been 17 at the time. It was the first climb we had succeeded on without our mother. For me, it still remained one of our best climbs together, a route that felt like we were performing as a team rather than trying to compete against each other.

'Come on, just us,' Papps said.

'All right.'

'What?'

'Alright, I said.'

'That's the way.' Papps leaned closer. 'It'll be okay, you'll see.'

'Anything to keep me occupied, eh?'

The hot chips arrived not long before Rally who had a knack for timing these things. He leaned over and reached for a fistful and dabbed them into the bowl of tomato sauce without waiting to be invited. Then he tried to get them into his mouth in one go and ended up smearing tomato sauce across his face.

'Anyone want another beer?' he said with a mouthful, spitting morsels of food and the sauce in all directions.

'Since you're asking,' Papps replied, making a deal of wiping himself.

'Same again,' I added. 'More chips too, you greedy beggar.'

Rally smiled over his shoulder as he walked to the bar.

'Must have hollow legs that one,' Papps said, watching our workmate weave through the crowd towards the bar.

I smiled. 'He certainly knows how to pack it away.'

Rally returned with the beers and then Geoff came up and put his fingers into the empties and took them away. He didn't say anything about Papps or me having to leave. Others arrived to gather at the bar and sit at the tables and laugh and clink their glasses together and search their pockets for more coins for the pool table. Everyone cursed the weather.

II

I'm a bit surprised how amused Zoe is at my pub story. That's probably for the best. She seems to have missed the fact I was carrying so much anger inside that I needed to lash out in violence when a situation arose. Instead of trying to calm things down I had wanted it to escalate. Maybe a part of me even embraced the prospect.

'Your workmates sound like fun,' she says.

'They were, well most of the time. Papps especially. He was someone you could rely on. We ended up doing some good climbs together. Afterwards.'

By the next day the rain had cleared, and an early morning mist settled over the town. It muffled the sound of my steps as I walked down the narrow gravel drive behind the glacier guiding office. I sat on the steps below the storeroom. Soon the thumping of helicopter blades could be heard from the south. For a moment I reflected on the times I had listened for that sound, hoping for the approach of help when I needed it. The racket seemed to pause overhead before easing down through the fog.

I looked up to see which helicopter it was, the call sign ZOE-14 painted on its underside eventually coming into view.

'Wait. What?' asks Zoe suddenly.

'What what?' I reply, purposefully being obtuse. I wondered if she would pick up on it.

'The name on the helicopter....'

'What about it?'

'You said "Zoe".'

'I did,' I reply, trying to keep the smile from my face.

'Is it…is that where my name came from?'

'What, you think your mother would name you after a helicopter? Really?'

'Well, did she?'

I could not help but laugh, probably giving the game away at the same time. 'Ah, you'll have to be asking her that one, Sawn Off.'

Beckett's braille-like flying never ceased to amaze me. Everyone who knew about these things reckoned she was the best pilot around. Some of the blokes talked a good game comparing themselves to her, but it was nothing more than sexism. If there was ever a difficult pick up on the glacier because the cloud had come in off the sea earlier than expected, I would request Beckett rather than risk it with one of the lesser capable or experienced pilots. Some of them were little better than cowboys.

I had my axe, crampons, and a small pack of provisions, and I left these at the bottom of the stairs. The key to the storeroom was on a nail beside the door. I grabbed a radio that had been charging overnight and returned outside, reaching the helipad just as Beckett touched down. She powered down the rotors and climbed out of the Hughes 500.

'How you doing?' she shouted against the din of the blades, giving a thumbs up at the same time.

I waggled my hand. 'Can't complain,' I called back.

'Sure you can.' Beckett walked over to the fuel drum and lifted the nozzle. 'Just you this morning?'

I pointed at myself and nodded. We both took a few steps further away from the machine, so it was easier to talk.

'Papps shacked up again? I'm presuming that's why he's not here too.'

I grinned, and then gave a suggestive wink. 'You know he only does it to impress you.'

'What's that?' Beckett replied, turning towards me and frowning.

'Proving his, um, prowess. It's you he fancies. Thought you knew.'

Beckett had a throaty laugh. I could understand Papps' attraction for her. 'Heard you both got into another dust up last night,' she said, changing the subject.

'News travels fast. Nothing to write home about. Just a couple of hot-headed tourists.'

'You want to be keeping your own noggin down. Papps can take care of himself. I mean look at the size of him. But you. You're not really wired for it eh?' Beckett tapped the side of her head. 'In here, I mean.'

It was my turn to change the subject. 'How's the weather looking up higher?'

'Clear after twenty feet or so. Light sou'west, blowing five to ten knots. Bit of cirrus out to the north. Might kick in later today.'

I nodded. 'Have you got much on?'

'Two lots of scenics after I drop you but not till later, then a pick-up from over the other side of the range mid-afternoon. If the weather holds, that is.'

'Reckon it will?'

Beckett grinned. 'You tell me, and we'll go buy a Lotto ticket.'

We climbed into the helicopter. The Hughie shook itself awake as Beckett hugged the joystick between her knees. 'Wind's getting up already,' she said through the headset as we lifted above the fog.

I adjusted my mouthpiece. 'I don't mind. A half day trip will do me fine.'

'If you're lucky! All hell would have to break loose before Brian calls any tours off. Has a nose for money, that man.'

I grinned, then turned to look out my side at the fog that hung over the lowlands. Tree tops poked through like lone sentinels, and ridge lines twisted their way towards the divide. The mountains sat well above the mist, clear and cold, and with a light dusting of fresh snow near the summits. Below the helicopter the glacier glowed an intense blue.

'That rain cleaned her up pretty good,' Beckett said.

'Yep and washed away all of my steps.'

The snaking sweep of ice squeezed down between eroding ridges, a latticework of crevasses opening through the troughs and closing again at the plateaus. I could not help but shudder. The sight of the crevasses, especially from this angle, made me think about the accident for a moment. Remember the look on Duncan's face and his outstretched arms. How close his hand was to mine.

I took a deep breath. 'Just up there'll do,' I said to Beckett, pointing at a flattish spot in the distance, further up the glacier.

'Right you are.'

I tried to make myself not do it. Look to the south, instinctively, across the snowy summits until I could see one in particular. For a few seconds we were high enough, and just before Beckett began spiraling the helicopter back down towards the glacier. I knew exactly which direction to check and beyond which ridge line. Maunga ō Hine rose over the horizon, distant and alone, its steepness a challenge and a rebuttal, as if a single chunk of ice and stone held the essence of capturing everything good and bad in my life in one memorial.

I didn't think Beckett had noticed me staring to the south. But she chose to bring the 500 around one more time before pushing the joystick forward, finally setting us on a jumble of moraine with the nose of the helicopter facing uphill.

'Take care out there Mr Williamson,' she said.

'Always do.'

I shut the door, checked the latch, and crouched low, covering my face against any grit stirred up by the rotor wash. I stood once the helicopter had lifted away, and gave Beckett a thumb's up as she swept past, heading back down the valley. Then I checked my watch. There was still another three hours before the first tour reached the terminal moraine, plenty of time to get the steps cut back down towards them. Further up, above the glacier, clouds of snow wafted off the high ridges and trailed to the northeast. Like feathery plumes, they drifted with the wind, settling again in the sheltered lee of the mountains.

I sat there and drunk a cup of coffee from my thermos, trying to draw my mind away from the emotions I had struggled with moments earlier. I turned and looked at the glacier, considering how easy it was to relate to this place through its human elements. How it went through good times and bad in terms of growth and how there were other influences, some like the bedrock beneath that it would strive against, but then others like the rising temperatures of the planet that could, ultimately, prove too much for its continuing existence. Much like the life of a person, I thought. Any life. My own.

I leaned back and closed my eyes, enjoying the growing warmth of the sun on my face and the quietly groaning ice beneath me. I lay there and recalled a story that my mother had told me years earlier regarding the name of the glacier: Tears of the Avalanche Girl, Hine, and what her love would cost her.

Like the tale, concepts of love and loss and a need to protect those I loved were connected to this place. The moods of the landscape seemed to affect anyone who chose its pathless opportunities, and in so many ways. Sometimes there could be comfort gained from knowing and understanding this. But, more often, the randomness of everything we did and what happened to us made me wonder if there could ever be any purpose in the world.

III

My mother was at the crib when I arrived back in the evening. She was sitting in front of the fire with Frank. They looked like they had been there for a while, quietly working through my supply of beer. My mother stood up and we hugged. Stags eventually dragged himself up from the mat by the fire to also say hi and for me to give him a scratch behind his ear.

'How have you been?' my mother asked.

'Okay. You know.'

She looked me up and down. 'Well it's nice to see you. Been a while.'

'It has. You're looking good.'

My mother laughed, and Frank chuckled from his seat. 'Yeah right,' she said. 'Flattery will get you nowhere. We always wondered if your eyesight was off. So, you been getting out much?'

'A bit.'

'Good.' My mother nodded and sat back down, gingerly rubbing her knee. 'You want to keep at it,' she added. 'Before you know, one day you'll wake up and wonder where it's all gone.'

'Where has it all gone?' Frank asked.

'Buggered if I can remember,' she replied, scratching the top of her head, and putting on a puzzled look. 'But I'll certainly drink to where it's come from.'

I laughed along with them, and then took a beer from the

fridge. I looked at my mother. She appeared to have lost some weight since last time I had seen her.

'I've got another trip up on the ice tomorrow,' I said. 'You should come if you want. You too Frank.'

My mother shook her head.

'No, no. I don't think so. Reckon those hill climbing days are best behind me.'

'You can still walk can't you?'

'Last time I tried.'

'Well, then.'

My mother looked at Frank for support of her argument, but Frank shrugged his shoulders.

'Do you need me to go next door and ask permission?' I asked with a grin.

'Cheeky sod,' Frank replied. 'Nancy will let me out. She always figured you as the careful one.'

For a moment Frank looked embarrassed. He took a drink from his beer. My mother and I glanced at one another to see if the other would respond.

'Well it's true,' my mother said. 'No point beating about the bush on it.'

I rubbed the back of my neck, and then stood up. 'Guess I should get some grub on.'

'Nancy has it sorted,' Frank said, waving his hand before looking at his watch. 'Actually. She'll be expecting us right smartly.'

My mother smiled. 'No offence son, but your cooking doesn't come a distant second.'

The three of us laughed again. The humour felt good. Natural. We finished our beers before going outside and pushing our way through the gap in the hedge to Frank and Nancy's place.

Nancy hugged my mother warmly at the door. She had a roast chicken with onions and potatoes and kumara in the oven, and Frank said he would find a bottle of wine that he had been aging in the wardrobe for a special occasion. I took a glass when offered but my mother declined.

'Prefer to stick to beer tonight if that's all the same to you.'

'Of course it is,' Nancy replied, fussing like she was mothering the three of us, and everyone enjoying the attention.

'More for the rest of us,' Frank added.

My uncle even made the effort to change into a collared shirt before dinner, and he attempted to get his beard under control. I wondered whether to give him cheek about it, but he caught me looking sideways at him.

'Don't even think about it unless you want some stories about how often you pooped in your nappies,' he said with a smirk. 'Up until the age of 10 or so if my memory serves me correct.'

Frank and my mother reminisced about how much better the old times were, and then Nancy suggested that perhaps their memories were not what they used to be.

My mother and I decided to take the long way back to the crib. Moonlight lit the beach in a pale glow, and we could see enough to make walking in the dark easy. I looked to the sky and the stars. I knew there would be no such thing as a good time to talk. The sea was unusually calm, as if the weather were pausing before the next storm surge. Only the smallest of waves crumpled against the shore with a hush, while further out the moon cut its rippling path like an offering of a way forward.

My mother cleared her throat as if to say something, but then she stopped. I could just make out her expression in the moonlight. I placed a hand on her arm, and she turned to me and smiled a thin, sad smile. She coughed again, before wiping the flat of her palm quickly over her face.

We took our time walking along the beach, the sand crunching beneath our gumboots. Drifts of wood loomed as oddly shaped monstrosities in the dark.

Finally, my mother spoke. 'I've been reading a book on how to deal with grief.'

'Is it helping?'

'Damned if I know, but least I'm processing better than I was.'

'How's that?' I asked.

'I'm still pretty angry about everything. Doesn't seem fair is all. Yep, I expect that's the crux of it.'

'You been seeing much of Kate?'

My mother nodded. 'At least once a week. Go round for dinner most Thursdays. She says to say "hi" by the way.'

'I spoke to her on the phone the other day.'

'She had mentioned that, and she told me how much she appreciated the call.' My mother paused. 'Did you get to talk to Tyler as well?' she asked, her face now a silhouette as she looked towards me.

'Not much chance of that yet, I don't reckon.'

We started walking again. At the entrance to the estuary we turned inland, crossing the grass paddock that some of the locals used as a landing strip, and then continuing past the campground which looked like it was empty for a change.

Stags whined quietly from behind the door of the crib as we approached, and he rushed outside as we entered. He sniffed pensively around in the dark before peeing against the wheel of my four-wheel-drive, and then he trotted back to where I was waiting with the door still open. It seemed our sombre mood had affected him. And all the while the moon continued its slow, jaded arc across the sky.

IV

Telling this story to Zoe, I guess it is protecting me as much as protecting her. At least I am getting to explain it the way I want to. The way I need to. Keeping the order of my memories so they make sense, and so that I don't get lost in my own self-pity while recalling them. Zoe deserves as much. The memory of Duncan, and of Kate, deserves as much too.

But Zoe is not a climber. Part of me wonders whether she really understands what drove us to constantly strive for altitude even if it meant courting risk.

'My mother would have bristled at being considered a flatlander,' I explain. 'Especially in her younger days. No, thank you very much, she was born into the high country.'

Zoe grins at my attempt at mimicking my mother's voice and the way she might hold herself while talking.

If you asked her up front, my mother would probably have admitted that her need for mountains was severe. Unhealthy even. She craved any opportunity to journey over snowfields with a pair of crampons strapped to her boots and an ice axe in her hand. When the sound of her boots upon the still-frozen morning snow was like biting into the crispest of apples. And the colours up there, in certain types of light and especially after a downpour of rain had washed the glaciers clean, colours trapped within the ice. To her it was like trying to climb rainbows. No surprises that the rest of us followed in her footsteps and felt the same way.

'You know, up in the mountains the air is so dry,' I recall my mother saying one time when Duncan and I were still young. I can still remember her making a deal out of taking a deep breath and then letting it out again. 'It smells so clean up there. Reminds you of nothing. Even gives you enough time to forget what's happening below.'

The steeper the country the better I reckon my mother identified with it. Blank rock walls. Pillars of ice. Even just the idea of them seemed to awaken something inside her, and despite what might seem to outsiders like the drudgery of such endeavor. My mother tended not to care what others thought.

'Up, always up,' she explained. 'Doesn't matter how slow you go. Just be sure to watch where you place your feet. Your hands.'

My mother got caught up in her storytelling, mimicking the movements a climber might make, part looking at us and part staring upwards as if she was studying the imagined terrain that lay ahead.

'Be particular about it, mind,' she said. 'One step, then another. And another. Each movement must be on its own, of its own. You get to rest only when you really need to. Only when it's safe.'

At the time it had felt like a sermon, my mother leaning close to us to accentuate each point, and her eyes wide with the excitement that seemed to be waiting. Up there. Then she looked at Duncan and me in turn.

'Teamwork is everything,' she said. 'Rope up when you have to, even if it slows you down and don't be afraid to put in an extra piece of protection. That might be the one piece that saves you in the end.'

My mother frowned, like she was unsure what to say next. 'Never have any doubts,' she finally added. 'It's the doubts that will kill you quick as anything else. Decide, trust your judgment, and then commit for all you're worth.'

The clients sat on their jackets on the piles of glacial moraine and they ate sandwiches and drunk from water bottles and then took photos of each other holding their ice axes in various assertive poses against the ice. The terminal face of the glacier dropped away a few hundred metres below where we all sat. Down valley, the river bubbled past Cyril's Rock in thick braids, silty and grey and with blocks of ice bouncing off each other. Past the bridge it ran straight and deep in a single torrent to the sea.

I had guided the small group up the terminal face in the morning. Light reflected off the ice as I chipped steps for the others to follow. At one stage three kea circled above us, calling out to one another or maybe even to us. I stopped to point out the mountain parrots and explain to the tourists their prevalence for mischief.

'Smartest birds in the world,' I said and some of the tourists nodded like they already knew this.

'At one of the hotels they had to design special lids for the rubbish bins,' I continued. 'Some film crew tried to document each of the birds as it worked out how to break into the bins and then show the other kea how it was done.'

'The blighters wrecked my car the other day,' an older guy said from the rear of the group. 'Stripped the rubber from the door and even broke my aerial damn off.'

I nodded. 'Yeah they can be like a bunch of unruly teenagers, that's for sure.'

I considered telling the clients that they were my favourite birds, that their antics and their attitudes were always a source of entertainment in the mountains. How a particular bird could take on enough human attributes and then carry them out with such an attitude that they became like a treasured friend. Or even a member of the family.

I glance towards Zoe.

'You know, Zoe would be a good name for a kea,' I tell her.

She looks back and grins. 'Are you trying to insinuate that I'm a troublemaker,' she replies.

'Well, aren't all teenagers?'

We all watched as the kea called out and swirled about on a light breeze that was pushing up the valley. Eventually the birds glided behind a spur that led up to the main ridge north of the glacier. Then, I suggested that the group should start moving again, and for everyone to keep a hand on the rope because it was there for a reason.

It had been a slower than usual ascent up the lower edge of the glacier. Frank was not the worst of the group. I knew that his leg must have been aching something chronic with all the uphill. But he said he was fine. Then he asked whether Nancy had put me up to all the fussing.

When we stopped for lunch, Frank walked off a polite distance to talk to a young woman from Germany who was over near one of the melt pools.

'Maybe I can encourage her to strip off and jump in,' he said cheekily to me. 'Isn't that what you guides do for laughs?'

'Go for your life,' I encouraged. 'Promise I won't tell.'

My mother had chosen to sit a small distance away from the other clients, like she needed the space. But she smiled and nodded as I moved closer. Finally, she spoke.

'You know you've got to come back and get everything sorted, one way or the other.'

I had been staring out over the glacier. I turned to my mother as if to say something and then looked away again.

'I can't say I understand what's happening between you and Kate, but what's done is done. And, on top of everything else, I can see how it must all feel too much.'

I took a deep breath. I stared at my mother for a long time and could see that she was struggling. I wondered how much of what had followed the service - what had and had not happened between Kate and I - that my mother knew about. I thought there was a fair chance she had figured it all out. Or maybe Tyler told her. The realization of that made me feel ashamed. Even though I thought she would likely understand the reasoning behind it.

'I guess, I'm not sure where to start,' I said.

'I know it. We could talk around this till we're blue in the face.'

'And?'

'And nothing. I guess everyone is still trying to deal with it in their own way. But running away solves nothing.'

I took my axe in my hands and started chipping at the ice. 'Yeah, I know. I just needed this, some space away. It was doing my head in over there.'

'Is it helping?'

'Some.'

'How much longer do you think you need?'

'I don't know.'

My mother put her sandwich down. 'You realise this is one of those times, don't you?'

'I guess.'

'We don't get to choose them. They just arrive. And they're never easy. God knows we have experienced enough of them lately. But it's not the situation that matters. It's how we face up to it.'

I stared up at the mountains. My mother looked where I looked and pointed to a snowy summit above the glacier.

'They're just objects, nothing more than rock and ice and beat up by the weather and the wind. But that doesn't stop us from placing our trust in them. They become something more important in our mind because we need them to be. But we still need protecting from them. And some of us do more than others.'

Frank was trying to glance up towards the two of us without

us realising. He made to walk closer but then stopped. My mother didn't seem to notice. She continued speaking, partly for her own benefit, it seemed, as much as mine.

'This, all of this, is nothing but a bunch of moments passing us by. There is no certainty to it, no more than the pretense of a new day providing a chance to start over. Everything matters. Every single thing. You can't afford to wait till tomorrow because who knows if it's even going to get here.'

I sighed. 'I read somewhere recently that we can't begin to make sense of a thing until we've lost all hope for it.'

'Pah,' my mother said. 'Hope is just some made up word. It's not what you have but what you do that matters.'

'I don't know. Maybe. Guess I'll realise that when I get there.'

'You won't. Waiting for it doesn't change a damn thing other than making what's already wrong seem a whole lot worse.'

I made to stand up, and my mother placed her hand on my arm. 'Look, if nothing else you need to talk to Tyler.'

'I will.'

'You need to. Soon. She's not right with all this, in the head. I'm not sure, but it's like she's angry. Yes, at you. At everything, even the mountains. And that's not good.'

'Is she climbing?'

'With some young guy. I don't know who he is or whether he's much cop but she seems pretty driven, almost like she's on a path for revenge or something.'

'What?'

My mother nodded. 'I've seen it before. There's a need to claim something back. You start to think the mountains owe you because of the loss you've experienced. I'm not saying it's right, just that it happens.'

'And you think Tyler is, what, being reckless up there?'

'Hell, I don't know. She hasn't talked to me about it and why would she? I am well past it these days. But Kate told me that she's now got a real bee in her bonnet about climbing mountains. Kate's worried and I reckon she's every right to be.'

I didn't say anything.

'I realise Tyler must be pretty angry with you about something,' my mother continued. 'But you're probably the only one she will listen to.'

'I don't know about that.'

'She loves climbing with you. She told me as much.'

'What if she doesn't listen to me? Then what?'

'Worry about that afterwards.'

I stood and walked away from my mother, down to where the clients were milling about and waiting for the tour to continue. My eyes met with Frank's. And then he looked away. More clouds were gathering to the west. It looked like yet another storm could be building on the horizon.

V

The wind swung half a compass and lifted. It tapered along the spur, stuttering across wooded flanks to the valley below, almost a mile down as the wind blows, to a brackish, sagging land where dark bush edged spindly-grassed paddocks and a mist lurked low over the flats. Through the middle a river ran its course fat and swift, peaty waters chased by the wind westwards to the coast, a day and a half away if the weather held.

The wind cooled my skin. The trees that enclosed me hushed to its rhythm. This was anonymous country. Faceless. No need for a name, a history or even a reason for being. Thoughts of those in my life and of one not long passed absorbed into the earth like a light rain falling through the forest. The wildness allowed me just enough sense to keep moving. To exist.

The old people, the people who knew the land like it was family or a lover, they believed mountain summits were places where spirits could pass to the afterlife. Look up to a particular mountain and it might resemble the face of someone from your whānau, your clan. But not the forests. Trees acted as an enclosure, their branches a mesh that trapped not only the dead but the memories of the living also. Within them there could be no perspective. No way to see. Only damp and the darkness.

The spur before me ended abruptly. It arched in slopes and drops, barely supporting itself and the thick-trunked trees, roots helping bind what was left to the bedrock. Some trees leaned obliquely to the earth. Small groves of saplings collapsed in tight clusters where the soil had fallen away to the valley floor.

I hunkered down and peered at the earth, touching it in places despite the tracks I had been following being obvious, perhaps half a day old and leading single file down the spur. It was the only means along this stretch of backcountry allowing a route to the flats.

Leaning my rifle against a branch, I cupped each hand to the sides of my head and listened. Like putting your ear to a conical shell to hear nothing but the hush of the wind, or the sea, but then came a faint crashing of bodies against undergrowth somewhere in the valley. Down where the farmer Reynolds had kept at his attempts to burn-back the scrub, the regrowth crackled and broke.

I figured I was listening to the same herd. Three days now I had been tracking the wild cattle, leaving my four-wheel-drive and open country thirty kilometres to the north, near where Reynolds reckoned he had last seen the old black bull, and then following their trail up a broad, forested shelf into the high country.

A few months had passed since I last spoke to my mother. And almost a year since I left Christchurch with a few hastily grabbed possessions. I tell Zoe how I can still recall many things so vividly. Sometimes it feels like it happened only a week ago, or even just a day. If I had my time again, I say to her, I wouldn't have run away like I did.

But, to my thinking back then, escaping to the Coast was the only thing I could do. Or could do right, it seemed. Standing there in the bush, the memory of it and the days before it and the anger I knew others must feel towards me threatened to overwhelm me again.

I stood beneath the old trees. For the briefest of moments, I thought of Kate. And then Tyler. There had been a thought nagging at the back of my mind. Something in the tone of Kate's voice when she tried to talk to me one time. Something that she figured I needed to know. But thinking too much about it only made my feelings of guilt and disorientation rise again, and I tried to force the thoughts from my mind.

With the coming dusk, the crashing below receded, the herd settling for the evening by the sounds of it. Reynolds would be pissed off if they bust through any more of his fences. Not that much could be done about it now. The old black bull might be running on instinct, but I figured that he would have some sort of a plan, maybe that it was finally time to turn and face up to whoever was tracking him. I envied him that decisiveness.

Light retreated from the earth. I took my foam mat from the pack and rolled it across a bed of leaves. Then my sleeping bag. I tied a nylon tarp between a kāmahi and a broadleaf sapling, enough to provide cover from the morning dew and any rain that might fall through the night.

I looked up when the questioning call of a bellbird fluttered through the branches above, and again. Then it stopped. I thought I saw the bird but could not make its shape against the coming darkness. Then I noticed a strange, musky smell in the air. There was movement in the bush. A faint blur. There, between the "y" of two branches, a form, perhaps human, a face in the shadows.

Unable to distinguish age or sex, hair, or skin, I stared back at the eyes, dark orbs watching me without blinking. Keeping motionless to show I wasn't alarmed or about to do anything sudden, I sniffed, trying to distinguish the aroma. For some reason I did not think to say anything or call out a greeting. My thoughts drifted, just in case, to where my rifle lay almost within reach. I barely glanced in that direction then back to where I had noticed the face. But now it was gone, if it had been there in the first place, leaving the two branches and the slight swaying of a fern.

I looked around to see if it had moved somewhere else. Had I half-dreamed the whole occurrence? I decided I wouldn't get up to check for tracks, but then did, moving first to where I had seen the face, crouching to the damp grass and mud and running my hands over the earth. From there I moved methodically outwards in half circles, but finding nothing other than a scuff of moss freshly dislodged from a dead branch. I stood still, eyes half closed, smelling, and listening at the stillness for minutes. But there was nothing, and before long the bellbird started up again overhead. Soon it was joined by another. A final chorus before nightfall.

I had heard talk of unusual experiences like this happening to others on occasion, but only after a few beers when no one could be sure either way and the conversation likely forgotten by daylight. The old people, the people of the land whom I sometimes met in the forests gathering herbs and leaves and hunting boar when the air was still and the mist patchy, occasionally they would kōrero with me about such things.

Of course, it could have been a deer. There were plenty of red about and a few wapiti in these parts, and some of the old stags could get a bit too nosy for their own good. But there was no sign left by them. And the smell had thrown me – wapiti especially had a distinct aroma and this hadn't been anything like it.

Frank always had theories on these kinds of experiences. He thought that the forests could trap spirits, holding them in the trees and sometimes even in the animals that lived among them.

'Likely the spirit was interested in you if it bothered to show itself,' he would no doubt reason.

Duncan had never believed any of this kind of stuff, and I guess his thoughts were no surprise to me. Black and white was just that to my brother's thinking. 'Dead is dead,' he would say. 'You're either here or you're nothing. There's no halfway about it.'

I didn't recognise the face in the darkness. But would I if they were no longer a face I could recognise? Was it my mind playing tricks, fatigue from this day and the days before not just overloading my body? The stress of my life and the hauntings of memories and decisions and bad timing combining to detach me from whatever grasp on reality I had left.

I woke sometime in the night, suddenly, grabbing at the air and taking a moment to realise where I was. Laying there in the dark, listening to a gentle wind push through the trees overhead, taking in deep breaths to calm myself, I wished many things. Lately, I had been using fatigue to deal with my grief, to allow me to sleep each night, but this didn't fix the darkness that remained inside. There were times like now when I wondered at the worth of it all, of even carrying on.

I don't tell Zoe this, but at one stage I thought to myself that a rifle shot would be awkward but quick. In the night I would not look at what I was holding, just feel the pressure of the barrel against my skull and take one long, final breath. I could be living one of Duncan's fateful stories.

I lay there, considering how the loss of someone so close could have led me to places and actions so unimaginable. I thought about Kate and I wished I could take back many things. I doubted whether Tyler would ever speak to me again. And then, with another pang of guilt, I realised how much I missed those few, secret, intimate seconds I got to share with Kate.

But, beyond all other thoughts, I wished that my brother was still alive. That I had been able to save him. That I had chosen not to run away, but to stay and fight for what I wanted.

VI

As I continue to tell the story to Zoe, I can see my decision to track down and face the black bull as a turning point. I was tired, low on food, and a long way from my vehicle. The weather appeared to be worsening. Part of me wanted to take the easier option to bail. I don't know if the apparition had any influence. Even now I have no idea what it was I saw that night. I like to think that, perhaps, it was the ghost of Duncan. Anyway, the next morning I decided I was going to get that bloody bull!

The wild cattle had been hugging the cover of bush. Their tracks crossed the stream below where it trickled over a bluff of bleached rock, and then back up another forested terrace. I followed their sign, climbing steadily into the low hills again, working hard against the altitude and through the tangle of the undergrowth. But I made no ground on them that day. Nearing dusk I stopped in a small clearing midway up the broad ridge that I had been ascending.

From where I lay, I could see past the tarp and through the thin forest canopy to a myriad of stars, to the endless constellations that promised much but provided nothing other than an overwhelming awareness of insignificance. I looked for the Pleiades but couldn't see them. Then I thought of Duncan again. In the darkness under the roots of an old and dying miro, tears came softly and silent.

I rose early the following morning and continued. It was mid-afternoon before I finally caught up to the cattle. I could hear them scuffing against the bush some way ahead and mooing softly to each other. Where I had come off the ridge was downwind of them. Through the bush they appeared, vanished, and appeared again. I stopped and crouched. Removing my rifle from my pack, I loaded the shells as quietly as I could and waited beneath the drooping fronds of a large ponga fern.

Birdsong drifted from the canopy. Branches creaked as the wind strengthened from the northwest. Minutes passed. A pīwakawaka flitted through the undergrowth, peeping noisily as it chased at the bugs that had gathered around me. I tried to shoo it away without making a sound or drawing attention to myself.

Eventually the cattle drew close. I stayed hunkered down, leaning against a tree to sight on the nearest of the beasts. There came the bull at the front where I knew it would be, thickset in the shoulders and its black hide scarred from old battles but also freshly torn in places. It was standing and sniffing the air. While the others plodded on aimlessly, it seemed to be the only one with any awareness that something foreign to the forest could be close. He was doing his best to protect the herd.

I took a quiet intake of breath, flicked off the safety on the rifle, and then slowly exhaled. All of the cattle jumped as if they've been shot. The bull stayed on his feet. I think I must have caught him in the shoulder. He spun around no doubt wondering what had just happened. I quickly ejected the empty cartridge, stood for a better angle, and fired again. This time I made sure that I had hit him in the head. Right between the eyes.

The other cattle crashed off noisily through the undergrowth. I picked up my pack and walked towards the old bull. Surprisingly, he was still alive. He lay there breathing noisily but not struggling. It was as if he had finally accepted his fate. His eyes rolled around and then stared at me as I levered another final round into the rifle. I held the muzzle to his head.

Afterwards, I sat beside him for what might have been ages. I lost track of time. I stared over the land that fell away beneath us. Thick cloud was pouring in from the coast. Wind blew noisily through the branches of the tree above me and which creaked and complained like the limbs of an old man who had been forced to move too suddenly. An old man who was being made to face up to what he could no longer control.

I placed a hand on the bull's hide. I had finished what I set out to do, but there was no sense of relief in the outcome.

Zoe is shuffling beside me. 'It's coming isn't it?' she says.

'What's that?'

'You know. About my mother.'

'Yes, Zoe.'

'Is it bad, remembering back?'

I scratch my chin. 'Not like with Duncan. Nothing as difficult as that. But, yes. It makes me feel….'

Zoe glances up at me. 'Vulnerable?'

'Remorseful.'

I look at Zoe. I wish I could tell her everything. Maybe there will be a day when I can, but I doubt it. It might bring peace to my own heart, but I don't think Tyler will feel the same way. Or Zoe for that matter.

What matters the most - what I understand now as my most important role in my last years - is that I help nurture Zoe through her life as well as protect her memories of her family. The love I feel for her and her mother is a contract with myself that I must keep.

VII

What sounded like shotgun pellets slapped against the window of the crib, a cold rain driving hard from the coast. Wind shuddered my home against its foundations. It sought gaps in the tongue and groove flooring and rattled the front door against the hinges. Earlier, storm clouds had been a dark blanket to the west, and the sea a warning calm before them. Then came the wind. The rain would wash everything, wash me clean. Blat blat the gunshots hit the roofing iron, falling from a great height until the racket of them melded into a cacophony, until the rain sounded like - I don't know what - loud, unrelenting, something trying to get in.

The wetness spread over the land, dirtying the estuary, pooling across the lawn, and leaking into the long drop toilet. With the land flooding the shit rose. There were things swimming round in the bottom of it. Don't look. I'd tell myself, don't you fucking look. But I did. I always do.

I sat there on the couch, drinking coffee in the dead light before dawn and absorbing the din. My mind drifted unreliably. My toast was cold and untouched on a plate on the hearth of a cold, untouched fire. Stags lay at my feet, his paws extended and his nose only inches from the plate. He kept glancing in my direction, his eyebrows going up and down depending on what he considered his chances were at being allowed the toast.

'Go on then. You can have it.'

The storm had been steadily building, the northwesterly wind and the black swelling of cloud over the ocean the afternoon before like a premonition. I had walked the beach, watching as the sea was stirred up and seabirds hunkered down among the sand dunes. Then the wind swung southerly in the evening, gusting to near gale force and bringing the rain with it. Sometime in the middle of the night I woke to the sound of roofing iron screeching as it was torn off the woodshed.

I tell Zoe that, deep down, I guess I figured this moment had always been on the horizon. I don't know how I knew, just that I did. Things couldn't have continued as they were. Something had to give. I realise that. But, even now, all this time later, I still wish that it would have been something that happened to me rather than to someone else I cared greatly for.

Later in the morning I hiked the wet weather track leading to the terminal face of the glacier. The route weaved along a terrace thick with bush a hundred metres above the valley floor. Flooded side streams careered off rocky bluffs above me. The spray from waterfalls lifted with the wind. Down in the valley the river roared, its banks spilling across the gravel flats on either side.

Brian had canceled all guiding trips for the morning due to the weather. And, I figured cynically, perhaps because no visitor in their right mind would choose to be out in these conditions. But he had still asked me to go up and check conditions on the glacier.

'In case the weather improves in the afternoon,' he said.

I changed my boots at the terminal face, tightened my crampon straps and stepped on to the glacier. Rain had washed all the aerated ice off its surface, the colour now the same blue as inside its deepest crevasses. A slippery blue. A blue that couldn't be trusted. My crampons would protect me.

Brian had instructed me to work through a heavily crevassed

area of the glacier, re-chipping a line of steps in the ice for clients to maybe use later in the day, and to check the ice screws and safety lines. Given the state of the weather, I doubted it was worth the effort. But it was something to take my mind off how I had felt back at the crib.

I had only just stepped on to the ice when the radio crackled. I instantly recognised Brian's voice.

'You there, Jase?'

'Where else would I be?'

There was a period of silence.

'Brian?'

'I'm here…. Look, you'd better get back down to the office.'

'Bloody hell, I've only just got here. What's going on?'

Despite the distortion of the radio static, Brian's voice sounded strange. 'I've just had a call from your mother. Tyler might have gone missing.'

'Missing?'

'In the mountains. She's on a trip with a friend. Over this way, apparently.'

'In this weather? I didn't even know she was here.'

'That's all your mother said. They are a couple of days overdue. Talbot has been notified already, but your mother still wants to talk to you.'

'Did she say anything else?'

'You should just get down quick as you can.'

'Which mountain?' I asked.

'What's that?'

'Did she say what mountain they were climbing?'

'Yeah…'

'Well?'

'It's Maunga ō Hine.'

VIII

Talbot Cameron was the local police officer, and also the coordinator for the area's Search and Rescue team. I'd met him a few times over the years. He seemed competent enough, although he would have been the first to admit he wasn't overly experienced when it came to the high country. He was more of a hunting and fishing type. This was something I couldn't get out of my mind, and especially when it came to his ability to manage decisions around a potentially difficult rescue.

I found Talbot sitting at his desk. He was studying a map, and which had a number of coloured pins sticking to it. Outside, the wind was making the window frame rattle. He stood and we shook hands.

'What's the plan?' I asked.

'We need to be ready for when this weather lifts,' he said, sitting back down behind his desk again. 'The chopper team is standing by. Beckett said she is ready to go whenever we are.'

'Good,' I said. 'You're not going to send anyone in by foot as a backup?'

Talbot shook his head. 'The river's likely to be too high. No way to get across. Best thing is to wait for a clearance and fly a search pattern.'

'I guess it's fine if your guys don't think they can get there without a chopper ride in these conditions.'

Talbot stared at me, picking up on the sarcasm. 'You think you can?'

'Maybe. I know the area well. I've been in a few times. You know that. I've probably got the best knowledge about the place and where they might be, especially if they are anywhere on the mountain.'

I knew it was Talbot's job to be cautious, to try to avoid all risks. 'What are you going to do about the river?' he asked.

'I'll worry about it when I get there. There's only a small catchment above so the water level can go up and down pretty quick smart depending on localized rainfall. It could change either way, and we wouldn't know it sitting and waiting here.'

Talbot stood up. He straightened his uniform before walking to the window to look out. He was making a final attempt to dissuade me. 'I know you want to help. I can understand it what with your niece being one of the missing. But going off half-cocked isn't going to solve anything.'

'I can't just do nothing.'

'Sometimes that's the best option. The only option.'

I stood and walked to the same window. We both remained there in silence for a few moments, staring outside at the rain.

Finally, I spoke. 'I don't believe it's the right call what you're planning. Not now. Not in this instance. You have no idea where they could be. What injuries they might have. You're sitting here blind.'

Talbot turned to me. 'So, you're going to head in there. In this weather? And then we might just fly right over you. You'll be a liability, not a help.'

I shook my head. 'I'm going. I have to go.'

I figured Talbot always knew what I was going to do. He sighed. 'There's no stopping you, is there?' Then he handed me a radio. 'At least take this. Monitor it and keep in touch when you can. Look, you'd better show me on the map where you are planning on heading and by which route. That way, at least, we can keep an eye out.'

We were both studying the map, and I was pointing out specific areas I had been to in the past and which way I thought Tyler and her partner might take, when Beckett walked into the office. Being focussed on the map, I hardly noticed her at first.

'How are you doing Jase?' she asked quietly.

I turned and looked at her without saying anything.

'It's your niece Tyler, isn't it?'

I nodded.

'I'm so sorry,' Beckett added. 'You know if there's anything I can help with.'

'Thanks. Sorry, look I've got to get going,' I said.

'I understand,' Beckett replied. 'I'll walk you out.' Then she turned to Talbot. 'I'll be back in a few minutes.'

Once outside, Beckett put her hand on my shoulder. 'You're heading in, aren't you?'

I nodded. We both stood in the doorway to the police station and looked skywards, at the dark cloud covering the valley and the forest and the rain falling from it.

'Today?'

'Soon as I'm packed.'

'Anyone else going with you?'

'Hadn't got that far. Maybe…Papps, but I haven't spoken to him yet.'

'Make sure you do.'

A car drove slowly along the main road, and we had to step back to avoid getting splashed from a puddle.

'What do you reckon about the weather?' Beckett asked.

'It'll get worse before it gets better,' I replied. 'But I think it should push through maybe end of tomorrow, next day at the latest.'

'Yeah, that's what I reckon too.' Beckett turned to look at me. 'I'll come in as soon as I can. You know that. Just stay safe in there, whatever you plan to do. You're taking comms?'

'I've got a radio. Not sure what the coverage will be like in there though.'

'Well, you get a message out and I'll come in as soon as I can.'

'Thanks,' I said to Beckett. 'It's good to know you've got us covered.'

Brian walked up to me as soon as I had returned to the guiding office. 'Are you okay?' he asked.

'I'm fine.'

'I'm sure things will sort themselves out.'

'How the hell do you explain that?'

The office phone rang. A relieved look came over Brian's face. 'Sorry, I'd better get it,' he said.

Papps was just coming down from the gear room.

'What are you going to do?'

'I'm going to bloody well get her.'

'It's alright mate. We'll work something out. Together.'

I looked up.

'You don't think I'm letting you go wandering off on your own. Miss all the excitement.'

'Thanks, mate,' I said to him in a low voice.

I took a map out of my pack and spread it on the table. We both leaned over it. 'Really, there's only one way in and out from this side,' I said, pointing at the contours leading to Maunga ō Hine. 'They have to use this river for access.'

'What if they are on the way up or down from the climb? Papps asked. Then he glanced at me. 'They could be trapped on the climb or, well, you know, on the glacier. Where you guys were.'

I swallowed. This was no time for sentimentality about the mistakes of my past.

'I know mate. Let's get in there and see what we see. Tyler has heard my stories enough about this bloody mountain. I'm sure she will remember them.'

Papps nodded. 'You're right mate. From what you've told me about her, she's a smart kid. Had one or two good climbing instructors by the sounds of it.'

I smiled back at my friend. It was a relief knowing he was prepared to come with me. We were much stronger as a team than me going in there on my own.

The phone rang again in the office. Brian called out. 'Jase. It's your mother. She wants to talk to you.'

'What are the rescuers planning to do?' she asked as soon as I had picked up the phone.

'Talbot's sitting on his hands for the time being.'

'Not surprising given the forecast, I suppose,' she said.

'Not surprising given he's out of his depth.'

My mother let out a loud sigh. 'He's just doing what he can.'

'What's the guy like that Tyler's gone in with?' I asked.

'Met him just the once,' she said. 'He'd climbed a few things or so he said. Talked a good game anyway. But who knows these days?'

I could hear the strain in my mother's voice. To lose a son to the mountains was a tragic waste, and probably something she would never fully get over. But then the possibility of her granddaughter also, that would surely be too much. But it hadn't come to that, not yet at least and which was why I was choosing to act.

'Papps is going to come with me,' I said.

'Watch that river, won't you? And crossing the pass. Imagine it'll cop a bit of snow with this front.'

'I'll be careful. You know that.'

'I know.'

'Guess I should get on with it. We want to get in there before dark.'

'Hang on. Someone else wants to talk to you.'

It was a few seconds before I heard Kate's voice. She sounded tired. Stressed. Anxious.

'Are you sure about this?' she asked.

'It's worth a go. We could wait around for the rescue guys but doesn't sound like they will be doing anything in a hurry. Not in this weather anyway. Even if there's the smallest of chances, I have to try.'

'I know,' she said in a quiet voice. 'It's just....'

'Just, what?'

'I don't know. Make sure you come back, okay?'

'Don't worry. I will, with Tyler.'

'I know, but that's not what I mean.'

There was a long period of silence.

'Okay,' Kate said. 'Okay. You go find her, Jase. I know you can.'

My vehicle stuttered up a short rise on the highway, wind gusts lurching it sideways as I drove over a bridge. I dropped into second and gripped the steering wheel with both hands. The windscreen wipers clunked back and forth, making little headway against the rain. It was early afternoon yet already quite dark outside, with low cloud smothering the land. I glanced at Papps. He was looking out the side window, lost in his thoughts. I couldn't blame him.

I tried to keep my mind focussed on the road, driving to the conditions and despite my own thoughts threatening to boil over. At least having a plan was something to cling to. I would do everything I could to find Tyler and get her safely back from the mountains.

If nothing else, the prospect remained a flicker of light, something to focus on, anything to keep the emptiness in my heart from finally becoming too much.

Not again, I said to myself, almost in prayer. Please. Not again.

IX

It was late in the afternoon by the time we reached the end of the road. I looked at the sky then at Papps. 'Are you sure you want to do this? Going to be pretty bleak in there.'

'Sure, I'm sure,' he replied, not meeting my eyes but staring back across the flats at the rain and thick cloud consuming everything around us.

'You don't have to come,' I added, noticing his hesitation.

Papps kicked a stone and watched it topple over a small rise.

'I know.'

He started to say something else but stopped, kicking at a bigger stone which refused to budge.

We grabbed our packs and started walking. The storm worsened. Rain came hard at the land, driven by a wind that screeched like some ungodly violin. The heavy wet raked woodlands and swamps, then up the rising country of ridges and spurs; higher still, to where the air cooled further, and the earth turned jagged. Trapped against towers of bedrock, the rain chilled to sleet and then snow.

'Might be a struggle going over the pass in this,' Papps said.

I nodded. 'Well, let's see how far we get before dark.'

I could remember the route and took the lead. The river was so flooded that in a number of places we were forced to wade through waist deep water. Being a big guy, Papps felt like an immovable force as we linked arms and made our way across. My legs became numb from the cold, and I hiked as quickly as I could to stop my core from following suit.

It was getting dark as we reached the start of the trail leading over the pass. We were both shivering. Papps cupped his hands, blew into them, and then rubbed them together. 'What do you reckon, mate?'

'Yeah,' I replied. 'I guess here is as good as anywhere. Don't fancy trying to push over at night. Especially given how much snow is likely to be up there already. It'll be a hard trudge in the dark.'

We found a flat area far enough away from the river to pitch the tent. A gust of wind almost snatched it from my hands as I threaded a pole into the fly. I made sure to tie it securely to a nearby tree as backup. Then we both climbed into our sleeping bags to warm up. I hardly had enough energy to boil water for dinner, and I swore when I spilled some on my bag.

Papps looked across. 'You alright mate?'

'It's so fucked. Everything.'

'I know. Let's just grab a few hours here and get going first light. It'll work out. We'll find them.'

I pulled out a map from my pack and studied it again, as if some hint of an idea was hidden in its details, something that I'd missed. Papps glanced across. 'Any thoughts?'

I scratched my head. 'I'm not sure, but I reckon Tyler will head for here if she can,' I said, pointing at a junction on the map. 'If I was her, I would get to low ground by the easiest means rather than the most direct.'

'Makes sense,' Papps said. 'Less risk that way, especially if they are getting tired.'

'But certainly I'd try to lose height to get away from the cold,' I continued. 'Tyler will reckon someone is coming by now, and will go to where she thinks they think she will be. If she can, at least.'

'That's a lot of surmising,' Papps said.

'I know, mate. But what else do we have to go on.'

Despite feeling tired and struggling to warm up, it still took me ages to go to sleep. What my mother had predicted a few months back was coming true. I hated that. I hated myself for not having the forethought to do something sooner. Now, it might be too late. What I was moving towards felt like the sharpened point of everything that had occurred since my brother's death. Before then maybe. Like it was a manifestation of our parents splitting up and the three of us moving to the Coast, then Duncan being too competitive and me wanting to keep up. And then everything else with Kate.

I was angry. At Duncan. At myself. At pretty much everyone and everything, I guess. Even the mountains. Especially the mountains.

I woke as light lifted sepia-toned across the land. There was a strange quietness around us, especially when compared to the storm that had raged through most of the night. Stifled from half-sleep by a dream that the night hadn't subdued, I lay there in my cocoon, listening for the mood of the day, to the silence and then a strange, bony rasping. I blinked, staring at the half light. Trying to register what the noise was.

I worked one arm out of my sleeping bag and drew a hand down my face, thumb and forefinger wiping across my eyelids and pinching the bridge of my nose. There was the noise again. Almost like fingernails on slate-hard glacial ice. Unzipping my bag, I leaned forward and peered out the entrance of the tent. A part of me expected or at least hoped to see the silhouette of a person standing there. Yet I knew the idea was stupid.

The dark smudge of a hebe waved like an apparition in a slowly rising breeze, scratching itself against a rocky outcrop a few metres away from our tent.

There was another rustle, this one much closer to me. 'How's it look?' Papps mumbled.

'Not too bad for now. Think the wind might be getting up again though.'

I rolled back into the tent, leaning across to get the stove which I'd stored in my pack.

'You want a quick coffee before we get going?' I asked Papps.

'Hell, yeah.'

'Better toss over your mug.'

We packed up the tent and our sleeping bags and started up the ridge. As I'd predicted, the wind picked up again and it swung to the north. A new band of cirrus cloud was hugging the horizon.

Papps was a few metres behind me. He was starting to breathe heavily from the exertion of moving so quickly up the steep hill. 'Hey JW!'

'Yeah?'

'What's the pressure doing?'

'Hang on.' I scrambled across a short rocky knoll to get closer to Papps, and then checked my watch. 'Dropped a chunk.'

'Won't be much fun when it kicks in again.'

'Yeah, mate. I know.'

Sure enough, soon we could hear the roar of approaching wind squalls. Cloud billowed and sunk, swallowing the land and immersing us again into its void. Rain started falling and the temperature plummeted. As we neared the top of the pass the rain turned to sleet and then snow. The new snow was piling up over the old snow and against rocky outcrops. Small avalanches began collapsing from under our feet. Difficult to make out in the low cloud, they were deep enough to almost take us with them.

Wind tore the snow from the top of the exposed ridge - the place where I had stopped all those years ago with Duncan and Frank and my mother, the place where I had first seen Maunga ō Hine. The snow seemed to somehow be twisting in the air, almost creating ghostlike shapes before falling to the land again, forming into huge pillows and smothering everything around us.

I tried to shout at Papps. But the windchill had become so severe that my mouth wouldn't work properly. I pointed in the direction I thought we should take, and my friend nodded. We struggled slowly through the deep snow, finally over the crest of the pass and then down, careful not to set off a big enough avalanche that would dislodge us. We were shivering and desperate for shelter. Both of us knew that no living thing should be out in these conditions or would last for very long without protection. Our minds were solely focussed on getting closer to the valley floor where conditions wouldn't be so dangerous.

Papps stumbled and fell. I heard his scream against the shriek of the wind. He was rolling around and holding his knee. As I moved to help him, he tried to stand. Then he fell again. He sat there for a few moments, flexing to see how bad he had injured his leg.

'I'm okay,' he yelled, grimacing. 'But I might need some help. Let's just get the fuck off here, eh?'

Hours later, both of us cold and desperate, we had finally descended enough to be below the snow and within the relative safety of the tree line. But Papps could hardly walk any more. At first he was able to use a broken branch as a walking stick, but as his injury became more painful I needed to support him with each step.

But he wouldn't stop. He insisted that we follow the next valley as far as we could, keeping mostly to its edge, past where I had spent the cold night with Frank all those years ago and finally reaching the point where we needed to scramble across a cliff. This was where Brian had fallen into the water on the trip I had taken with him and Duncan.

Papps had his arm draped over my shoulder and I supported him as best I could. I knew we were pretty much done. I didn't say anything to Papps, but I figured he would probably need flying out of here too.

Stopping before the cliff, I couldn't help but think back to the climb with Duncan and Brian, and then desperately hoping that this wasn't going to follow the same outcome in some horrible and twisted quirk of fate.

'There's no way,' I finally shouted, pointing at the cliff. 'The river is way too high.'

Papps nodded. I set him down against a log and then started looking around for a clearing in the scrub. We were trapped. All I could do was pitch the tent under a stand of beech, far enough away from the flooded river to be safe if it rose any further. And then to get Papps inside out of the weather.

I was cold and shivering. But I still spent the next few minutes staring across the river, searching the clearing on the other side for a tent or any sign that Tyler and her partner might be close.

This was a place where I thought Tyler would try to reach. If they weren't here, they could be anywhere, and I doubted we would find them. Not alive anyway.

Papps sat and watched me pace back and forth. There was nothing to say. No need to remind each other that anyone caught out in this weather, if they didn't have warm shelter nearby, would not likely stay alive for very long. I mumbled a few quiet, pleading words to any deity who might be listening. My niece was stubborn, a fighter. She'd keep at it for as long as she could. Long enough for us to find her. I told myself that over and over until I actually started to believe it again.

Low cloud hid everything, and I could only see a few metres in any direction. Meanwhile, Papps gave up trying to get through on the radio.

'Maybe they're not monitoring it at the moment,' he said.

'Doesn't surprise me. Talbot didn't seem that on to it.'

'Yeah or there's not enough coverage for a signal in here,' Papps replied. 'Come on, Jase. Best thing is to get in out of the weather, have some rest and start searching first thing in the morning.'

Exhausted, and without hope for anything other than our own survival, we had no energy even to cook dinner. I barely managed to eat half a muesli bar. I wanted to check Papps' leg but he had fallen asleep with his boots on. I leaned across and pulled his sleeping bag up over his shoulders.

'You must have been totally exhausted,' Zoe says to me.

'Yes, I was. But I still lay there, awake in my sleeping bag for quite some time,' I reply. 'For some reason my thoughts drifted to Duncan. More specifically, to how useless I had felt when I realised that I couldn't rescue him from the crevasse.'

I glance across to Zoe to try to judge her reaction. She doesn't say anything. 'I guess I had been carrying the guilt of failure around with me all of this time. My brother had been relying on me and I had let him down.'

'I'm sure you did everything you could,' she says.

'Who really knows?' I reply. 'I mean, really, short of me not making it out either how would I know that I had tried hard enough. Whether I should have stayed with him.'

The look on Zoe's face tells me that she doesn't agree with what I am saying.

'Anyway,' I add. 'I was damned if I was going to let that guilt hold me back. This time I would be sure to do everything that I could. I didn't care what it might cost me. I guess I was going to succeed or die trying.'

X

Fragments of a dream remain, flashes of falling snow, of being in a place so bright that I can't see my own hands. The intense white swallowing my shouts, my body, my very existence. I feel myself falling, and then the jolt of an imagined impact.

I woke with a start. It was still dark, and I looked at my watch to check the time. I tried to work out what had stirred me. Something was nagging me, something from my dream.

Then I reached for the radio: our only link out. I started tapping out Morse code. I had no idea if it would work, but there might just be enough of a signal here – not enough for talking over the airwaves but enough for this. Someone might be listening at the other end. It was worth a try. My memory of the Morse alphabet wasn't very good, but I could recall enough to tap the first part of Beckett's call sign: Z…O…E… I tapped, over and over.

I woke again, blinking my eyes because the light was a weird dishwater grey inside the tent. Outside, the wind was still blowing. The walls of the tent were flapping, and beech trees overhead creaked and groaned. At least it seemed that the rain had stopped for the time being.

I felt an urge to get up. Maybe it was the inertia of staying inside my sleeping bag and the tent that encouraged me. Anyway, I needed to see what conditions were like. I knew Papps wouldn't be going anywhere, but maybe I could get around the edge of the river or find a place somewhere to cross it. But there was something else in the back of my mind. I didn't know what it was, but it gently prodded me. Papps kept snoring as I dressed.

The first thing I noticed was right outside the tent door. There were tracks in the mud, fresh bird tracks. Straight away I realised they were from a kiwi. Sometime in the night, it must have paid us a visit, inquisitive enough to prod around a strange shape in its backyard, wondering what the hell it was doing here. Despite everything that had happened, and the prospect of what might lie ahead, the imagery of the kiwi wandering around with its plump body, whiskers and comically long beak made me smile for a second.

The cloud still swirled above us, but higher now. It hid the tops of trees further up the ridge line, and made the valley feel like it was trapped in a void detached from the rest of the world. Which, at this point, probably wasn't too far from the truth. I walked down to the river edge to see if the floodwater had receded enough to try to cross, and I checked the marker stick I had placed the previous evening. It looked like the level of the water had dropped by a metre or so. I started thinking about whether I could try to traverse the cliff.

I clambered back up the hill behind the tent to try to get a better perspective. See if there was anything I could spot. It was quieter up there, being further away from the river, almost peaceful. Eventually I reached a point well above the cliff that I had traversed all those years ago with Duncan and Brian. The hill opened out beneath my feet, and I had a clear view of the forest and hills on the other side of the river.

I took a deep breath, and then shouted out as loud as I could: 'TYLER!' My shout echoed up the valley. I cupped my ears and listened. Nothing. I tried again and listened again. I sat for a few minutes before continuing. At one stage I thought I heard something muffled, but I couldn't be sure. I listened for ages but didn't hear the sound again.

After the fifth attempt at shouting and listening to the returning echoes I stood up and slowly made my way back down towards our campsite.

Back in the valley, I poked my head into the tent to see whether Papps was awake.

'Anything?' he asked.

I shook my head. 'How's your leg?'

'Yeah,' my friend replied, pulling a face.

'It's okay mate. You're fine here.'

'How are you?' he asked.

I shrugged my shoulders. 'Not really sure,' I replied. 'Anyway, do you need anything? Some water?'

'Nah, I'm all good, thanks.'

I grabbed my empty water bottle and closed the tent door. I was at a loss what to do next. I could probably get past the rock face to search further up the river. But I wasn't sure that I should leave Papps. I thought about my mother's advice around making good decisions. And then I remembered how guilty I felt leaving Duncan.

Something caught my eye, movement over past the opposite bank of the river, near the edge of the forest. There, slumped against the base of a beech tree, a form. Something. At first, I thought it was an oddly shaped bush, but the colour didn't quite fit. Then it stirred. It moved, and eventually rose to its feet. I rubbed at my eyes.

I couldn't believe what - who - I was staring at. I couldn't take my eyes off the form. An apparition come to life, and one that would surely vanish if I turned away, even just for a moment. My excited shouts were swallowed by the noise of rushing water. Tyler looked around as if trying to work out where she was. She must have come down from the forest. Maybe she heard me shouting earlier.

I could see blood on her face. The front of her jacket was torn, and she hobbled badly, wincing and clutching at her side with each step. She wasn't wearing a pack and there was no sign of her climbing partner.

Eventually, Tyler looked over in my direction. Surely, she must have seen me flailing my arms. I pushed the hood of my jacket back and took my beanie off so she might recognise who it was waving at her. It seemed like an age, but she slowly raised a hand. I saw a half smile. Her lips moved. I shouted again, as much a release from a sudden energy surge as an effort to communicate with her.

Tyler took another half step towards me. She was quite close to bank of the river now. But she didn't seem to be aware of it. Her smile was stronger. I was sure she recognised me, and I gave her a double thumbs up to show that everything would be okay. That she didn't have to worry about anything anymore.

I knew I should rush back to wake Papps. And to try the radio again. But how could I get to Tyler? I wondered for a moment whether using a rope to try to cross the river might work. But then I figured the water was still too deep and swift.

I couldn't make myself lose sight of Tyler. As if she might be nothing more than a ghost, vanishing back into the forest as soon as I turned away. Then she seemed to sway on her feet. I watched in horror as she staggered sideways, recovered, before collapsing to the ground less than a metre from where the rushing water could sweep her away at any moment.

I shouted or screamed more likely. Even though I knew the roar of the river would hide it. But Tyler didn't move. Not even a little bit. I stepped forward without really thinking, downwards and into the shallows of the river to try to see better.

Despite the water only rising to my knees the pull of the current was still strong. I could just make out Tyler again, but not easily because of the turbulent water. She hadn't stirred. Now her legs were in the water. I screamed, at Tyler, at the swollen river, the sky, anything that might listen, my frustration so intense that it was forcing me to move further and further into the water. I didn't notice. I didn't care. To lose Tyler when I had come this close was not something I could face dealing with. Life wouldn't be worth it.

A partially submerged log had become lodged against the bank just downriver from where I stood. Without stopping to assess the risk, I started pushing against it, figuring I could maybe use it to float across. But I couldn't move it. It was stuck fast. I started swearing again, struggling against the gravel and the drag of the river's current, not realising how close I was to being swept away.

Two firm hands gripped my shoulders, holding me in place, slowly but firmly pulling me back to land. My only instinct was to fight this new resistance, ignoring the voice in my head, a voice shouting at me. Insisting.

'Jase. Stop. JASE!'

My legs buckled under the strength of the grip from my friend, both of us collapsing onto the bank behind us. Papps had managed to get up and hobble out here. He kept his arms around me, hugging me to his chest.

'It's all right, mate.'

I tried to speak but couldn't. I relaxed enough for my friend to ease his grip and then eventually let me go. We both stood up, my friend perched on his good leg.

'Hang on a second,' he said, holding both hands up in front of me as he looked across towards Tyler's slumped form. 'Let's just think about this.' I nodded like I understood. But in my mind, I couldn't wait. I'd waited all of my life. Without thinking, I lunged towards the river. Next thing I was in the water. The impact knocked the air from my lungs. And the cold. The cold that enveloped me like a vice. My whole body submerged for what seemed like eternity before I struggled back to the surface. I tried to get a breath, but only managed to swallow a mouthful of water. Then I got dragged under again.

I was immersed in a cacophony of noise and cold. Fighting against a far superior force. Something I could never win against. But through all of the confusion, of the whining wind and the slopping water, I thought for a moment that I could hear a voice.

'Swim, Jase. Swim for shore.'

I was struggling against the current and the standing waves and trying to keep my head at the surface. Swept downstream at an alarming rate while fighting to make the other side. In my mind it was all that mattered. Stroke after stroke, arms and legs heavy from the cold. An incessant pull against my will.

Even now, as I tell all of this to Zoe, I can hear something in my head that sounds like the cry of a karoro, a bird of the sea. Then there is the voice again. A clear, strong voice telling me to keep swimming. Keep fighting.

I swam like I had never swum in my life. Arms flailing for all I was worth. I could see land rushing by, and I thrashed towards it. I kept being dragged under and had to fight to get back to the surface each time. I was getting colder. I could feel myself slowly but surely slipping away. Come on, Jase. Come on.

I hit something. It took me a moment to realise it was the bank on the other side. I used my numbed hands to drag myself out of the water. My legs wouldn't work properly. But I forced myself to stand, falling back down but then trying again, staggering step by step back upstream as quickly as I could.

For a second, I caught sight of Papps across the boiling, rushing water. He was hobbling around and pointing. The look on his face suggested I might be too late.

Then I saw Tyler. She was still on the riverbank. Water was at her waist, lifting her body and dragging it slowly into the main current. I grabbed for her with both hands. Trying to get them to work well enough so I could get hold of her before she was swept away. Inch by inch, I managed to drag her from the river.

I was shivering uncontrollably, but Tyler was worse. She was unresponsive to my touch. I shouted at her to wake up, enveloping her in my arms, hugging her cold body as if this alone would be enough to bring her back to consciousness. To life. I searched for a sign from her. Anything. I imagined I could hear her breathing. And then moaning. Did her lips just move? Yes, I was sure of it.

Then her arms. They were lifting slowly and grasping me. Her eyes remained closed, but she was trying to draw me closer. Both of us embracing so tightly that we could never be prised apart again. I knew she wouldn't likely hear my words. But the act of doing it seemed enough.

'Everything's going to be alright,' I said to her, not knowing what I could do next but needing her to feel safe. Protected. 'You'll see. I promise.'

And then the beating of wings came.

XI

They say that time heals all wounds. What a load of codswallop. Maybe we become used to it. The suffering. The guilt. The self-loathing. The grief. The fear and the love. We try to keep it shut in a room in a dark recess in our mind. A room that we keep guarded for all we're worth. But we know that it's never going to be enough.

Kate has been gone for five months now. I keep waking every morning hoping to see her sleeping form again in the bed beside me. Instead, my tired body tends to remind me that maybe it won't be too long before we are together again.

Tyler and Zoe have been slowly sorting through her possessions. I'm happy for them to keep doing that if they want. And there has been some of my brother's stuff as it worked out.

I didn't for a moment think they would actually find anything. Especially not something that leads me to sharing so much of this story with Zoe. A quirk of fate? Maybe it was meant to happen all along. Pre-ordained by some so-called Great Almighty. Old age does that to you, makes you think about the what if's. About the afterlife and so forth. Even if just in a few moments of self-indulged weakness.

Blah. Kate just held on to some of Duncan's stuff as keepsakes is all. That's what's happened. And that's why all of this has come to light, and why Zoe's head is filled with so many questions.

Zoe likes to use the hole in the hedge between what has been

Kate's and my home and what used to be Frank and Nancy's place. Their crib had been left to me after they both passed away. Years ago now, of course. But I could never bring myself to sell it, and it remained empty for ages. That was before Tyler asked if she and Zoe could perhaps move in.

Tyler split with her own partner not so long ago. A few months back if I remember correctly, just after Kate's passing. The symmetry is startling in its closeness to my family's move here all of those decades ago. I guess the Coast can do that to you. Offer you something that other places don't or can't. Maybe we were always meant to be drawn here, eventually, one way or the other. As if the sun's gravity had pulled us.

For a moment I try to remember the bloke's name that Tyler has split with. Zoe's father. Nope. It's gone. Ah well. Anyway, good riddance, I say. What a prat!

It has certainly been cathartic for me to retell this story to Zoe. To shape the narrative of our family in a way that protects their memories as well as Zoe's impression of them.

It's late in the day and my voice has grown hoarse from talking so much. 'How about we go for a walk before dinner?' I suggest. 'Along the beach if you'd like. It should be calm.'

'That sounds great,' Zoe replies.

We walk for a bit, and then stop so I can rest on a large piece of driftwood that has washed ashore. We stare at the sea.

'So it was that pilot, your friend Beckett, who came and found you in the end,' Zoe says, surmising. 'Your Morse code trick must have worked.'

'That's right. I had confidence she would find us either way. The weather had cleared enough for her to fly the line of the valley we agreed upon. All she needed was a head's up. And, yep, her timing was perfect.'

Then Zoe frowns. 'But what happened to Mum? And her friend? How did they get in that situation in the first place? Needing to get rescued. Was it just the weather that caught them out?'

'You'll have to ask her.'

'I did, but she's pretty cagey about it. Keeps putting me off. You must know, like did her climbing friend make it?'

I gave a smile that could be taken either way. 'Ask her again,' I suggest. 'Tell her how important it is for you to understand. Everything.'

'But what did you find out? Afterwards, I mean.'

'It's better coming from your mother. It's her story to tell after all, not mine.'

Zoe looks away. I wonder if she has accepted my reasoning or if she is wondering how to ask the questions in a different way. I guess I'll worry about that if and when it comes.

The evening is about as warm as it gets here on the Coast. My skin tingles from the heat. I close my eyes, and I listen to the sound of the water gently lapping against the shoreline and the cries of gulls as they fly overhead. Somewhere inland there is shouting and laughter and a bellbird singing its sweet song.

'Can I ask you something?' The tone in Zoe's voice makes me open my eyes and turn to her. The look on her face makes my stomach tighten again. Oh no. Now what? What else is on her mind?

'It's important,' she adds.

'Of course it is,' I reply, my voice cracking a little. My mind races. There's really only one thing it can be. One final secret.

Zoe takes a deep breath. It looks like she is about to confess something that could be really bad. 'Is Granddad Duncan my real grandfather?'

There's a squawk of a lone gull somewhere nearby. It's my turn to take a very deep breath. I start to think of some way to sidestep. Like I've been doing all of these years. But no. I'm done with it.

'How long have you known?'

Zoe shrugs her shoulders. 'I've wondered for a while. That's why I asked Mum whether we could go through all his and Nanna Kate's things.'

'You're pretty sharp. Hunting for clues eh?'

My granddaughter nods. 'I had figured it was you in that photo. Not at first, but the more I looked and thought about everything that I knew or suspected. It all made sense in the end.'

'Does your mother know too?'

'I don't think so,' Zoe replies. 'Not yet anyway. Well, not that she told me. But you know what she can be like. Just like you, with her secrets.'

And then Zoe smiles. She doesn't say anything else. She just takes my hand in hers and looks out over the sea.

Of course, I feel an urge to turn and glance over my shoulder, to see what is happening inland. I watch the clouds passing over the mountains. They have varied shapes. Some are curved like upside down saucers. Others scatter like washing blown off a clothesline or become stacked like music written on a page (what would that sound like, I wonder). Some are hiding the mountains, but others hover just so over the tops, like they're responding to each other. Like they are aware of being watched. Like they are watching back.

It starts and ends with falling, and with lies, and the colour blue. Blue used to be my favourite colour, but not anymore. If I see a certain shade, it makes me shiver. Reminds me of the emptiness that lurks inside, and how that emptiness feeds off the cold. A stabbing, unrelenting cold.

Eventually cold will dull the pain. Maybe that's the answer.

But so does love. Love keeps the pain at bay. Love and loss, intertwined so that they make me feel happy and sad, nostalgic, laconic. Lucky, I guess, to feel anything so strongly, especially at my age. Anything to keep the melancholy at bay. Feeling something binds with it the will to keep going, just a little longer. To be here for Zoe, not that she's probably going to need my aged advice anymore. But one never knows.

I turn back to the sea. The horizon is as blue as blue can be. It's almost the same colour as the inside of a crevasse. I give another involuntary shudder. But this blue has just enough light shining into it that the darkness and the emptiness and the cold recedes.

I tell myself that everything is going to be okay.

Protection

Paul Hersey

A Few Words, and Thanks

I started jotting down notes for this story back in 2014, during the final days of a failing expedition to Eastern Nepal. Partly it was to pass the time while being stuck in base camp through endless bad weather. But, mostly, it was to help me deal with loss. A few months before the start of our trip an early climbing mentor was killed by an avalanche on K2. Weeks later, one of my best mates also died in a mountaineering accident, leaving behind his partner and young son.

Grief is a constant reminder of the cost of mountaineering. We can't escape loss. We just find ways to deal with it as best we can.

I discovered the fine line between escapism and adventure at an early age. My father took me hunting. My mother encouraged me to embrace nature. My brothers grew to treasure (or dread) the words 'Let's take this shortcut home'. Adventuring became a way of life, a way of experiencing life, of letting me see the value of challenge, of journeying, and then of simply being in the outdoors.

Here's to slogging up-hill with heavy packs, cold bivouacs beneath the stars, nervous alpine starts, and those knife in the chest cruxes right when you least expect them. And here's to those who chose to share in such adventures.

In essence, this - as well as remembering - is what I wanted to celebrate by the writing of 'Protection'.

There are people to thank for helping tackle my clumsy ideas and shape them into something that others might actually want to read. First up, and a big one, double thumbs to Matt Turner. I probably would have dragged myself there in the end but getting that initial 'yes' was such a shot in the arm. Matt, I love it that we remain friends a few books and years later, and that I can call you up out of the blue and pick your supremely knowledgeable publishing brain.

Laurence Fearnley, you're a rose among thorns, or is it a thorn among the roses. A veritable literary heavy weight when there seem to be so few genuine ones left. Your gentle guidance has been a constant, calming influence through my creative highs and lows. Coffee and cake has much to answer for.

Jerry Auld, we finally got here after a couple of false starts. I appreciate your straight shooting and your nose for the narrative thread. I like how we might live on opposite sides of the world but can connect as if residing just down the road from one another.

Thanks also to Ross Cullen and the New Zealand Alpine Club publications committee for a funding grant. Every bit helps keep the proverbial wolves from the door and yours is sincerely appreciated.

Finally, Shelley - climbing buddy, mountain biking buddy, surfing buddy, life buddy - forever known by: 'Can I come?'

About The Author

Paul Hersey lives in the South Island of New Zealand, next to the sea and close to the mountains. His previous jobs have included newspaper reporter, ice climbing instructor, fisheries enforcement officer, surf lifeguard, photographer, sea cave kayaking guide, and outdoors retail store manager.

An award-winning author and journalist, Paul has written seven non-fiction books, and is a contributor to *Alpinist*, *New Zealand Geographic*, *The Surfer's Journal*, *North and South*, *White Horses*, and *Wilderness* magazines.

Protection is his first full length work of fiction.

Other Titles

Where The Mountains Throw Their Dice
High Misadventure
Searching For Groundswell
Our Mountains
Merino Country
New Zealand's Great Walks (with Shelley Hersey)
To The Mountains (edited with Laurence Fearnley)

9 781777 242107